MEDICI
Supremacy

MEDICI
Supremacy

MATTEO STRUKUL

Translated from the Italian
by Richard McKenna

HEAD
ZEUS

First published in Italian as *Un uomo al potere*
in 2016 by Newton Compton
First published in the UK in 2020 by Head of Zeus Ltd
This paperback edition first published in 2021 by Head of Zeus Ltd

9 7 5 3 1 2 4 6 8

A catalogue record for this book is available from
the British Library.

ISBN (PB): 9781786692153
ISBN (E): 9781786692122

Typeset by Silicon Chips Services Ltd UK

Printed and bound in Great Britain by
CPI Group (UK) Ltd, Croydon CR0 4YY

Head of Zeus Ltd
5–8 Hardwick Street
London EC1R 4RG
WWW.HEADOFZEUS.COM

To Silvia; to Leonardo

FEBRUARY 1469

1

The Joust

Lorenzo drew in a deep breath of the cold air.

He could feel the tension building within him as he sat there in the saddle. Beneath him, his beloved mount Folgore, his coal-black coat glossy and lustrous, turned in circles and pawed at the paving stones of the square. Lorenzo struggled to hold him still.

Like a prayer, a murmur rose from the tribunes, boxes, loggias, balconies, windows and porches, and Lorenzo's eyes met those of Lucrezia Donati. She was clad in a magnificent dress that day: a gown of indigo which seemed to melt into her obsidian eyes. Her pearl-grey *gamurra* was studded with gems and hinted at the curve of her bosom, a white fox fur stole encircled her beautiful pale shoulders and Lucrezia's rebellious mass of black hair, which resembled the waves of some nocturnal sea, was magnificently dressed.

Lorenzo wondered if he would manage to be worthy of her.

He raised his fingers to the scarf he wore around his neck. Lucrezia had embroidered it for him herself, and as he inhaled its scent of cornflowers he felt as though he were sinking into the embrace of Empyrean.

His thoughts turned to his arrival at the tournament a few moments earlier, to his brother Giuliano – looking splendid in his green jerkin – and to the host of two hundred men dressed in the colours of spring as though to calm the warlike minds of a city which had been drowning in blood and corruption until practically the previous day. A city that his father, Piero de' Medici, had worked hard, despite his ill health and the gout that consumed him, to save from the rebel families who plotted in the shadows against the Medici and who had set ambushes for them on more than one occasion. Piero had handed down to Lorenzo a weary and exhausted Republic on the verge of collapse that was struggling even to remember its identity.

But despite the blood and torment, the day of the jousting tournament held in honour of the wedding of Lorenzo's good friend Braccio Martelli had arrived. It had cost ten thousand florins – a fortune – and for a while at least would wash away the fears and the rancour.

Lorenzo raised his head: in front of him was the wooden barrier that ran to the opposite end of the square. There, sealed up in his plate armour, was Pier Soderini, his tight-fitting helmet made even more threatening by its lowered visor. In his bent arm he held a long lance of ash wood.

At the entrance to Piazza Santa Croce, the roaring of the crowd was deafening.

Lorenzo looked down to check his shield one last time and saw the colours of the Medici, bright against the saddlecloth of his steed, reflected in a puddle: the five red balls with, upon the sixth, the lily conceded to them by the King of France as a symbol of nobility. They hung there threateningly.

This waiting, this feeling of responsibility... He felt as though it were driving him out of his mind.

He closed his visor, its eye slit reducing the world outside to a gelid strip, then lowered his lance and put his spurs to his mount.

Without a moment's hesitation, the horse leapt forward, as fast as a gust of wind, hurling itself towards Pier Soderini.

Lorenzo felt the mighty musculature of his darting beast and heard the mud-splashed saddlecloth flapping in the breeze. Soderini had just set off, while Lorenzo had already covered almost half the distance. He raised his shield to better protect himself and aimed his long lance at his target.

The crowd seemed to be holding its breath.

From up on the wooden platform, Lucrezia kept her eyes fixed upon Lorenzo. She wasn't afraid, she simply wanted to impress the moment upon her memory. She knew how hard her beloved had prepared for this joust and how extraordinarily courageous he was. He had already proved that. And she wasn't going to think about the fact that he was now promised to Clarice Orsini, the Roman noblewoman his mother had chosen for him. She wouldn't hide her passion for him, and neither would Florence and its people, who looked indulgently upon the pair of lovers. They hated the fact that Lorenzo's mother's scheming meant that the man appointed to lead the Signoria had asked for the hand of a Roman, even if she was of noble rank.

But that day there was no time to waste on such thoughts. The horses' nostrils steamed in the freezing air, the tempered steel plates of the armour glinted and the banners flapped in a blaze of colours.

Finally, the impact came: a crash of wood and steel like a thunderclap.

Lorenzo's lance found its way through Pier Soderini's guard and struck him in his breastplate. The lance shattered into pieces and Soderini found himself thrown out of the saddle by the impact.

He hit the ground of the square with a loud clang while Lorenzo rode past him. The indomitable Folgore galloped on, rearing up with a whinny when he reached the end of the lists.

The crowd exploded in a roar of amazement, crying out in jubilation, and the Medici too shouted at the top of their lungs, the men applauding thunderously and the women beaming with joy.

Lorenzo was even more surprised than the rest of them. He could barely believe it – it had all happened so fast that he hadn't been able to take it in.

Attendants and squires were already rushing to the aid of Pier Soderini, who must still be in one piece because he was standing up. He had slipped off his helmet and, red in the face, was shaking his head, partly in annoyance and partly in disbelief at having been unseated.

Her hands on her bosom, Lucrezia's beautiful face lit up with a dazzling smile.

Lorenzo removed his own helmet and iron gloves and almost instinctively touched the scarf. He could smell her perfume, light and intoxicating and full of promise.

He loved her with a burning passion – the same passion that he tried to express in his clumsy sonnets. Many acclaimed his compositions as magnificent, but he knew that all the words in the world would never be able to do justice to what he felt in his heart.

Lucrezia made him feel so alive, and when she looked at him with those eyes of hers, whose long onyx lashes seemed almost able to trap shadow, he felt blessed. He could think of nothing more beautiful.

The crowd seemed to notice the looks that passed between them, and exploded in a second roar of applause that was even more deafening than the first. Florence loved him, and so did Lucrezia. She had conceded him no more than a fleeting glance, but when he caught it, Lorenzo knew that he would love only her and that even if his mother had already chosen for him a Roman bride – a noblewoman who would offer the family useful alliances and pacts – his heart would be for one woman alone: Lucrezia.

While he was absorbed in these thoughts, the herald communicated the result, proclaiming Lorenzo the clear winner of the joust. His noble friends and dignitaries could wait no longer: Braccio Martelli was the first to jump down from the platform and run over to congratulate him while his squires removed his breastplate and the tassets from his legs.

Braccio was so happy that he began shouting Lorenzo's name, and the crowd joined in.

Giuliano, the younger of the two Medici brothers, smiled down from the highest tribune. He was tall and elegant, and his subtle and refined features were very different from those of his older brother, which were stronger and more defined.

Lucrezia gave a cry of admiration and, not content with the scandal she had already caused, blew her champion a kiss and threw him a handkerchief of fine linen.

Lorenzo caught it, and the perfume of cornflowers almost overwhelmed him.

The city embraced its favourite son. And yet among that festive crowd there walked a strange figure, swaying like an insect's antenna.

He had the features and form of a young man – and a good-looking one, at that. But something in the sneer that arched his thin, blood-coloured lips was horribly out of place.

Soon, thought the silent spectator, all that harmony would be shattered.

2

Riario

His uncle had been absolutely right.

And his uncle would soon become Pope. There was no doubt about it: it was only a matter of time.

Girolamo Riario looked at the boy. He had deep blue eyes and mahogany hair, and his thin lips were curled into a cruel smile. In him, Riario sensed a wickedness which his features – refined, but sharp enough to be severe – barely concealed.

He sighed.

The skeleton of a project consumed his thoughts. It was not fully conceived – indeed was little more than a vague hypothesis, barely sketched out and in all likelihood difficult to implement. And yet he did not despair.

Motivation was the most important thing that a man could possess, and as well as being of proven seriousness, the young man who stood before him possessed plenty of it.

Girolamo's grey eyes flashed as he smoothed a long lock of his hair back into place. He knew that this little serpent had its own diabolical intelligence and he, who was always so very reckless, had no wish to allow himself to be outwitted.

'Are you certain of what you say?'

'I have no doubt of it, my lord,' replied the boy.

'And did you see them?'

'As I see you now. All of Florence applauded that exchange of gazes.'

Of course it did! Lorenzo de' Medici's love for Lucrezia Donati was no secret, and, however improper it might be, it was not so deplorable. Not openly, anyway. His uncle would not have approved of it, and neither, perhaps, would the Pope, but there was nothing new about that. And anyway, a look was not sufficient grounds for excommunication. Marriages of convenience were a custom and the fact that Lorenzo nurtured a love – be it courtly or carnal – for the young Donati meant nothing. Indeed, his city openly supported his romantic infidelity.

Those damn Florentines, he thought.

'What else did you see?'

'Florence, my lord.'

Girolamo raised an eyebrow.

'Florence?'

'The city adores him.'

'Are you serious?'

'It pains me to admit it, but it is so.'

Riario gave another sigh. He had to do something, but what? Was he certain that the idea that he had dreamed up was really so very cunning?

'Speak with Giovanni de' Diotisalvi Neroni.'

'The Archbishop of Florence, my lord?'

'Who else?'

'Naturally. But to what end, if I may ask?' the other replied, one of those strange smirks of his appearing on his face. Though the question was a legitimate one, it irked Girolamo. How dare he? But in truth he was not sure how to answer the lad. It was that damned habit of his of talking too much – he had dropped Giovanni de' Diotisalvi Neroni's name in the hope that some inspiration, some suggestion, some flash of genius would follow.

But there was nothing.

Despite all his bluster, Riario was intelligent and self-aware enough to know that he wasn't good at coming up with brilliant ideas, or at least, not the kind of brilliant ideas he needed. Ideas like those which, providentially and punctually, emerged from the diabolical mind of that youth. He had already seen it happen in the past.

Neroni might have his finger on the pulse of things, though. Certainly more than he, Girolamo, who was stuck here between Savona and Treviso waiting for his uncle to ascend to the papal throne.

'If nothing else, you will familiarize yourself with the mood of the nobility and see first-hand the frustrations and anger of the Medici's enemies.'

It was a lucid thought – as precise as the edge of a blade.

'Might I make a suggestion?' asked the diabolical youth.

Riario nodded. He didn't know where all this talk was leading, but if it meant coming up with a plan to get rid of the Medici – the perfect, flawless plan that he was seeking – then it would be worth it.

'I'm listening,' he said encouragingly.

The young man seemed to concentrate.

'Well, the idea of testing the waters is a fascinating one, my lord. One might even say brilliant—'

'Get to the point!' interrupted Riario.

'Very well. So... if, as you rightly claim, Giovanni de' Diotisalvi Neroni, Archbishop of Florence, is in a position to identify the most powerful family hostile to the Medici then it might be advisable to prompt them into orchestrating a conspiracy against Lorenzo in order to have him and his brother exiled. Spilling blood is never a good idea, but exile – removal, as happened with his grandfather Cosimo – might be the ideal solution.'

'Are you certain of that?' asked Girolamo.

'Very much so. You see, my lord, Lorenzo is in a sense consubstantial with his city: deprived of it, he is deprived of all his power. And let's be honest: his father Piero is a poltroon who has done much to weaken their family. Lorenzo could cause us problems, but if we act now while he is young and inexperienced we might have a good chance against him, and that would open the way for a family which would be more attentive to your wishes.'

'Ingenious, my young friend – ingenious but vague. What accusations might allow the banishment of which you speak, I wonder?'

'In truth, my lord, there are many possibilities, but only one which would discredit him so much that it would legitimize the sentence.' The youth spoke so much like a skilled politician that it gave Girolamo the unpleasant sensation he must have been born directly from the loins of some demonic creature.

'And what would that be?' he asked, his voice betraying his impatience.

'High treason,' answered the youth promptly.

Girolamo Riario raised an eyebrow.

'You see, my lord, there is in Florence an artist who is as yet little known but who is endowed with an extraordinary personality: he is also an engineer and inventor, and there is no man in the world of equal intelligence and spirit. He is still very young, of course, but people will soon be talking about him, and if we could prove – or rather, if an allied family could do so – that Lorenzo and this man are collaborating in order to invent a weapon so powerful that it would be lethal if it were used to attack the surrounding states, that would reflect very badly on the city of Florence and make it hated and feared by all... And at that point, I believe, again with the help of some friendly family, we would have no difficulty in overturning the Medici party and making the city yours. We could in all probability accuse Lorenzo of high treason and even of heresy for the extent of his blind faith in war and science, which exceeds the boundaries imposed by the Church.'

With those words, the youth fell silent.

Eyes wide with amazement, Girolamo stared at him.

'Magnificent, my boy, magnificent! A complex plan and full of unknown factors, certainly, but for this very reason it must at least be considered. So yes, you should go and put our project into action. But don't hurry: we have time – my faction has yet to come to power. In the meanwhile, let's identify the family who will help us, and then we will assemble the elements necessary to entrap the Medici. When we are at the height of our powers, then we will strike. And we will do it in such a way that it will no longer be possible for the Medici to pick themselves up again. Tell your mother that I greatly appreciate her son's suggestions, and as proof, I beg you to accept a token of my undying esteem.'

And so saying, Girolamo Riario pulled a periwinkle velvet purse out of the drawer of a mahogany table and threw it to the boy.

Ludovico Ricci caught it neatly, eliciting from inside the purse the unmistakable clink of silver.

'You are very generous, my lord,' he said, and then headed for the door.

'One last thing, Ludovico.'

The boy stopped and turned to face his lord.

'What's the name of this genius of whom you were speaking?'

'Leonardo da Vinci,' answered the young Ricci.

3

Lucrezia and Lorenzo

'She has large eyes and a strong character. I believe that you will like her and that she will satisfy your every desire, my son. More importantly, she will guarantee alliances and friendships which had previously been closed off to you, and God alone knows how much our family needs alliances and friendships in this moment.'

Lorenzo's mother Lucrezia was singing the praises of Clarice in a veritable flood of words, as though the girl were the herald of a new life for Florence.

Lorenzo was not convinced, though. Not at all. He understood the needs of the state – he was no fool. But on the other hand, what people had told him about his future bride did nothing to endear her to him. She sounded like a pious woman, meticulous and careful:

virtues which were certainly not to be despised, but not ones which interested *him*. How would they get on?

With all the diplomacy and courtesy of which he was capable, he attempted to point this out to his mother.

'What you say makes me happy, Mother dear, and I am infinitely grateful to you for what you have done. Yet I wonder whether you feel that Clarice has also those qualities, such as lively intelligence and an attractive appearance, which are typical of young women of her age...'

On hearing this, Lucrezia gave her son an icy glare. She was an elegant but severe woman, and the features of her face could become implacably hard when necessary.

'My dear Lorenzo, I prefer to speak now and to speak only once so as not to have to return to this topic. I know of your absurd infatuation with Lucrezia Donati. I do not say that the girl is not worthy of your attention, but let this be clear: it must stop, and quickly. I know your temperament and, worse still, I know hers. That girl has fire inside her, but it will bring you no good, you can take my word for that. And in any case, from this day on you will no longer be able to indulge your fancies. Clarice is coming from Rome and she is an Orsini, one of the noblest of families, and that is enough to make her irresistible. I know that it will take Florence some time to accept her, but if you lead the way, the others will follow. I want no foolishness about this. In due course you may think of permitting yourself some distractions – I know something about *that*, after accepting the daughter of another woman into our family and forgiving your father for what he did. But there is one thing you must get into your head. Your father suffers from fragile health and a disease that no longer allows him to be the man he was. Your time has come and there is no point in you trying to shirk the leadership of the Republic. And the leadership of Florence comes through marriage with Clarice Orsini. So the sooner you accept that, the better it will be for all of us.'

Lorenzo knew all too well that his mother was right, and also knew the thousand challenges she had faced, first in Rome and then in Florence, to seal the agreement between the Medici and the Orsini, overcoming barriers of caste and getting into the good graces of the Capitoline nobility. But Lucrezia Donati's sensuality, her eyes, her shapeliness, her way of dressing and walking... everything about her was pure charm, seduction, mystery and adventure, and he needed it to feel alive, desired and invincible. But he also knew that was not what his mother wanted to hear.

'I will do as you ask, and you will be proud of me,' he said. 'I will be wary of my enemies and will keep faith with the teachings of my father and my grandfather before him, and thus with the sense of moderation which is the raw material that shapes decorum and consensus. But nobody will ever make me forget Lucrezia Donati.'

His mother sighed. Once again, she met her son's gaze.

'My dearest son, I understand you and, believe me, what I want is your happiness. I am happy to hear you say these words, and no one asks that you should forget your Lucrezia. But ready yourself to honour Clarice Orsini as wife, because the destiny of Florence is linked to her. And another thing: you must do your utmost to ensure that the city welcomes her as she deserves. I am certain that this diffidence towards her is the result of your reckless attitude, so try and temper it and convince our people to honour her like a queen. She will be your lady and it is as such that you must treat her. You have to understand that an alliance between Rome and Florence is all the more necessary now – the good pontiff Paul II may favour us, but it is not certain that his successor will do the same, and we must be ready. But with the Orsini family on our side, perhaps – perhaps, I say – we will have a better chance, even if the eventual new appointee does not look too favourably upon us. Do you understand me?'

'Of course I understand you,' replied Lorenzo with a hint of irritation. 'I know perfectly well that Pius II was behind the appointment of Filippo de' Medici as Archbishop of Pisa and that it was made possible thanks to the pressure of Grandfather Cosimo. Just as I have no doubt that the current Archbishop of Florence is, instead, against us... The facts have amply demonstrated it. I was the one who prevented them carrying out the ambush on the road to Careggi, do you remember?'

Lucrezia nodded.

'And it was the Archbishop of Florence who was behind that wickedness. Therefore it is obvious that he is hoping for a scandal upon which to crucify me...' Lorenzo paused a moment, then continued. 'Listen, Mother, I want one thing to be clear: you have no need to worry about my conduct; I will be an exemplary and attentive husband. But do not ask me to love her. I will not be able to do that. Not immediately, at least. I know my duty and I have no illusions about how ruthless my enemies are, but I do think that my character grants me some influence over people. The other day, at the joust in honour of Braccio Martelli, I had the feeling that the peasants, the people and even some of the nobility were with me. In short, I don't wish to give up what I am. There is in me a fire that, if I keep it properly under control, can be of some use for our family – that, at least, you must admit.'

'Come here and let me embrace you', said Lucrezia when she heard these words, 'and do not think even for a moment that you have disappointed me. What I say is for your own good and because I hold you in such great esteem that I believe you and only you, my son, can guide the Medici to the glory they deserve, continuing the work of your father and, above all, that of your grandfather Cosimo, who loved you so much when he was alive.'

'And who I miss so very much,' concluded Lorenzo.

He went over to his mother, who had risen from her chair, and embraced her with such fervour that he almost felt as though he were embracing a lover.

4

Leonardo

Leonardo breathed in the cool air of that February morning.

His long blond hair ruffled by the wind, he looked at the fields of brown earth, encrusted with iridescent sheets of hoar frost.

There was a power in nature so extraordinary that it took his breath away each time he witnessed it. It made him feel so small and insignificant that he was overcome with a sense of wonder and gratitude for what the world seemed to give him every day.

And yet, men seemed not to care. Even he had found himself working for war, for that cruel and senseless conflict that set human beings against one another in the name of a shameful goal: the conquest of power and territory. Because that was that was precisely what denying others their freedom was.

It was shameful. That was why he had decided to work for Lorenzo de' Medici – because in his eyes he had perceived the spirit of an intelligent and stubborn man, but not of a tyrant or a warlord. From the beginning of their collaboration, Lorenzo had asked him to work for the Medici, refining his knowledge and his experiments for the construction of war machines that would be used exclusively for defensive purposes. Never, he had told him, would he use his weapons to attack another city. Following the teachings of his grandfather and father, Lorenzo was convinced that the future of Florence lay in peace, prosperity, art and literature. Certainly not in conflict.

Under these conditions, Leonardo had agreed to lend his talents to the Medici. He hadn't left the workshop of Andrea del Verrocchio because he still had much to learn, especially in relation to what was at that time his principal passion: painting. However, thanks to his ideas about military engineering he received a hundred florins a month and therefore managed to live in greater ease – and also, if truth be told, to put aside something so that one day he might have a workshop of his own.

That morning, while he was musing on all this, he had watched Lorenzo arrive with his host of guards. The horses galloped along the dirt road and soon arrived at the top of the hill where he was standing among the cypresses, gazing at the ploughed fields, and where the invisible currents of wind blew sharp and cold.

Lorenzo climbed down from his horse. He was clad in a magnificent doublet and cape of dark green, and his strong features gave his gaze an uncommon determination, illuminating it so intensely that his every action seemed to possess rare vitality.

He squeezed Leonardo's hand with contagious vigour and gratitude, and Leonardo could feel Lorenzo's warmth and almost disarming sincerity. He would do well not to disappoint a man like that, he thought. But he was confident that he would not, because he had a great surprise for him that day.

'My friend,' said Lorenzo, 'seeing you always gives me great joy, because I always think I am about to witness a miracle.'

'Come, sir, you are too kind. And in any case, it remains to be seen whether what I have for you will actually surprise you.'

'I have no doubt of it.'

While Lorenzo's men dismounted, Leonardo began to explain his project.

'My magnificent lord,' he began, 'as you can see, I have had some straw men set up in order to make the most of this demonstration.' As he spoke, he gestured to some scarecrows that had been arranged a few hundred paces from them.

'You will agree,' he continued, 'that the crossbowman is a fundamental soldier in any army. We all remember how the battle of Anghiari was won: without the formidable Genoese crossbowmen who attacked the flank of Astorre Manfredi's army from the slopes of the hills and put them out of action, we would perhaps not be here speaking today.' He paused to let his words sink in. He was a skilled orator who knew very well how to present a discovery or a project in a powerfully dramatic fashion, adopting the appropriate rhythm so as to arouse the listener's curiosity – he put as much work into the presentation of his work as he did into the work itself. 'As we know,' he continued, 'the crossbow is an ancient weapon and its purpose is to increase, where possible, the range and power of the bow, of which it represents an evolution. Its efficiency, combined with its power and precision, is its chief virtue.'

As he spoke, Leonardo had gone over to a table he had placed in the clearing and, with a gesture not wholly devoid of theatricality, raised a sheet of rough linen, revealing several crossbows of polished wood.

'We are speaking about a sophisticated and highly strategic weapon, but one whose efficiency is gradually being lost thanks to the construction of increasingly powerful models whose loading procedures are so complex that they compromise its effectiveness. The introduction of steel bows has certainly improved performance, but has also led to undeniable problems when in use, as they are so difficult to pull back that the crossbowman can no longer get the string into the loading position even with both hands. So we are forced to resort to levers, winches or ratchets, which mean wasting a great deal of time and putting the crossbowman's life in constant danger.'

'Without even mentioning,' cut in Lorenzo, 'that all the various devices the crossbowman must carry with him reduce his mobility in the field.'

'Precisely.'

Leonardo paused for a moment, making his listeners wait for him to conclude his explanation.

'Which is why I propose to you today what I have called the "fast crossbow". In essence, this is a crossbow whose loading system has been made much more rapid. As you can see, the butt of the crossbow is divided into two parts. The lower one, connected to a sturdy hinge, is opened thus...' Leonardo snatched up one of the crossbows from the table and in a fluid motion pulled down the bottom part of the butt like a lever. 'And a system of internal levers brings the nut down to the string in its resting position, then catches it and slides it back into the loading position.'

At that point there was a click, and Lorenzo and his men saw with amazement that the string was already stretched tight and ready to welcome a bolt to fire.

Without wasting another moment, Leonardo nocked the bolt and aimed his weapon in the direction of one of the straw men tied to the branches of the trees in front of them.

He pulled the trigger and the bolt flew out, whistling through the air with a sinister, deadly hiss and piercing the scarecrow's head from side to side.

The Medici guards stood open-mouthed, and even Lorenzo could not hold back a gesture of enthusiasm. The entire operation of loading the crossbow had taken no more than a few moments and while they were staring in amazement at the straw man, Leonardo had already reloaded the weapon and fired off a second dart.

Another whistle and another head punctured by the tip of the dart.

'Incredible!' cried an ecstatic Lorenzo. Unable to resist the charm of this incredible crossbow, he grabbed one from the table and opened and closed the tiller, loading the weapon without touching the string or using any external objects: it was simply incredible.

'Do you not find that loading in this way makes the process extremely fast, my lord?' asked Leonardo.

In answer, Lorenzo fired the dart he had loaded and it pierced the heart of the third scarecrow.

'Nicely done, my lord!' exclaimed the commander of the guards who had accompanied him on that early-morning ride.

'Wonderful, Leonardo,' exclaimed the young Medici. 'You are a genius, and the pride of our city! This project of yours makes the crossbow a weapon which is not only powerful but also rapid and efficient.'

'Perfect for an effective defence, in the case of attack,' pointed out Leonardo, and a shadow appeared briefly in his blue eyes. It was only a moment, but Lorenzo saw it clearly.

'Of course, my friend – my word is my bond. We will use it only to defend ourselves from possible enemy attacks.'

Leonardo nodded. He had needed to hear it said.

Words were nothing but air, of course – but the words of a man like Lorenzo could make the earth tremble. Leonardo knew this well and was even more grateful to his friend because he was certain that, despite his young age, Lorenzo would not allow temperament, which he certainly did not lack, or the impetuosity typical of his youth, to yield to the flattery of violence and aggression.

He smiled. Though he was a few years Lorenzo's junior, he had never been interested in war, conflict or the battlefield. He knew how to defend himself when necessary, but fighting was not one of his priorities. On the contrary, he found it so stupid and pointless that he couldn't understand why by the lords of neighbouring states couldn't see it for themselves.

Yet there it was: Florence, Imola, Forlì, Ferrara, Milan, Modena, Rome, Naples, Venice... all of them saw in war and in conflict a way of affirming their existence.

It almost seemed as though they actually needed it to perpetuate themselves.

He shook his head.

Suddenly, he felt someone embracing him. It was Lorenzo. There, it had happened again – he had got lost in his thoughts.

'Leonardo,' Lorenzo was saying, 'your friendship and your talent honour me and contribute each day to the glory of Florence. You will be rewarded for your immense contribution. And now I want to invite you to return to the city with me. My men will bring back these specimens of yours, and if you would be so kind as to work with my engineers, I'll commission you to make at least two hundred of these incredible crossbows.'

'Have this one from me,' said Leonardo, handing him one. 'It is the best and the most beautiful of those I've made so far.'

'I could ask for nothing better,' said Lorenzo, his voice evincing all the pride and joy the gift gave him. 'But now, come back with me to the city – I need to speak to you of something which is very close to my heart. I think that you might like it.'

'What is it?'

'I will explain it to you in due course. Trust me.'

5

Lucrezia Donati

Lorenzo was lost in that river of dark onyx that smelled of mint and nettle. Lucrezia's beauty was such that it cancelled out the rest of the world.

He heard the embers sizzling in the fireplace, the sparks rising like glowing red fireflies.

Lucrezia looked at him, her eyes dark, shining and wild, her gaze penetrating deep inside him, gripping his heart. He couldn't take his eyes off her. She was not only beautiful: there was about her something almost like nature itself, an ancestral charm, arcane and inextinguishable, that held him bound.

Her breasts big and full in the light of the candles and her hips moving sublimely, Lucrezia flung back her head and arched her back, sending Lorenzo sinking deeper yet into that whirlpool of pleasure until he lost all consciousness of space and time – until nothing mattered. Such was the power of their wild passion that it consumed in an instant any need or desire which was not that of the purest pleasure.

He abandoned himself to her sex and let himself be overwhelmed, his member ready to flood her with his humours.

Lucrezia gasped with pleasure as she continued to ride him until she finally let out a cry and, her arms pushing against his chest and her nails scratching his nipples, they came together in an orgasm so violent it seemed almost to break her in two.

Lorenzo fell into a swoon and Lucrezia slowly lowered her body on to his, her breasts resting against his chest, her arms over his arms. For a moment, the room – and his mind and emotions – seemed to spin like a carousel.

They lay in that embrace, silent and lost as though they wanted to remain forever protected by their love, far from the sounds of a world which made no concessions to their passion.

That was why Lucrezia was crying, her tears bathing Lorenzo's face. As the contours of the objects and the boundaries of the walls and ceiling and the geometries of everyday life began to re-emerge, the injustice of their forbidden love became overwhelming.

After a time, Lucrezia spoke. Perhaps because she wanted to hear her voice, wanted a tangible, earthly affirmation of what they had just experienced. As though words could confirm that, even in the real world, their feelings would survive.

She demanded it.

'Swear to me that you will love only me,' she told him.

'I swear it.'

Lorenzo didn't need to think about it. With Lucrezia everything was so simple and wonderful. She knew exactly what he wanted. There could never be another like her. He felt for her the same awe and gratitude that filled his heart when the night was illuminated by the glow of the stars. A passion so naked – so brash, almost – frightened him, but that fear was a luxury that he could and wanted to allow himself. When the time came, he would behave accordingly. He would protect Lucrezia.

It was the only thing that really mattered to him.

'Even when Clarice arrives?' she asked.

'I swear it,' he repeated.

'And will you love me even when I'm old and have white hair and my skin is like parchment?'

'Even then and even more.'

'And will you be ready to defend me if necessary?'

'I will.'

'I ask nothing more of you, Lorenzo. Yet I know for sure that it will not be so. You swear now, but who knows how time will change you? Who knows what you will become. Now, this room seems like heaven, but soon it will be too cramped and bare and I will be only one of the many women you have had. I know that.'

He took her face in his hands. 'Don't say that, not even in jest!'

Lucrezia's lips curved into a bitter smile.

'You are destined to be the lord of Florence, Lorenzo. Soon you will have the city at your feet. More so than it already is. You will have to deal with power, *real* power, the kind that generates pain and death. You will have to face ruthless enemies and accept compromises for the good of your people and your city. And what will you remember of me when your heart is heavy and your hands are stained with blood? When war is your only thought since it is the only way to defend what you hold dear from the cowardly attacks of men obsessed with greed and plunder?'

'I will still love you,' he replied without hesitation, because he believed deeply in the power of that feeling and knew that one way or another it would never end. 'We are so busy listening to the voice of today that we forget what we had yesterday. And what we had is no small thing: too often we allow the present to cloud the past and obscure that which urged us to want to be better. I will keep this love of yours in the strongbox of my soul and I will not let anyone see it. It will be mine alone and I will cradle it like a child: on days of celebration and on days of pain. And this love will give me strength and torment, joy and bitterness, but it will remain alive and unforgettable.'

She raised her head. Her tears stopped falling.

'What beautiful words,' she said. 'How wonderful it would be if it could actually happen.'

'That depends on us, Lucrezia, and on nobody else. Whatever happens, we will have to remain firm in our principles and in our feelings. If we do that, our love will live. If we lose it, it will be our fault alone, but at least we will have had it once. For that alone, I am grateful.'

For a long time, Lucrezia looked into his eyes. They sparkled, despite their darkness.

And then she wept, for she knew that what is too beautiful cannot last forever.

APRIL 1469

6

The Music

The tables were richly arrayed and the serving staff known as the 'officers of the mouth' presided over them, ensuring that the dishes were always full and appropriately arranged. Stewards, carvers and cup-bearers were busy cutting red and white meat, serving wine and filling glasses, laying upon the plates imposing slices of pies and flans, or perhaps simply displaying, in a swirl of aromas and flavours, the many fruits that would delight the palates of the guests. And then there were the sweets and cakes, tempests of colourful confections ordered by Lorenzo for his mother from some of the finest pastry chefs in Florence.

That feast, one of the many that Lorenzo organized at the Palazzo Medici in Via Larga during the year, brought together some of the finest minds and the fullest purses in Florence, and Marsilio Ficino certainly belonged to the first category.

As was often the case, he wore a red robe. Not overly tall, his slim yet robust form embodied the lucid intelligence and the equilibrium of a man consecrated to the love of knowledge. His many accomplishments included having produced translations which had been fundamental for the Western world, including those of the texts of Hermes Trismegistus and Plato.

Francesco de' Pazzi indubitably belonged to the second category. A member of one of the fastest-rising families in Florence, he always dressed in black, displayed almost excessive resolve and was ever quick to respond to provocations, both real and imagined. His was an arrogance dictated by a combination of wealth and personality, yet in its flashes of violent lightning his haughty and sometimes crude behaviour hinted at the storm which was gathering in the sky above Florence better than a thousand speeches.

Lorenzo and Giuliano certainly did not fear the Pazzi. Though intelligent and privileged representatives of a noble and wealthy family, they remained confined to a background which, however golden, would never become centre stage.

Francesco, in contrast, didn't bother to restrain his impulses and made no secret of the lack of sympathy he felt for his hosts. His grim eyes, so intensely black they resembled ink, darted from one salon to the next, as if storing up useful information to use later against Lorenzo and Giuliano.

The halls of the Palazzo Medici were full of ladies and gentlemen, each of them intent on flaunting their power or their charms.

And yet, when Lorenzo suddenly heard music, so sweet that it almost ravished his ears, every face, every dress, every light suddenly seemed to fade and grow indistinct.

It was like a whispering waterfall of honey that drew him towards it, depriving him of his will and dominating his very being. For a moment he could barely breathe, bewildered as he was by that stream of notes. It was as if he were floating in some unknown dimension, as if everything around him – the decorations, the halls, the guests – had suddenly been wiped away.

Lorenzo closed his eyes and listened. At first, he didn't even wonder who the composer of the magnificent melody was. Listening to well-executed music was a pleasure he rarely enjoyed and on this occasion he had no intention of missing it.

Too often, in an attempt to control his feelings, he had entrusted what he felt to words, but he had never succeeded as he would have liked. It was like moulding ice into shapes that failed to reflect what was in his soul. For that reason the sonnets he composed seemed to him a distortion – a false, deformed image of what he felt in his heart.

In the same way, words would never be enough for music as beautiful as that.

He smelt the scent of cornflowers. It was an aroma he knew well.

Tears began streaming down his face.

He couldn't stop himself. He couldn't explain what was happening, but he didn't care: it was so nice not to have to explain, not to have to understand.

The music soared and then descended again, its melody carrying his emotions to new peaks. At first insistent, it became soft, almost supple, and Lorenzo sensed its irrepressible, irresistible sensuality.

The strings of the lute were plucked so lightly that one might have thought they were playing themselves.

For a moment, the music seemed to falter and there was a pause, then it resumed, but this time sad and bitter, and filled with a whispered melancholy that revealed something about the woman playing it. Because in that moment, Lorenzo was certain that it was a woman.

He savoured it, relishing it like sips of a cordial with an irresistible aroma, and anticipating the joy of discovery.

He opened his eyes wide and then, since the heart understands what the eyes only later perceive, he realized he already knew who the musician was.

Before him, blindingly beautiful, was Lucrezia.

Her slim brown hands barely touched the strings of the lute she held in her lap, and her head was bent slightly over the instrument, not so much because she needed to study the strings but rather because she seemed as lost in that melody as he was.

Abandoned to the music, her cinnamon-coloured skin seemed to blaze with pure sensuality and the irises of her dreamy black eyes were lit with flashes of lightning.

Lorenzo had never suspected this talent of Lucrezia's, who sat, passionate and beautiful, in the centre of the room cloaked in fiery flame-red velvet. He was almost blinded by her, while his mother once again glared with anger and fear at this latest affront, this time in her own home.

In spite of his promises and oaths, Lorenzo could not repress his admiration for what he had just heard. And evidently neither could the guests, who, as soon as the music ceased, exploded in thunderous and sincere applause.

In any case, her talent was as undeniable as it was awkward: Lorenzo might be about to take a wife, but what he had heard could in no way be ignored.

At first he wasn't even able to applaud. It seemed disrespectful of what he had heard. He just stood there staring at her in silence. For a moment, he clearly sensed his soul touching hers. He felt a covenant between them that meant there was no need for him to speak.

Ignoring the enthusiastic applause of the others, he shared his silence with her and simply stood there looking at her.

But suddenly he felt that something was compromising that bond, like an invisible crack in a sheet of glass that gradually spreads until it suddenly shatters.

He looked around him and realized that Francesco de' Pazzi was staring at him.

It was then that Lorenzo realized how foolish it was to expose Lucrezia to such danger.

He would protect her, he said to himself, even at the cost of losing her. But in his heart he feared it was already too late.

JUNE 1469

7

Clarice

The sun shone high in the sky, bathing in its golden light the roofs of the houses and the calm stone of the facades of the palaces and churches. It sparkled on the slabs which paved the streets and squares of Florence, lighting up Lorenzo Ghiberti's Gates of Paradise and the red dome of Santa Maria del Fiore.

Clarice had travelled to the city escorted by fifty knights. She had arrived on horseback like a virgin warrior, to emphasize the noble Roman line from which she descended, but also to challenge, on her home ground, this woman of whom there was so much talk: Lucrezia Donati. As though to underline that she would be taking Lorenzo for herself.

The murmurs of the people snaked between statues and tabernacles, architraves and epigraphs, seemingly waiting to see how that challenge would end.

Giuliano accompanied her, riding at her side. Along the way from Santa Maria del Fiore to the Palazzo Medici in Via Larga, all was a succession of colourful carts, decorated tables and ensigns and banners bearing the Medici coat of arms: the red balls on a golden background.

That carnival of colours and shapes was a show of splendour and strength – displaying how Lorenzo had inherited the glory of his grandfather Cosimo and his father Piero, who was now tired and ill.

As soon as he saw Clarice, he noticed how beautiful she was: her long hair was the colour of ancient gold, her deep green eyes were powerfully seductive and her lips were like corals blossoming in the waves of the sea. She wore a light dress that left her shoulders uncovered, like Diana when hunting.

His mother had chosen well, thought Lorenzo.

Yet, despite the grace of her figure and the pride in her face, she seemed cold and distant, imprisoned in her role. Just like him. He sensed a profound and ineluctable sadness in her. Perhaps it was this feeling of being obliged to perform which was most troubling – it exacerbated an inner conflict that was nourished day after day by the tension between reason and instinct, convention and freedom.

The procession reached the courtyard of the palazzo and the servants rushed to help Clarice dismount but, almost disdainfully, she pre-empted them and climbed down by herself. The nobles and guests who would be taking part in the feast arranged themselves around her to welcome her, and not a few of them scrutinized her to try and assess the woman's temper.

Others cast looks at Lucrezia Donati, who wore an elegant gown of an intense light blue with a deep neckline and braided sleeves studded with precious stones to enhance her tawny complexion. She could not moderate the fury in her gaze, and many were amused by her reaction.

Lorenzo knelt in front of Clarice, whom Lucrezia Tornabuoni, his mother, had already led to him, and took her hands in his.

'I have waited for you for a long time, my lady. Finally you have come to me. I am delighted to see that you have had a good journey and that your beauty is even greater than I had expected. For this, I am doubly grateful to my brother for having watched over you so effectively,' he said, gesturing to Giuliano. He felt as though he were playing a part, reciting a monologue written by a court jester who was amusing himself by damning him forever. But then he remembered the look on Francesco de' Pazzi's face and all his regrets instantly disappeared. He had to think of Lucrezia and guard against exposing her to danger and to the dark plots of his enemies. He could not allow that.

Clarice invited him to rise and she held his hands in hers.

'My beloved Lorenzo, I will confess that when I left Rome I feared the unknown. I had never been to Florence, but now I have seen her incredible beauty. Your mother was right once again. Giuliano has been magnificent and I am happy to finally hold your strong hands in mine. Before me I see an authoritative, handsome man, and it gives me infinite joy to see our families united.'

Lorenzo kissed her hands while his father descended from the great staircase, unsteady on his feet but with a spirited gaze full of wise determination.

He was clad in a purple doublet and pantaloons, and his face was tired, but his lively eyes flickered like those of a hawk across the large gathering of guests who crowded the courtyard.

Clarice and Lorenzo waited for Piero at the foot of the stairs, and when he arrived, he embraced his future daughter-in-law. More than one of the onlookers smirked: Piero must be particularly fond of this girl, since she had brought with her a dowry of six thousand florins, refilling in a instant the embattled coffers of the Medici which, thanks to him, were now half-empty, even though Cosimo had left the family drowning in gold.

And furthermore, the marriage also protected him from dangerous enemies who only seemed to have been deterred from acting by the fact that Pope Paul II remained on his side.

But how long would Piero continue to enjoy such support? Rumours abounded that the pontiff was not in good health and that the opponents of the Medici were sharpening their knives in preparation for the moment conditions became more favourable.

He was certainly no friend of the Archbishop of Florence, who had been forced to make the best of a bad lot, nor of the Pazzi and the Pitti, who were only counting the days until they could find some way to have the Medici thrown out of the city.

But this new alliance with the Orsinis closed the ranks and allowed Piero and Lorenzo to look to the future with confidence. Lucrezia Tornabuoni's masterstroke had been achieved thanks to her brother, the bank's steward in Rome who was well connected with the local nobility.

It was this that was on everyone's minds, but as Piero smilingly embraced Clarice like the most precious of women, he couldn't help shooting his son a warning look.

Lucrezia Donati would have to accept the situation. Too much depended on this union.

Lorenzo noticed the shadow in his father's eyes and understood.

His eyes met Lucrezia's, which burned with resentment and anger. They looked at each other for a moment, but it was like not seeing her at all.

Her words came back to him.

Was that all it had taken for him to change his mind? Had it only taken a few seconds for him to bend to the needs of the state?

No, truly!

He looked back at her, but now she refused to meet his gaze.

Patience, he thought. He certainly couldn't blame her. One day she would understand: what mattered was not making her a target.

He must keep that in mind.

He returned his gaze to Clarice, took her by the hand and followed his parents as they set off towards the gardens. The guests followed them to the loggias around the green-paved courtyard, where magnificent tables lain with refined foods and delicious wines awaited them.

Laura looked at herself in the mirror.

The years had passed for her too, and they had not been kind. Although she was still a beautiful woman, her skin was not as smooth and supple as it once was, and her beautiful long black hair was streaked with white.

Her thirst for revenge, however, remained the same – indeed, it had become even more intense.

And that was why she had raised her son to hate the Medici.

She had never been able to forget the one man who had loved her: Reinhardt Schwartz. And the Medici had deprived her even of him. They had killed him, and she had never forgiven them for it.

Then she had met a minor lord and had become his favourite, and he had given her a son: Ludovico.

Who stood before her now.

He was back from one of his trips to weave alliances into a deadly conspiracy against the most powerful family in Florence and its champion: Lorenzo.

Thanks to the affections of Filippo Maria Visconti, Laura had succeeded over the years in earning herself a title and a small fief and for some time now had been the lady of Norcia, where she dwelled as mistress of those lands.

'Well, my love,' she said, looking at Ludovico, 'what do you think of Girolamo Riario?'

'Actually, Mother, I think the man hates the Medici more than you do, if that is possible. His hatred seems to be rooted in envy and a desire for personal affirmation. I can't tell if he is an astute man, though my instinct would be that he is not, as his solutions are sometimes clumsy. But he is certainly ready to accept advice and form alliances.'

'Just as I imagined, my son. Girolamo is a powerful man and, above all, is the nephew of a cardinal who many say will be the next Pope. For this reason you must become one of his acolytes so you can be at the side of one who, sooner or later, will surely be the greatest antagonist of the Medici. If you advise him well, he will be grateful and will allow you to obtain the position in the world that you deserve. After all, you have no other choice: being a child of minor nobles is almost worse than being a child of the plebeians, because, in a sense, we are permitted to see the glow of power in the distance but can never touch it. Under Riario's wing, you would be able to elude such barriers of class and make your way to the top of society, I am sure of it. A long time ago, I knew such misery and deprivation as you cannot imagine, and there is nothing more horrible. That is not what I want for my son.'

'You are my light, Mother – my beacon in the night. Your love comforts and supports me, and I will of course follow your advice. As you know, Girolamo asked me a few months ago to question the Archbishop of Florence, Giovanni de' Diotisalvi Neroni, because if there is anyone willing to fight the Medici it is he.'

Impatient to learn the details of that meeting, Laura raised an eyebrow. 'So?'

'It's soon told: after the Neroni and the Pitti failed, it seems that it is now the Pazzi who most ardently desire the downfall of the Medici. Francesco is certainly the most suitable of them – he has a fiery temperament and is prone to anger, and he possesses the qualities needed to pull the strings of a conspiracy. But it still feels premature: on the one hand, according to the archbishop, the suspicions that Soderini and Neroni's conspiracy against Piero de' Medici raised are still alive, and therefore that diabolical family has its eyes wide open and its ears bent to hear the smallest sound; and on the other, the Pazzi do not yet seem so powerful that they can seriously trouble the lords of Florence.'

'That is a pity, because they are vulnerable at the moment: Piero is devoured by gout and Lorenzo is simply a youth with strong appetites. This would be the perfect time.'

'I am simply telling you what the Archbishop of Florence believes. It is true that, precisely because they are in difficulty, the Medici are locked up in that fortress-like palazzo of theirs. Wherever Lorenzo goes, he is surrounded by guards. Their mother, Lucrezia Tornabuoni, has forged an alliance with the Orsini, thanks to Lorenzo's marriage to Clarice.'

'That damn viper!' spat Laura, a flash of anger lighting up her still-beautiful face.

'I love you as I will never love any other woman,' said Ludovico suddenly. Her anger had almost seemed to ignite in him a passion unsuitable for a child. 'You are beautiful.'

'Don't talk nonsense,' she said bitterly. 'You should have seen me years ago when I was in the service of Rinaldo degli Albizzi, or later, when I had become a tarot reader for Filippo Maria Visconti, the Duke of Milan. I was truly beautiful then.'

'I find your beauty extraordinary – irresistible,' insisted Ludovico, and as he spoke his eyes glowed with an admiration which had about it something dark and perverse. Ludovico adored his mother, and obeyed her in all things. Something about her deranged his senses yet at the same time shaped his will to the extent that he would protect, defend and even avenge her if necessary: his dedication to her knew no limits. Laura knew it and in the face of her son's devotion, could not help indulging her licentious affection. She stroked his cheek, then took his hands in hers and raised them to her lips, kissing them in a way that was decidedly unmaternal.

'You are my champion, Ludovico. Never disappoint me. Swear it.'

'I will do anything for you, my mother. Order it and I will obey you, whatever you tell me to do.'

'Then give your mother a kiss.'

Ludovico approached her and placed his mouth against her red lips. Laura's tongue flickered lewdly against his.

He felt her fingernails on his chest, her soft tongue on his nipples and then even further down.

His penis hardened until it hurt.

'Take me now,' she whispered in his ear, 'I want you inside me.'

8

The Portrait

For some time now she had been feeling neglected. She had expected that – in fact it was exactly what she had predicted to her incredulous lover – but the arrival of Clarice had reduced the opportunities for her to meet with Lorenzo in a way she hadn't imagined.

So when he had decided to commission Leonardo to paint her portrait, Lucrezia had welcomed the attention with pleasure. She knew how friendly Lorenzo was with the young artist.

The day had finally come and Leonardo had arrived at her home. He was a young man with his own peculiar beauty and a lively and intelligent gaze: his long blond hair and slim beard framed a face with elegant but delicate features which were of almost feminine, or even angelic, refinement.

The way he spoke was fascinating and Lucrezia was equally enchanted by his eyes, which exercised upon their interlocutor a sort of tacit magic that, combined with his persuasive voice, left her hanging on his every word.

'Dress in blue,' Lorenzo had told her, knowing how Leonardo loved that colour and that at the same time it brought out Lucrezia's sultry, wild beauty.

She had thus presented herself in a gown the colour of the sky which made Leonardo's eyes sparkle.

The day was bright and clear. He had asked her if she would go over to one of the windows in the largest salon of her house.

They found themselves in a medium-sized space. Lucrezia was the daughter of minor nobility and her house could not compete with those of the Florentine aristocracy, but the room was furnished with good taste and, more importantly, was flooded with light thanks to the row of large windows.

Leonardo had wasted no time, rapidly preparing his painting materials and then setting to.

Lucrezia did not know how he would portray her but it was clear that his intention was to capture her crowned with light, almost as though the sun were a diadem on her jet-black hair.

Leonardo had spoken little, and now wasn't speaking at all. Lucrezia tried to keep her eyes focused where he had asked her to. She held her forehead high, her expression almost impudent, in an attempt to display her 'haughty and dazzling beauty', as he had termed it. Lucrezia could not hold back a smile. She was not a woman who liked to boast of her beauty, but what lady would *not* have been delighted to receive the compliments of a young yet established artist like Leonardo?

And besides, those words meant more to her than a compliment. When Leonardo spoke, his words were as direct and clear as an edict.

Leonardo was a bright but elusive young man who defied categorization: airy and other-worldly, and happy to observe life. In his eyes, a desire for personal success was no more than a distasteful charade, capable only of sullying the perfection of a reality that deserved to be contemplated, not bent to the foolish ambitions of man.

And yet, perhaps precisely for this reason, he succeeded in doing what others thought impossible. Lorenzo had often lauded his achievements in architecture and engineering, the extraordinary solutions he adopted in the construction of his first flying machines – was it actually possible for man to fly? – or his defensive weapons.

Leonardo looked at her furtively. She truly was a woman of rare beauty.

But it wasn't just that which struck him about her.

He saw in her an indomitable spirit, a stateliness that could not be conferred by titles or bloodline but only by nature, which in her was proud and wild. Precisely for this reason, and with the assistance of the blue of that simple gown, he intended to play upon that contrast of opposing elements. The light that flooded the room would allow him to create a harmony of opposites between reason and sentiment.

He smiled at the idea.

He was happy with what was emerging from the canvas.

He had always loved working with greens and blues, but he also adored dark colours and her bright complexion with its warm, enveloping tone.

Fire and ice, light and shadow: he would work that dualism without holding back. His brush flew across the canvas in an attempt to capture the spirit of the woman and portray it as authentically as possible. There was something special about her, he sensed – a peculiar fury unrestrained by docility or convention. And he himself had little time for either.

When he looked at her, so beautiful and haughty, it struck him how clever Lorenzo had been to insist that they meet. As if Lorenzo was, after all, able to look into people's souls.

He had underestimated Lorenzo, he thought: in future, he would give him more credit. Not that he didn't hold him in esteem – he owed the man everything: his fortunes and the commissions he was receiving were entirely the result of Lorenzo's generosity and intelligence. Lorenzo was too sure of himself, and that was a weakness. He knew he was no ordinary person, but made every effort not to be arrogant. Even so, his confidence in himself sometimes misled him, making him think that the people he dealt with were always and only engaged in politics. In this, Lorenzo was certainly skilled, but his talent came from his ability to grasp the deepest essence of a human soul.

As Lucrezia's portrait began to take shape, though, Leonardo couldn't hide from himself a touch of disquiet.

Just how far would a man with such gifts be willing to go?

DECEMBER 1469

9

The Medici Legacy

Winter was coming. It almost seemed that autumn had decided not to show its face that year, so cold and sharp had it been. It was as if, by denying the year a mild season, even nature itself wanted to participate in the pain that racked Lorenzo over the death of his father Piero.

The Palazzo Medici was empty and cold, and it seemed that everything had declined after the departure of the patriarch: the colours of the paintings were less bright, the lights no longer sparkled, the garden was bare and sad, and snow had fallen, covering all their souls with a layer of ice.

Lorenzo was sitting in front of the fireplace. The flames burned but the room was gelid. For the last few days he had not been able to eat. The pain had thrown the family into despair, and each of them had chosen to face their suffering in solitude.

Lucrezia, his mother, had closed herself up in her rooms and had not left them for at least three days, until in the end Lorenzo had urged the servants to check on her, fearing she might commit some madness.

Giuliano had taken refuge in books, and Clarice in prayer.

His grandmother, Contessina, had retired to Careggi, where she took long walks, thinking about her lost son.

The pain had divided them and each of them was trying to put together the pieces of their life without Piero.

His father had left a huge void. He had been loved by all, because he was a good and intelligent man, a cultured lover of art and a generous patron. In the years he had governed, not all citizens had been on his side, but he had in any case managed to maintain the hegemony of the Medici in Florence.

But now the power vacuum required Lorenzo to assume responsibility.

He had known this day would come. Until this moment he had benefited from the advantages of being considered lord of Florence without actually *being* it. It was a promise, a wish, something that existed on a purely theoretical level but not in reality. But now, what frightened him was not only realizing that the day had arrived, but also that he had to live up to expectations.

Would he be able to fulfil the task that was being laid out for him?

How would he manage without the benevolent guidance of his father who, with his indulgence and kindness, had taught him so much? Lorenzo knew how extraordinary and unique his example had been. He owed everything he was to him. And to his mother, of course – but now Piero was gone and the mere fact of not hearing his voice, resolute, but still lively and full of enthusiasm, was crushing.

He looked into the heart of the blood-red flames that failed to heat the room. Would he too be like that? Inadequate? And above all, was this really what he wanted for himself and his future? To become the lord of Florence and give up everything else? He loved Lucrezia Donati so much and knew that deep down in his heart what he really wanted was to run away with her. That would mean dishonouring the memory of his father and his whole family. The idea was pure madness, a stupid dream which he indulged because he wanted to delude himself, at least in his mind, that he was still a free man.

And had he not promised himself to protect Lucrezia? Sworn to himself that he wouldn't try to see her again, even though it was a daily torment?

It was when the servants announced that there were visitors to see him that he realized that even the last shreds of his dream were about to be torn apart for ever.

Shortly afterwards, Gentile de' Becchi and Antonio di Puccio Pucci were led into the room. Both had been close friends of Piero and allies of the Medici. Gentile had been Lorenzo's tutor and adviser, while Antonio was the son of Puccio Pucci, who had been with his grandfather Cosimo when, together with his brother Lorenzo, he had been exiled first to Padua and then to Venice.

Gentile was as elegant as ever: he wore a dark brown doublet and a grand cloak of the same colour, closed by a magnificent diamond brooch. On his head he wore a green velvet hat. Antonio was dressed more soberly, entirely in pearl grey.

Gentile knew how much Lorenzo was suffering, but had no intention of failing in his task.

'My dear, beloved Lorenzo,' he said, 'I know how vast the loss you have suffered is, and I fully understand your state of mind – I can see how sad and full of bitterness you are.'

'You cannot know how much,' the young Medici replied.

'But that said,' replied Becchi, 'everyone can see how much Florence needs you, especially at this moment. And that's why I'm bringing you the petitions of the highest lords of Florence – allies of yourself and your father, and of Messer Cosimo before him – so that you may claim what is yours: nothing more and nothing less than the leadership of the Medici and the government of Florence.'

Gentile de' Becchi hadn't wasted any time in broaching the issue.

'Yes, my lord, that is what everyone in Florence expects,' echoed Antonio Pucci. 'Although it may seem premature and indelicate, we are here today to ask you to accept the honours that were your father's and your grandfather's before him because, whether you desire it or not, you *are* Florence.'

Lorenzo remained silent, his hands clasped and his eyes staring at the hearth.

So the moment had come, then. He was being asked to put everything aside and to dedicate himself to the city, to power, to politics.

He had known in his heart that it would end that way – his mother had warned him of it well before his wedding to Clarice and, in a sense, it was the task for which he had been bred: a mission that had already been entrusted to him years earlier. But that didn't make it any less difficult.

He wasn't certain that he wanted to accept, wanted to surrender all his freedom, because once he took that path he knew he could never go back: it would change him forever.

Was he willing to sup from that goblet? He wasn't at all sure that he was.

He tried to express his doubts as best he could.

'My dear friends,' he said, 'you speak to me of guidance and government and call me "sir", and that

67

makes me look for my father's face in the mirror. Are you not perhaps more suited to such a task? Wiser, more experienced in statecraft than I am? I'm only twenty years old. I understand why you're here, but do you think these objections of mine so very strange? Be honest, I beg you.'

Gentile de' Becchi looked at him benevolently.

'My dear boy, we understand your reservations, which are valid and sensible. What? you think. Your father just gone and here we are already asking you to lead your house? What men worthy of the name would be so cynical and indifferent to others' feelings as to make such a proposal at a time like this? We understand your doubts perfectly. However, we must remind you that we're in a volatile situation. The most powerful families in the city – the Pitti, the Strozzi, the Pazzi, the Bardi, the Capponi and the Guidi, to name just a few! – have always been at one another's throats, yet despite such rivalries, one of these families managed to rise to the top, forging through skill and good governance a unity which has endured: that family was the Medici. More than thirty years ago, they, and only they, managed to do the impossible. I do not deny that there have been ups and down, but your house was the only one able to restore order to Florence. And so, no matter how difficult what we're asking you is going to be, there is no one else in the city we can turn to.'

Lorenzo sighed. 'You're very eloquent, Gentile. I knew of your skill as an orator and it is as charming as it is effective. And yet I ask myself if it is not soon – if we couldn't wait a little longer.'

Becchi looked at him fondly. His trust in Lorenzo was unshakable, but so was his determination, and precisely for that reason he would never give up. His kind eyes harboured an unbending resolve.

'And that's exactly what must not happen,' he said. 'We cannot allow our enemies to take advantage of this moment, otherwise we might as well give up immediately. We can't wait, my boy. It is precisely now that we must show our strength. Your opponents are ours too, and it must be made clear to them that the death of Piero does not mean the end of the Medici and their hegemony. But to do that you need to accept this task now, and not in a week, a month or a year. Each day that passes will be mistaken for hesitation – and hesitation for weakness. As great as your father's political legacy is, I must tell you that the situation is not as favourable to us as it was in the time of your grandfather Cosimo.'

Lorenzo reflected.

He knew that he could not escape the fate which had already been decided for him. He had no choice, however much he might try to convince himself of the contrary. He stood up and crossed the hall in great strides. The lamps illuminated the large, beautifully furnished space:

the beautiful armchairs lined with velvet, the wonderful paintings by Paolo Uccello depicting the battle of San Romano and to which Lorenzo was so attached that he was considering having them hung in his own rooms, the tables in precious wood, finely carved and decorated.

The light of the candles made the silverware sparkle and its reflections glinted in the large windows that gave on to Via Larga.

Patiently, trustingly, Gentile de' Becchi and Antonio Pucci were awaiting a sign. Lorenzo was deeply struck by the fact: it was strange, though certainly not unpleasant, to see how loyal these men were. Just for a moment he felt clearly the pleasant flattery of power. He knew that he could have considered the question for a whole day, and that Becchi and Pucci would still have waited for his answer.

He was ashamed of the pettiness of the thought, and yet was not entirely indifferent to it. It was as though there were something in him that was happy to accept the compromises and rules of politics founded on power and money.

Eventually he looked back at them.

'Very well,' he said. 'I will be the man you want me to be. But remember from this moment on that if I must lead you, then I will not be like my father or my grandfather before him. I will be a leader, but in my own way: take it or leave it.'

This time, it was Antonio Pucci who spoke.

'It was exactly what we hoped to hear you say,' he answered.

'That may be, my friend,' answered Lorenzo, 'but let me tell you now that one day we will perhaps regret it.'

And as he said those words, Lorenzo felt he had signed his own life sentence.

APRIL 1470

10

The Question of Power

He remembered the words of his father, and of his grandfather before him. The aim of the death penalty was not to punish criminals. Justice had a twofold function: on the one hand, the sentence itself helped legitimize contested power, while on the other an eventual reduction of the sentence could be used to foster support.

Power was a careful balancing of tools like these which had to be used carefully, without going too far in one direction or the other. The real talent lay in distinguishing the exact moment in which a sentence or pardon should be applied, and a true man of power would not allow himself to hesitate.

Such hesitation meant exposing one's flanks to revolts and conspiracies, a lesson Piero had learned all too well.

Therefore Lorenzo could not allow himself exceptions, unless he wanted to lose his dominion over the city before it had even begun.

And Bernardo Nardi certainly deserved no pardon. None at all, given that only a few days before he had entered Prato at the head of a group of armed men and had taken up office in the Palazzo del Comune, occupying it by force and taking the Podestà, Cesare Petrucci, prisoner.

That action had been all the more despicable because it had been conducted without honour or decency and with the sole purpose of inciting hatred against Florence, since it was the first step towards challenging the city by setting it against one of its vassal towns. Except that Bernardo had not foreseen that, far from granting him their support, the many Florentines who had gone to live in Prato would instead fight him strenuously. And so Giorgio Ginori had put himself in charge of a handful of men of honour and had routed him and his louts and delivered the rebel into the hands of Lorenzo and of Florence.

There could be no mercy for a man like Bernardo Nardi.

To grant it would be like admitting weakness and allowing all and sundry to flout Florentine authority as they pleased.

And that was not possible.

Lorenzo was not happy about having to pass a death sentence, but he knew that the people had been demanding it for days. Ever since Bernardo had been taken to the prisons of the Palazzo del Podestà.

And now he could no longer put off the moment.

Nor could he avoid being present for it. There was no excuse. And so here he was.

At the centre of the courtyard surrounded by porticoes, whose vaults seemed to multiply the horror which was about to take place, the gallows had been erected. Six loops hung wearily from the beam and at the centre of the platform, right in the middle of as many stools, a black wooden block had been placed.

Clad in a black hood and a tunic of the same colour dotted with steel studs, and brown boots, dirty with mud, that reached up to his knees, the executioner looked at the crowd that filled the courtyard around him. He was leaning on the long handle of the axe. The blade, wide and sharp, reflected the pale flashes of sunlight that filtered through the veil of clouds.

From the balcony, Lorenzo looked down at the hellish scene. Along with the others from the criminal magistrature of the Eight of Guard, he was waiting for the prisoner to be brought.

The common people, the middle classes and even the nobles murmured expectantly, and their subdued muttering sounded like the threatening rumble of a pot in which the devil was simmering some unholy stew.

It was a horrible yet all-too-real vision of what the administration of power meant. If he wasn't ready to face a test like this, how could he expect to lead a city like Florence?

He shook his head, as though to clear his mind.

To tell the truth, he actually felt less disturbed by it than he would have been willing to admit. After all, Bernardo had been the architect of his own destiny and had only himself to blame. And Lorenzo had to take advantage of this opportunity to consolidate his power. He had no intention of turning the Republic into something different – he would never have turned it openly into a seigniory – but everyone had to know that there was one man alone who made the decisions.

Naturally, he had maintained the institutions, just as his grandfather and father had done, but it would have been deeply hypocritical to claim that the political decisions they took were not influenced by his men and by those loyal to his party.

He intended to continue to behave discreetly, just as both Cosimo and Piero had done, but only as concerned outward appearance. Because within himself he felt the fire of an ambition that consumed him and which, if properly governed, might be just the weapon that would allow him to triumph over his enemies.

He had no intention of extinguishing the flames of that ardour – on the contrary, he planned to feed them.

He realized, therefore, that that initial feeling of confusion was the result of the choice he was about to make and of the path that, from that moment on, he would take.

He swore to himself that he would never be afraid and would never shirk his responsibilities, and that he would face the tasks which life held in store for him to increase the prestige, honour and supremacy of his family.

And thus resolved upon a line of conduct, he raised his arm to motion for the guards to lead Bernardo out.

11

Hierarchies

Clarice was furious. Since she had entered this house she had been subjected to every kind of indignity and humiliation. Primary among them the fact that her husband loved another woman, for whom he had nurtured a burning passion before she even arrived in Florence.

Lorenzo had done nothing to disguise his feelings. Not that they prevented him from fulfilling his duties as a husband, but his attentions towards Lucrezia had proved unbearable to Clarice. Day by day, that slow torture was consuming her.

Especially because she had no idea how to fight it.

Weeping, she looked into the mirror of her dressing table and felt her nails scratching at its wooden surface. Anger filled her like poison filling a cup. And the more the anger grew in her, the more she felt the bitterness caused by her impotence almost overwhelming her. She wanted to tear off the beautiful dress. Or slash her face. And it wasn't the first time.

She had covered her arms with cuts as she tried to suppress the frustrations that devoured her during the day. In her need to expiate her ineptitude, her inability to keep her man bound to her, she had even tried to bury herself in prayer – and succeeded. But despite all the lies she insisted on telling herself, none of those occupations had achieved the desired effect.

She could have taken a lover, of course, but others did not interest her. She wanted Lorenzo, but could not satisfy him. Not as she would have liked. Not as she needed.

And even recently, when he had perhaps been seeing Lucrezia less often, he had not stopped writing and thinking about her. Maria, her favourite lady-in-waiting, had been spying on him and stealing information for Clarice, stoking inside her the fire which deprived her of sleep and life.

She had therefore decided to confront her mother-in-law Lucrezia Tornabuoni, because she wanted to make clear to her how unacceptable that situation was. She was an Orsini and could not tolerate such an affront, and if it proved necessary to use her name, she would not hesitate to do so.

After all, these Medici flaunting all their pomp and power were nothing more than upstarts – wool merchants from Mugello who had made a fortune with their bank but who certainly could not boast a noble and ancient lineage.

She stood up, left her chamber and went to Lucrezia's apartments.

She hadn't had her arrival announced – she was hoping to find her unprepared. Or at least taken off guard.

When her mother-in-law brought her into the parlour which served as an antechamber, holding a lamp whose faint, reddish light reflected off the walls, Clarice was ready to pour out of all of the resentment and anger she had been repressing for months.

And she did. She didn't even sit down, but remained standing as she poured out all that she had to say.

'I am tired, my lady. Tired of putting up with it. Of being treated like a woman without spirit or passion. I did not ask for this marriage and, even if my opinion is worthless, I want you to know that I do not intend to put up with your son's behaviour, which dishonours and humiliates me every day, and is completely inappropriate, if I may say so, in one who is in all respects the lord of Florence.'

In the feeble light of the lamp, Clarice had the distinct feeling that her mother-in-law was smiling. She hoped she was wrong. Lucrezia sat down. She did not open the curtains to let the soft light of the afternoon filter through but left the two of them in shadow, allowing the little lamp to illuminate her ambiguous gaze.

After sitting in silence for a long time, she finally answered.

'My dear, I have listened to your words. In what way, if I may ask, does Lorenzo disrespect you? For, in spite of the talk, as far as I am aware he has never betrayed you. If you're referring to the gossip around Florence, I say to you that you'll simply have to get used to it, since there is no woman who is more envied than you at this time, I can guarantee you that.'

But her words, kindly and attempting to calm the waters – indeed, to deny the evidence – only had the effect of making Clarice's voice even more shrill.

'If you think that will suffice to placate my anger, perhaps you fail to grasp who it is that stands before you. Gossip, you say? Do you not see how many poems Lorenzo dedicates to that slut? And of what *kind*? She who, moreover, is not even a noble! My ladies-in-waiting have told me that even before the wedding, Lorenzo had eyes only for Lucrezia Donati! He even dedicated his victory in the tournament at Braccio Martello's wedding to her! And I am supposed to endure—'

'What my son did before your marriage is none of your concern,' Lucrezia interrupted abruptly. 'I asked you for proof of his infidelity and you have given me none. And even if he lacks in respect, which I do not believe that he does, I would ask you to be careful of the accusations you make against him. You are in Florence,

Clarice, and you are loved and respected. Perhaps you could content yourself with the thousand opportunities this life offers you, instead of complaining about ghosts and gossip.'

Clarice was speechless. Despite all that she had promised herself she would say, Lucrezia's indifference and hardness had left her feeling hollow, disappointed and shocked.

Was it just her imaginings, then?

Was she nothing but a deluded ingrate?

For a moment, it seemed to her she had lost everything she believed in. And Lucrezia wasted no time in taking advantage of her insecurities.

'I would not want to have to remind you that in this family there is, one might say, a sort of hierarchy. Your role was clearly defined and agreed upon with your father long ago. Entering our family as Lorenzo's wife, it is clear that you became a Medici. Now, I do not wish to be harsh, but there is something rather peculiar about you coming to my rooms to tell me about your fantasies. Worse still, it is completely lacking in respect for Contessina, my mother-in-law, because your attitude risks relegating her, in a manner which is totally unjustified, to the position of a woman of little importance.'

Things were going in the worst possible way. Clarice was the injured party, and if her urgency had been mistaken for rudeness, well, she would not allow herself to be misunderstood.

'Never, even for a moment, did I mean to be disrespectful towards your mother-in-law. I'm here because I have been shamed and can endure it no more. If it is necessary that Contessina be informed of this—'

But once again Lucrezia Tornabuoni interrupted her.

'I understand the reason for your visit. What I can tell you, my sweet daughter-in-law, is that from what I have heard there is no reason to accuse my son. Nor to disturb Contessina: on that, I agree with you. My words were only intended to make you understand this family's hierarchy. The sooner you realize that you are on the lowest rung of the ladder, the better it will be for you.'

Clarice hoped that she had misheard, but realized that she had not. Lucrezia continued.

'If I remember correctly, our beloved Gentile de' Becchi gave you that beautiful book of prayers with a dark cover, decorated in silver and crystal, and entirely written in gold letters on a blue background. Is that not so?' Naturally, Lucrezia did not wait for an answer. 'What I therefore recommend, my darling daughter-in-law, is that you concentrate on prayer and upon the primary task which has been entrusted to you: that of producing children. And, since it does not seem to me that Lorenzo fails to visit you, let alone to fulfil his duties, I suggest that you think of yours, which consist first of all of supplying him with heirs.'

Clarice could not believe her ears, but at this point she was no longer able to retaliate. She had convinced herself that she could take Lucrezia Tornabuoni by surprise, but instead it had been Lucrezia who had stunned *her*, wounding her without hesitation or empathy.

A hierarchy, then!

And she was only the bottom rung of the ladder!

From that day on she would be buried alive, she realized. Called upon to provide the children who had not yet arrived like some bitch or brood mare.

'And now, please go,' said her mother-in-law, dismissing her and, without waiting for a reply, withdrawing to her chambers and closing the doors behind her.

Clarice remained where she was.

Even more bitterly than before, her tears began to fall.

12

Bernardo Nardi

Six men hung from the gallows like rotten fruit from a tree.

Now that their death spasms were over, their faces were black and rigid and their tattered garments hung like ghostly cloaks.

The people crowding the courtyard around the corpses gave deafening cries of joy, because the executions clearly demonstrated Florence's strength. It was as if those hangings could silence those who would endanger the delicate balance in which they knew they lived – like tightrope walkers.

Because of the future, the *real* future, made up of plans and hopes and dreams, they had no certainty at all.

Bernardo stared wide-eyed at the scene, an incredulous light glinting in his eyes as though he could not actually believe what was about to happen.

Lorenzo had not hesitated. He had to nip these attempts to overthrow the order in the bud, before it was too late.

He looked at the six hanged men staring at him with eyes as dull as marionettes in some macabre dance.

Without further delay, he nodded his head, and from under his hood, the executioner nodded back. Bernardo's hands were tied behind his back, the knotted rope cutting into the skin of his wrists, and his head placed on the block like a piece of wood ready to be split open.

The executioner raised the huge axe.

The sun broke through the clouds and the blade glinted ominously in the sunlight.

It was truly a lovely day to die.

A rumble came now from the crowd, seemingly keen to prevent any last-minute attack of conscience. In that subdued roar, they found the courage to feel that they were all brothers, and as such, demanded – in an increasingly threatening way – the blood of the man who had dared to endanger the whole community.

It was, after all, a ritual: a demonstration, a compelling, bloody spectacle whose power lay in its symbolic value.

Crows flew over to the gallows from which the dead men hung and perched upon it, their croaking litany announcing the advent of death.

Bernardo wept.

Another moment, and then the axe fell.

It hissed through the air and came down on Bernard's neck. Severed from his body, his head gave a dry thud as it hit the wooden planks, then rolled forward, bouncing twice before coming to a halt.

Scarlet blood gushed out as though from a spring while, to the applause of the people, Lorenzo stood up.

The other magistrates followed suit.

The Palazzo del Podestà resounded with shouts and cries cursing Bernardo Nardi's name. And in that moment Lorenzo understood the power of fear and capital punishment. He had chosen not to grant the traitor the honour of decapitation with a sword, for there had been no glory in the way that this enemy of Florence had attempted to rebel against them.

Now that he had seen it for himself, he realized that his decision had been a wise one.

He had taken everything from the man, even those shreds of dignity that a knight's blade would have given him. The axe was barbaric and ruthless. There was no nobility in it, only fury and violence, and Bernardo had died in the same way that an animal or a tree might have.

The crowd below had understood this perfectly, and now it was roaring its approval.

From his balcony, Lorenzo stared at his people. Even though that gesture had been necessary, something in the innermost corner of his heart had been corrupted. He only felt it a moment, nothing more than a twinge, the glimmer of a sensation. He could not have described it, but it was as though the violence and ardour had ignited a small flame that, if fed, could devour him.

And although the feeling was soon drowned out by the triumphant cries of the crowd, yet it did not abandon him.

Lorenzo pushed the tiny tongue of flame back into the corner from which, for a moment, it had seemed to expand and spread. He was convinced that he would be able to keep it at bay – that he would never feel satisfaction or, worse still, pleasure at that sense of revenge that had peered out from the recesses of his soul.

He waved to the men and women who thronged the courtyard and heard them loudly shout their support.

'Medici! Medici! Medici!' they roared, underlining that it had been Lorenzo rather than the Eight of Guard who had decided upon the punishment for Bernardo Nardi's arrogance. None of them had any doubt of it. The other magistrates looked at Lorenzo with a mixture of fear and envy, and in more than one of them he sensed the germination of the seed of anger and acrimony; a seed which was rapidly hidden behind a veil of opportunism. But he had noticed those feelings, which sprang up like weeds in the eyes of his fellow townsmen.

He let it go. It was certainly no surprise, and if he had to execute all those whom he suspected of treason, he would most likely have gone on cutting heads for a whole year.

He felt that he should say something.

While the roar of the crowd continued, he raised his hands and spoke to the people.

'My beloved fellow citizens,' he said, 'I know how much the execution today has freed our hearts from fear. Speaking on behalf of the College of the Eight of Guard, I can say that, despite its brutality, what you have just witnessed was necessary, or better, *proper* for restoring the peace and harmony which Florence seeks, and to guarantee the prosperity we feel we deserve. I more than any of you wanted to avoid what happened today! But it was not possible to tolerate the rebellion in Prato – if we had, then all the other vassal towns could have done the same. But we believe that it is in the union of Florence with its sister cities that the Republic realises its full potential. So go back home with happy hearts, because I guarantee you that with one act of justice today, we have avoided the many wars of tomorrow!'

Upon hearing his words, the Florentines exploded in an approving roar of catharsis that extinguished the last sparks of fear, confirming once again Lorenzo de' Medici as the city's champion.

And while the executioner picked up the head of Bernardo Nardi so that the guards might stick it on the tip of a pike, where it would serve as a warning to all those who even considered putting the safety of the Florentines at risk, Leonardo da Vinci, his face concealed by a long black hood, began to shake his head.

He was so saddened at the sight of that metamorphosis that he could barely believe it.

Yet something was changing in Lorenzo.

It wasn't simply the way he acted but also the way he spoke; lacking his sincerity of old, it concealed a kind of subtle ambiguity.

He hoped he was wrong, but he knew how all men, even the best of them, could change. And much had happened since the death of Piero de' Medici.

Florence had asked Lorenzo to become the man it needed.

And he was doing as she asked.

MAY 1471

13

The Golden Ball

For the whole night, Leonardo had observed the perfect copper ball, glowing with golden light, which stood under the high ceiling in the centre of the workshop.

Andrea, his teacher, had made it using sheets of copper he had gradually shaped, eventually assembling the six metal segments and rejecting the casting process that had already proven itself incapable of guaranteeing the desired result.

The challenge was enough to make your hands shake: it had proved too taxing for those who had preceded him, first among them Giovanni di Bartolomeo and Bartolomeo di Fruosino, who had created the wonderful copper 'button' which was to be the base upon which the ball should rest. Even they had given up trying to create the sphere after experiencing first-hand the ineffectiveness of casting.

Once the six different parts had been joined together, Andrea had covered the ball with a shower of gold dust.

Leonardo had worked hard to help his teacher, and he and Lorenzo di Credi, his good friend, had sweated to build parts of the winches that would be necessary to hoist it on to its housing at the top of the lantern of Santa Maria del Fiore. And that wasn't all: they had also checked the strength of the ropes and helped create other mysterious tools and bizarre machines to move and lift heavy weights.

It had been magnificent, and extremely rewarding.

Leonardo enjoyed learning the secrets of engineering almost more than he did grinding coloured powders, preparing glazes, mixing the components for the plaster and tracing out the faces in chalk.

For him, the workshop of Andrea del Verrocchio was a realm of wonders: he loved the place. The great hall with its forge, and then the bellows and anvil to work iron and bronze. The gigantic wooden scaffolding and trestles which were used to sculpt statues of colossal dimensions, much larger than the actual size of the models themselves. And during the day, a tempest of light poured in through the huge skylight in the ceiling.

Beyond that incredible workshop began the dark labyrinth from which opened off all the other smaller rooms, dedicated to frescoes and inlay and crowded with workbenches for carpentry. Then there were the stores of wax and plaster, that soft white powder which, when kneaded with warm water, became as malleable as clay, but once dried was harder than stone itself.

He felt his heart beating hard in his chest.

While the night had flowed past to make room for the pearly dawn, Leonardo had completed some drawings on sheets of parchment paper. They depicted several large pulleys which Andrea del Verrocchio had had built – on the basis of models by Filippo Brunelleschi, the extraordinary architect who had conceived the dome of Santa Maria del Fiore – to hoist the ball into position.

Leonardo had also jotted down calculations and descriptions.

Over the course of those days, not a few of Andrea's other pupils had spied on him with a touch of envy at his bizarre way of writing that went from right to left and contained many anagrams.

Leonardo wanted to leave his post as apprentice to someone else and he intended to do so as quickly as possible; it had been clear for some time now that he was no longer an apprentice.

The respect Lorenzo de' Medici felt for him had not gone unnoticed and, even if his comrades and his maestro were unaware that the lord of Florence had commissioned him to execute a lavishly paid assignment, his qualities were evident to all. Yet regardless of his recent successes, Leonardo continued to apply all his energies to learning as much as possible, watching as the new information unravelled itself for him in the air before his staring eyes. Then he had only to write them down, taking care to make them his own and maintaining the secrecy that was the basis of all success in art, just as in engineering and architecture.

He was amused to see how Lorenzo di Credi, as well as the older apprentices, were left open-mouthed by that magic he had invented. Writing back-to-front and mixing up a few words had been a good idea – and had even managed to irritate the most promising and expert students like Perugino and Botticelli.

He laughed; then returned his gaze to the giant ball.

The occasion was so important, and the expectations so high: Leonardo hoped everything would go perfectly. Andrea certainly deserved it, because his work had been extraordinary.

So when, early that morning, along with the other students, he followed his maestro to the square in the cart transporting the golden ball, he felt a powerful twinge of emotion in his heart.

A crowd had gathered to watch the miracle.

Andrea seemed confident. He had done the calculations necessary for hoisting the ball into position a thousand times, and had prepared the iron chains for the cross which, a few days later, would sit on top of the ball.

When they arrived, Leonardo climbed down from the cart and stood to one side. He had brought several sheets of parchment paper with him.

He stood there to watch.

'Do you think I'll remain silent while that woman tries to take you away from me?'

Clarice was furious.

And her fury made her beautiful.

Lorenzo had to admit it. Though slim she was shapely, with large, white breasts and flame-red hair, and her anger made her irresistible.

She was an intensely proud woman and could not accept being second choice. Over those two years, not only had she laid claim to her position, she had even stood up to his mother, who was certainly not a woman lacking in character. And her temper – fiery and almost authoritarian but not openly impudent – had not failed to please him.

In those two years, Clarice had proved herself a woman capable of personifying the very concept of contradiction. One moment she was passionate, a moment later coy, and her emotions alternated in an alchemy which was impossible to decipher. Lorenzo knew all too well that her mood swings were actually the result of his own attentions and shortcomings: Clarice was simply responding to his singular way of being her husband, when his heart actually belonged to one woman only – Lucrezia Donati. And she certainly had not failed to make heavy weather of it.

In every sense.

But it wasn't as if Lorenzo had actually been *ignoring* Clarice. In fact, his attentions towards her had even been meant to protect Lucrezia, given that the many duties he had to perform and the threats he received almost daily would certainly make her a target. And that was the last thing he wanted.

Because he loved her.

'I love only you, Clarice,' he confirmed hastily, though not without a flash of amusement in his eyes.

'Do you mock me, Lorenzo?'

'Not at all.'

'Your expression says otherwise.'

'It pains me to hear you say such a thing.'

'No more than it pains you to find out that they are serving chicken instead of wild boar for lunch,' said Clarice with a gesture of irritation.

'That's not true. In any case, what can I do to make you forgive me?'

Clarice raised an eyebrow.

'Are you serious?'

'Absolutely,' nodded Lorenzo.

'Swear to me you'll never see her again.'

'I cannot do that.'

'Ah! See? And what am I supposed to think after hearing an answer like that?'

Each time, Clarice pressed him with an insistence that occasionally bordered on anger. He realized that they couldn't go on like this. He had to reassure her.

'Don't misunderstand me, wife...' said Lorenzo, and as he spoke, he approached her and gently caressed her neck with the back of his hand. Clarice's eyes flashed and she stiffened, almost as though she were trying to make her flesh resist. 'What I mean is that Lucrezia Donati is still a noblewoman of this city and therefore it would be impossible for me to keep such a promise. Not inviting her to parties would only create pointless scandal.'

'You won't get out of it that easily,' Clarice replied icily. 'And in any case, she belongs to the *lesser* nobility.'

Lorenzo snorted.

'Come now, don't be too hard on me. I promise you that I will not see her again except during dances or festivities. And always keeping an appropriate distance.'

Clarice couldn't hold back a sigh.

'My beloved husband, you know how much I care about you. I know that I am jealous and, at the same time, it is clear to me that I cannot demand obedience from the lord of Florence. Who am I, after all, to give orders? The fact remains, though, that I am an Orsini and deserve the same respect that I show you.

I recently discovered that you not only commissioned a portrait of Lucrezia from the young Leonardo da Vinci but that it now hangs in your rooms. Needless to say, this discovery has caused me great pain. If you think that a few caresses will suffice to placate my heart then two years of life together have clearly not sufficed for you to understand who I am.'

And without another word, Clarice left the room, leaving Lorenzo alone with his thoughts.

DECEMBER 1471

14

Captain General of the Church

Finally, his stars were guiding events on a fortuitous course.

Captain General of the Church: Girolamo Riario could have asked for nothing better. As head of the troops of the Papal States, he finally had a large number of armed men to do his bidding, and since – thanks to his uncle, the newly elected Pope Sixtus IV – his appointment had been announced, he had made good use of them.

Drunk on violence and ambition, he smelled the scent of death the way a wild animal would.

The torched houses were reduced to black ruins and sparks dotted the night air, which was heavy with the sweetish stench of the blood that soaked the streets.

Heretics.

And Girolamo had not hesitated to put the village to the sword, looting the herds of animals, letting the women be raped and cutting the men's throats.

He smiled.

Power, that was what he needed. And a grudge to feed on forever. He would fill himself with both, and with them finally break the back of the Medici – one village at a time, if necessary, and with the protection of the Piscatory Ring. What more could he wish for? Below him, orange flames lit up the night and tongues of fire enveloped what remained of Castel Dell'Orso.

Noticing two men running in his direction as they tried to flee, he stuck his spurs into the flanks of his horse and set off towards them like a wild beast. As he reached them, he pulled out his sword and sliced off their heads. Severed from the bodies, they rolled along the paved alleys, to be eaten by dogs.

'May God have mercy on you, you accursed sodomites!' he thundered, prey to an uncontrollable mania. 'Spare nothing and no one, men! Let these beasts feel the iron of the cross and the wrath of God, for they have dishonoured the Church!'

'My lord,' shouted a voice behind him, and the Captain General of the Church turned his mount – a magnificent roan which had been a gift from the Pope – around.

Before him was the young man who always accompanied him and whose unbounded loyalty Girolamo had learned to appreciate.

'What is it, Ludovico?'

'Shall I spread the word to sack Castel Dell'Orso, my lord?'

'Listen to me well, my boy,' replied Riario, 'I don't just want you to sack the city, I want there to be no stone of this den of scum and rapists left standing. The heretics must know the wrath of Our Lord and his emissary on earth, the holy pontiff. Mercy must never encourage others like them to raise their heads. So spread the word and let nothing remain standing of Castel Dell'Orso, do you hear me?'

'Yes, my lord!'

And, so saying, Ludovico turned his horse towards the entrance to the village and set off at a gallop back to what was left of its houses and towers to make sure that nothing remained alive there.

When he was sure his young friend had gone, Girolamo Riario's thoughts returned to his own goals.

He wanted Lorenzo de' Medici to hear about him and his growing power. Within two years, he swore to himself, the lord of Florence would know his name.

In this life or the next.

Rome must finally expand its dominion, and he would be its sword. While the thought warmed his mind, he looked at the snow around him.

In the midst of that white expanse, Castel Dell'Orso, smoking like some fireplace of the underworld, was dying.

*

'This business with the alum will be the end of us!' snapped an exasperated Giuliano. His dirty hair fell over his face. He had hurried back from Volterra to warn his brother.

'Calm yourself!' said Lorenzo. 'What have we to fear? Florence can manage Volterra.'

'Oh, can it now?' snapped Giuliano, unable to hide his sarcasm. 'That's easy enough to say, but quite another thing to put into practice. You haven't seen how people in the city are reacting!'

'And why, dear brother, do you think I sent you on this mission?' Lorenzo was getting annoyed – he didn't like Giuliano's tone.

'In that case, perhaps you should pay more attention to what I say, since you were the one who sent me.'

'Very well! Explain to me on what basis you make such statements, then.'

Giuliano looked at him grimly. He threw his heavy cloak on to a chair then went over towards the large fireplace and stretched out his hands to warm them near the flames. The fire lit up his face and his eyes gleamed.

He was silent for a time, as though gathering his thoughts.

'It all started when those damned alum quarries were discovered...' He sighed. 'You know how it went: the most powerful families in Volterra were at each other's throats trying to get their hands on what would be a source of enormous wealth. The Municipality decided that the contract for the mines must be assigned to a company whose owner was the person who discovered them: Bennuccio di Cristoforo Capacci, from Siena. But precisely because it is a company, the proceeds of the mines belong to the other owners, namely Gino di Neri Capponi, and Bernardo di Cristoforo Buonagiusti, who are Florentine citizens, as well as to Benedetto di Bernardo Riccobaldi and Paolo d'Antonio Inghirami, known as Pecorino, from Volterra. And it is they, not the citizens of Volterra, who will get rich. But all that matters little now, because the situation is descending into chaos and since you decided to take Inghirami's side, the flames of anger that the agitators are fanning have swept the city.'

'I know that, but what else could I have done?' demanded Lorenzo. 'It was the people of Volterra themselves who implored me to resolve the issue. Even the Municipality of the city agreed to make me arbiter.'

'In Santa Maria del Fiore in January of this year. I remember it perfectly. But you don't know how things have changed. Volterra now cries betrayal and tramples all over your decision.'

'I know that. Tell me something that I do *not* know – something that justifies your going there.'

'Since you press me, dear brother, I shall. Paolo Inghirami, whom you defended from his fellow citizens when they wanted to tear up the contract that deprived them of the profits of the mine, ended up drowned in the fountain of the Palazzo del Podestà after locking himself in the tower and defending himself valiantly. Someone threw him through a window and he plunged all the way down into the fountain. His head was smashed like a pig at a slaughterhouse. What's more, I saw the locals dragging his body through the streets of the city.'

'How did they dare?'

'The severed heads of his men were stuck on pikes on the walls of the city for all to see.'

Lorenzo felt himself being overcome with anger in a way he never had before. He threw the glass of wine he held against the wall, where it shattered. His voice trembled with the rage mounting inside him.

'If it's true, I'll declare war on those impudent fools!'

'I don't think that would be wise, brother,' said Giuliano, trying to calm Lorenzo's rage.

'I understand why you think that, but I can no longer tolerate being at the mercy of Volterra's tantrums. They couldn't come to a sensible agreement about how to use the mine, so all the worse for them: I will send in the soldiers. Federico da Montefeltro will convince them to behave with more civility.'

'You know perfectly well that it will make a section of the population hostile to us.'

'I don't care; we can't stand by and watch. To hesitate now would be to offer our political adversaries yet another excuse for thinking us weak and hesitant. Our father has been dead for two years! Volterra is asking to be taken, and I am tired of waiting.'

'I fear that many will see it as an excuse to attack and silence an entire city.'

Giuliano's sincere eyes appealed to his brother's finest virtues: his fairness and clear-headedness. Though he feared they might have been compromised after the events in Prato the year before: Lorenzo had never been the same since the execution of Bernardo Nardi. He wouldn't admit it, of course, but Giuliano knew.

On the other hand, he understood that ignoring the affront would make Lorenzo look weak. It was a serious problem and Giuliano was aware his brother had only two alternatives: wait or attack.

But Lorenzo could no longer afford the luxury of being seen to let affronts go unpunished. Like Prato, Volterra was a vassal city, and if Florence accepted the decisions of its subjects they would be paving the way for not one but a hundred revolts.

It was a difficult decision, but one which now had to be made.

'I will think about it, I promise, but I'm afraid we have little choice.'

The moment Lorenzo said those words, the air seemed to tremble. It was as if something had broken: Giuliano could not have said exactly what it was, but he knew that nothing would be the same as before. His brother had crossed an invisible line and would never return. He knew that Lorenzo was intelligent enough not to lose himself in the flatteries of war, but the light that sparkled in his eyes frightened Giuliano. It was as though Volterra was intensifying the malady he had contracted with the execution of Bernardo Nardi. Giuliano sighed, aware of his failure and of how much that decision would cost his brother.

Lorenzo had chosen power, this time irrevocably. He'd had no choice, because all of them – Piero de' Medici above all, but also his mother Lucrezia, who had favoured his marriage with Clarice Orsini, and Gentile de' Becchi, Antonio Pucci, Braccio Martelli and all the others – had wanted him to lead the city.

And he had become what everyone had wanted.

In a way, it was the Medici heritage. And it was a heavy cross to bear. Lorenzo would have and then lose everything. Being the lord of Florence meant it was unavoidable. Giuliano hoped at least that the now-inevitable campaign against Volterra would one day end in a glorious victory.

But he doubted it.

15

Winds of War

'I thought I had been quite clear. I have no intention of discussing it.'

Leonardo's disappointment at what he had just heard was enormous – he couldn't understand it. Lorenzo was making a serious mistake. The lord of Florence seemed no longer to share the values which had been the basis for their friendship. Yet Leonardo had always been crystal clear on that point, and there was no explanation that justified such a course of action except what he sensed was the real reason for the change in his friend: that he had been seduced by power. Because regardless of what Lorenzo kept stubbornly telling him, it was obvious that a thirst for dominion dictated his actions. But Leonardo would not be his accomplice.

Lorenzo, however, continued to insist.

They stood there, surrounded by the drawings, strange instruments and incomprehensible calculations scratched on the walls that made the place look more like some madman's cell than a workshop.

It was a basement room in Oltrarno where the artist kept his creations and worked on his ideas. It was not ideal, but a little at a time he was realizing his intentions. Of course, it would take money to buy the other floors of the building, but with time Leonardo was sure he would succeed.

He knew that, in order to build his little kingdom, he had accepted the florins offered by Lorenzo after the commissions he had entrusted to him, and that made the conversation even more difficult, as Leonardo was well aware that not even he was free of hypocrisy, nor even of guilt.

But that was not a good reason for repeating the mistake.

'Leonardo, please. I know what we promised ourselves,' Lorenzo went on, 'and I implore you to believe me when I say that Florence is the victim and not the aggressor. You must understand that Volterra's attitude is one of open challenge to me. If I do not respond now, my hesitation will be mistaken for weakness!'

'And what if it is? Do you believe that strength is measured in the number of deaths that a man can cause?'

The words came out filled with rage and he spat, to show his disgust at the conversation, then with one hand swept away the alembics and tools that crowded a wooden table, sending them crashing to the floor.

'Would it not be better to show magnanimity and mercy? Or is it that which frightens you? Because to judge by how you have been behaving lately, that's the way it looks! Has it taken so little for you to lose the guiding light of reason? And do you think that your recklessness and your lust for power will not condemn you? I saw you that day at the Palazzo del Podestà in front of the decapitated body of Bernardo Nardi! I heard the words you spoke! And now you think you can come here and convince me by pouring a little honey into my ears?'

There was something about Leonardo's words which reminded Lorenzo of what Lucrezia had prophesied.

He snorted with frustration and fatigue.

He wished the people who loved him would take his side, at least at a time like this. Instead they were all so busy criticizing his mistakes that they were blind to the difficulties of his position.

'You don't understand, Leonardo! There is no room for feelings of pity in a man with my responsibilities! I cannot afford to be an idealist. You and Lucrezia are the same, damn it – you live in a world of fairy tales, and talk as though I were free to choose what to do. But I'm not! I have obligations, do you understand? Responsibilities! It's easy for you to rage against war and violence, but you don't have to protect our city!'

Leonardo shook his head.

'And what is it that you are protecting her from? Let's hear it! Because I don't see how Volterra poses a danger to Florence!'

'Do you really not understand? Volterra is the principle. If I let one city do what it wants without reacting, they will all think that they can attack me and my family. And I cannot allow that.'

'I can't join you in this, don't you realize? I don't want to. I have no intention of standing by the side of those whose actions go against my principles.' Leonardo sighed. His heart was aching, radiating a metallic pain that he felt weakening him a little at a time. His voice grew quiet. 'I'm sorry, Lorenzo, but I have to ask you, if our friendship is at all dear to you, not to use the crossbows I had prepared for your army. Remember? Some time ago we told ourselves that they would be used only to defend, not to attack.'

'I remember it all too well. We were friends, then. And now?'

'I do not know what we are,' Leonardo said bitterly.

And it was true. Because that poisonous conversation had revealed to him an entirely new and, in some ways, unexpected truth. It was hard for him to become attached to people, and yet it had miraculously happened with Lorenzo. Or at least he'd believed it had. What a disappointment to find out now that it hadn't at all.

'Are you blackmailing me?' said Lorenzo.

'Not at all, but I must keep my word.'

'So will I.'

'That comforts me, at least in part.'

'It doesn't mean that I will not attack. Only that I will not use your crossbows.'

'I realized that,' said Leonardo, a hint of resignation in his voice as though for a moment, in spite of what had been said, he had hoped for a different answer.

'So our paths fork?' he said eventually.

'Not by my choice, but I cannot beg you. No more than I have already done, at least. You must choose.'

'As though in the end it was all just a matter of pride.'

'Isn't it?' asked Lorenzo.

'No, not at all.'

'So what is it, then?'

'A matter of principles,' said Leonardo.

'Now you are speaking my language. A matter of principles, of course. But principles don't count for me, do they? There's no principle involved in accepting the role one has been given and trying to live up to it.'

'I don't see how that means attacking a weaker city.'

'Your words wound me.'

'They are the only words I can find today. And I would beg you to consider the contract that binds me to your family terminated.'

'Don't say that,' said Lorenzo. 'And anyway, I would never consider it such. You can come to me whenever you want.'

'Very well,' said Leonardo.

On his face, though, was a harsh expression of disappointment which cut Lorenzo to the quick.

'I give up, my friend. But I can't understand why you and Lucrezia don't try to see that this is my destiny, not something I chose for myself.'

Leonardo's gaze did not waver.

'Then that means that your destiny is also to be hated by your friends,' he concluded; and he turned his back on Lorenzo and waited for him to leave.

16

Federico da Montefeltro

The garden of the Palazzo Medici was white with snow. Winter showed no sign of loosening its grip, and the frost which covered everything with a frozen veil seemed even to have imprisoned the hearts of the men who stood there talking despite the bitter December cold.

Federico da Montefeltro looked at him with eyes as cold as the snow that cloaked the garden.

'At your command, seven thousand men will march to the walls of Volterra,' said Lorenzo. 'We will wait for spring to attack, but you should start preparing yourself now. I do not want the city to suffer anything worse than a siege and a defeat. I will not authorize looting or violence. Let it be clear: you will be well paid, but woe to you if the situation gets out of hand.'

Federico nodded. He was lord of Urbino: a man of arms and of few words.

'It shall be as you say, my lord.'

'This attack gives me no joy, but I have no alternative. For this reason I do not intend to permit savagery. I will hold you personally responsible for any wickedness carried out against the inhabitants of Volterra. I don't want a hair of their heads hurt!'

Federico da Montefeltro stared into Lorenzo's eyes and then, reluctantly, spoke.

The few words he uttered seemed to cause him inexpressible pain.

'My lord, it is my intention to obey your orders. I will be responsible for keeping the men in check. But I cannot help but notice that you seem troubled. It will be a war and, however we wish to dress it up, there is no way of making it better than it is. It will be dirty and bloody, and there is nothing anybody can do to change that, not even you. Therefore I ask you: what makes you say this?'

Lorenzo sighed.

Federico was right and he was wrong. But his heart was heavy because of the friends he had lost. Although, he still hoped, not forever.

'Being lord of Florence is pushing everyone away from me as though I were a plague. I have no friends, Federico; I have a family, of course, but how much of what is happening in my life did I actually choose?'

'You are a powerful man. No one will show you mercy. Instead you must guard yourself from the multitudes who envy you and desire in their black hearts to overthrow you. I am not a man of many words, but I can give you one piece of advice today, and it is this: do not hope that your enemies hesitate. Strike first, Lorenzo, and when you do, strike to kill. And now, if you will permit me, I would take my leave.'

Lorenzo nodded his consent.

Montefeltro's words echoed in Lorenzo's ears while the man departed. The sound of his footsteps on the flagstones of the courtyard left leaden echoes in the air while Lorenzo's soul sank in the cold of the morning.

The sky was as grey as if it were carved out of slate and the bare trees looked like omens of death.

There was something wrong with the whole story and she had to talk to him and put him back on the right path. Were those alum mines really precious enough for him to give up everything he had?

Lucrezia could not believe it. She felt Lorenzo withdrawing further and further away from her, and now he had even refused to listen to Leonardo.

She had spoken with him the night before and what she had heard left her in no doubt. And it was all in the name of a war which would bring nothing but pain and death.

How long ago they seemed, those days when she and Lorenzo had lain in bed, embracing one another and talking about their love!

She had to talk to him.

Attacking Volterra like that was pure, unadulterated madness. She understood that a vassal city could not be allowed to rebel against Florence with impunity, but lust for blood would not increase support for Lorenzo in the city. They would paint him as a ruthless nobleman, ready to exterminate anyone who got in his way.

Was that what he wanted? To be feared? It was the easiest and most direct way to govern, but was it the best? The Lorenzo she knew would never do such a thing – he preferred dialogue and diplomacy, and would have sought a different solution.

Where had that sensible young man disappeared to? Lucrezia no longer knew.

She walked briskly through the cold evening air. She had set off at sunset, and now the whole city was wrapped in the shadows of night and fires flickered in the square of San Pulinari.

Lucrezia wore a large, dark cloak, its hood pulled down to conceal her face. She did not want to attract unwanted attention. It had not been wise to go out at that time. She could have waited for Lorenzo to send her a carriage, as she usually did when they were to meet, but tonight she had preferred to take the initiative.

Suddenly, as though in confirmation of her fears, she glimpsed a figure standing in the shadows. It was only for an instant, but when she turned, there was no one there.

Shaking her head at her foolishness, she carried on – though at a faster pace.

She knew where to find Lorenzo. She knew his habits all too well.

He would be in the church which bore his name and where all the Medici were buried. He went there to spend time among the tombs of his loved ones whenever he had the opportunity. It helped him take the decisions he had to make, he claimed, so she was in no doubt that she would find him there.

She knew that surprising him like this would feel like an ambush, but she had to do something. She could not bear the idea of not being able to see him, and even less of watching him pushing everyone away from him.

She had almost reached her destination when she sensed something behind her. Before she had time to see what it was, a hand clamped itself over her mouth and she felt a blade, as cold as ice, pressed against her throat.

'What are you doing in the streets at this of night, my lady? Looking for trouble?'

Lucrezia almost fainted when she heard that gruff voice. It was true, then – someone *had* been following her, and now she was paying dearly for her imprudence.

She tried to scream, but the sound died in her throat. Her terror mounted.

'Don't speak,' continued the voice. 'It would serve no purpose except to get you killed.'

Without another word, the man dragged her into a darker corner of the alley where the only light was that of a distant torch and her plight was even less likely to be noticed. There he would be able to do whatever he wanted, completely undisturbed: rob her, rape her, kill her.

She saw the heels of her boots scraping on the ground, her legs kicking in a desperate attempt to resist.

But in spite of how youthful his voice sounded, the man who had attacked her was no weakling, and easily managed to drag her where he wanted.

She had to react and do something, and now! If she waited any longer she would have no chance.

It would be too late.

So she did the only thing that came to mind: she bit down on the fingers of the hand covering her mouth as hard as she could.

17

The Crossbow

On that day, he had decided to leave the church earlier than usual. Something was tormenting him, even if he could not say exactly what. That conversation with Federico da Montefeltro, above all. The difficult decision to attack Volterra. And then what had happened with Leonardo.

So absorbed in his thoughts that he was only dimly aware of his actions, he had somehow found himself in a narrow alley that was as dark as sin, the only light coming from a torch on the wall.

And in that moment he heard a cry, as disquieting and cruel as that of a man in a battle. Before he even realized what was happening, he saw something that took him completely by surprise: just before the point ahead where the alley turned to the left were two silhouettes. At first he could not work out what was happening, but then he saw one of the two figures break away from the other and run awkwardly towards him. Even in the dim light, Lorenzo recognized Lucrezia's face. Her long hair floated like black tentacles in the night air, and her sparkling eyes glittered with terror. He saw that her beautiful lips were smudged with something dark. He wasted no time.

He untied the crossbow that was fastened at his waist and in a flash had aimed it at the attacker and pulled the trigger.

The dart hissed through the air and struck the hand of the attacker, who gave a second cry which was even more terrible than the first. But despite the bolt sticking out of his flesh, the man didn't give up.

He held something in his hand and Lorenzo saw the gleam of a blade reflecting the flame of the torch. He was getting ready to stab from behind the woman who had dared escape him.

While Lucrezia stumbled towards him, Lorenzo drew a second dart from a small quiver and opened the tiller, returning the string to its loading position. He loaded the bolt in place and fired.

The missile pierced the man's neck and the attacker clapped his hands to his throat while a dark river of blood poured down his chest. He fell to his knees and then collapsed on his side.

And a moment later, Lucrezia was in Lorenzo's arms, where she fainted.

*

When he saw her smile, Lorenzo went over to her. Lucrezia lay on a bed, between clean sheets and warm blankets.

He had brought her a steaming bowl of fragrant broth.

'Drink, my love,' he told her, 'it'll make you feel better, you'll see.'

She took it in her hands.

'You shouldn't have been so rash. You know how much I care about you. If it hadn't been for Leonardo's crossbow, something terrible could have happened.'

He spoke with a feverish urgency, the words filled with such sincere concern that it almost surprised him. He knew he had practically abandoned her and he could not forgive himself for it. If something happened to Lucrezia, it would be entirely his fault.

'Leonardo's crossbow has brought us all together for a moment, has it not?' she said in a quiet voice which broke with fear and emotion but held no trace of blame. 'Thank you for saving my life, my love. I had come looking for you, because I could no longer stay away from you.'

Lorenzo felt an infinite misery descend upon him. On the one hand, he wanted to tell her how much he too suffered in her absence, but on the other he knew that if he encouraged that feeling, he would put Lucrezia's life even more in danger than it already was.

'My love...' was all he managed to say. But then he summoned up his courage. 'You cannot be near me, because everything I touch burns like a cursed fire. I cannot allow that. Don't you see? Even today when you came to see me, you risked being killed.'

'I don't care,' replied Lucrezia. 'If I'm not in your arms then I don't care.'

She was so beautiful, he thought, her face suffused with pugnacious grace, as though she were a virgin warrior atop some mountain.

He grabbed the bowl from her and placed it on the small wooden table, then took her face in his hands and kissed her for a long time.

His love for her was so intense that he could not resist it. Let him be damned. If that was the price he had to pay for such a privilege, he was more than ready to pay it.

He felt her tongue flicker between his teeth and lick his lips, and he embraced her hard.

Lucrezia offered herself to him, and he could wait no longer. He undressed her as she undid his doublet, and when she was naked, she took his hands and laid them on her large, full breasts.

Lorenzo became more ardent and as he teased her dark nipples she felt an ecstasy she could barely believe possible. She felt his tongue darting against hers and flickering across her teeth and lips, and then Lucrezia felt herself being lifted up and found herself on all fours with Lorenzo's tongue exploring between her legs, savouring her sweetest fruit. The sensation entranced her with an irresistible uncertainty. She wanted him, and as though he had guessed the exact moment when the intensity of her excitement had become intolerable, he penetrated her.

Lucrezia welcomed him inside her with all of herself, arching her back and thrusting her hips at him.

And he filled her with everything he had.

JUNE 1472

18

The Sack of Volterra

Every day at dawn, the cannons had thundered ceaselessly, shattering the walls and decapitating the towers.

And after the smoke and the terrible roar of the barrage, the soldiers had descended on to the plain. Counting for its victory upon the bombardment and upon its sheer force of numbers, a torrent of armour and swords had poured down on Volterra.

The rising sun painted the armour of the soldiers pale pink while the irregular profile of the hill upon which the city was perched seemed to be draped with a gauzy curtain that softened the shape of its sharp rocks.

But when the cannons had finally gone silent and the soldiers had found themselves at the walls of the fortified city, the crossbowmen in the battlements had not hesitated and had fired down upon them a hail of iron that had thinned the ranks, leaving the clearing outside the gates of Volterra bloodstained and covered in corpses.

Screams of pain, the rattling of broken swords, red lifeblood that flowed away, helmets rolling in the dust, hands gloved with iron that clawed the air as their owners drew their last breaths: it had been a massacre for the Florentines.

The pink morning sky had been filled with the agony of the dead, and the corpses had soon made it darker than ever.

Captain Federico da Montefeltro had watched as so much of his men's blood had soaked into the ground that it had become red mud.

Sweating beneath his mail, he looked through eyes blurred by fatigue and shortness of breath at the bodies which covered the battlefield all the way to Volterra in a single, silent expanse of death.

Thus the attack had been quickly neutralized.

The Florentines had returned to their camp, exhausted in body and soul.

Federico had given the order to intensify the firing of the cannons, and more days had passed, but Volterra had not fallen.

Hoping to take the city in another way, the captain had had his men build an underground road. He had ordered them to cover themselves with mud and slime like pigs in order to dig a tunnel from the Florentine camp to the city walls. But that enterprise too had failed.

Thus, after a month, the besiegers had achieved nothing. Tired, wounded and humiliated, they sat in their camp waiting for something to happen.

And in the end, something did.

Something unthinkable which, in its shameful inhumanity, suddenly deprived Federico da Montefeltro, lord of Urbino, of everything: victory *and* honour.

It had happened in the darkness of the night, when the sky was still preparing for the ivory hues of dawn. The time when traitors are best able to carry out their plots.

Under cover of darkness and silence, Sienese and Venetian mercenaries had opened the Porta Diana gate, and, moving like spectres, the Florentine soldiers had swept into the city.

Before dawn, all hell had been let loose, and Federico had discovered too late what had happened: despite his orders, the men were coming down on Volterra like wolves on a flock of sheep, and now it was impossible to stop them.

Dishonour and misfortune – for him, for Florence, and for Lorenzo de' Medici.

As he mounted his horse and left the camp for the slopes of the hill and the Porta Diana, he wondered what had happened to dignity? What had happened to valour and honour?

The last shreds of discipline and piety had been torn from rules of war.

And he alone was the herald of that massacre and of the ignominy that would haunt him for years to come – the ignominy of not having been strong enough to stop the killing.

With tired eyes, Federico had looked upwards for a piece of blue sky, but the flames and smoke seemed to have consumed it all. The high walls of Volterra had not fallen, but deceit had opened its gates. No Trojan horse or brilliant strategy had been necessary: the betrayal of a few turncoats and the anger of many had been more than enough – those soldiers left to rot in the winter camp and then positioned like scarecrows in front of the walls for thirty days. They were to blame, but not as much as the commanders who had failed to hold back their hounds.

Opened with fraud and deception, that breach had unleashed the besiegers. Blinded by their losses, their privations and the scarcity of their booty, they launched themselves upon the city as if that was what they had been waiting for. Federico had shouted, threatened, ordered... but had come up against a wall of indifference. And even worse, had come too late, because by the first light of dawn, when it was clear that his soldiers were inside the city, he had entered Volterra to find it reduced to a crucible of agony.

Smoke enveloped the burning houses, which were now only dark, smouldering piles of rubble. Such had been the fury of the flames that the grey stones looked like blocks of sulphur. He looked on in silence, terrified that the victims of that massacre might recognize him, and curse him forever.

Even in his worst nightmares he had never seen anything like this – he had never witnessed such blind violence.

He saw children, their faces smeared with soot and snot, screaming silently, overwhelmed by the silence of their dead fathers.

He saw men run through with swords or slipping and sliding on the blood that flooded the streets.

He saw women whose eyes had been gouged out, and old people crucified at the entrances of their hovels.

He saw horses lying dead on the ground and storerooms looted of all they contained.

Not even locusts could have ravaged a city as quickly.

As he advanced through that nightmare he saw one of his men: half naked, the white curve of his back looming over his victim, her face pushed into the dirt and her long brown hair filthy with blood and sweat.

Disgusted by the sight, Federico snatched up a polearm which was sticking out of the body of a dying soldier and rammed it into the rapist's back.

The man grasped at the tip of the weapon which now protruded from his chest and staggered to his feet, abandoning his victim. Staring in shock as he realized that it had been his own commander who had taken his life, he took a couple of steps then collapsed sideways, falling onto the shattered remains of a cart.

As he closed his eyes, the woman who had been beneath him remained motionless. She was on all fours, trembling violently. Tears and blood and humours covered her in a single sheath of horror.

Slowly, Federico went over to her. How could he possibly remedy this wrong?

He pulled the cloak from his shoulders, wrapped it tightly around the woman and helped her get up. She couldn't stop trembling and sobbed desperately. Her face, which had been pushed into the mud, was filthy.

Federico saw a bucket of water, half full. As if by a miracle, someone had left it behind at the edge of the main street. He tore off a piece of his cloak and wet it in the clear water, then wiped clean the woman's face and picked her up.

She remained silent, her body jerking with the violence of her weeping.

It began to rain.

The sky had finally taken mercy on Volterra, thought Federico da Montefeltro.

The rain washed away that obscene spectacle – in part, at least. It fell ceaselessly, like a prayer, extinguishing the fires that the soldiers had set and making the embers sizzle.

With the woman in his arms, Federico walked through the carnage.

He held on to her as if the salvation of his soul depended upon it while the drops of rain bounced off the plates of his armour, stained with blood and dust, mud and betrayal.

Its children reduced to stray dogs, forced to wander among the ruins of a world that had been overthrown by the army of Florence, Volterra cried out in pain.

Never again would it rebel against Lorenzo de' Medici.

Never again.

19

The First Accusations

'Volterra will be the end of the Medici,' thundered Francesco de' Pazzi, 'heed my words. And even if we are now celebrating the taking of the feudal city that dared to rebel against its master, I believe that the favour which Lorenzo presently enjoys will soon vanish.'

His face was inflamed with rage and his forehead beaded with sweat, and his hands flailed in the air as if his gestures could strengthen the wild hatred he already felt for the Medici.

He was attempting to whip up the other nine members of the Council of Ten of War against Lorenzo, but it was not easy. Luca Pitti and Pier Soderini were certainly on his side, but the same couldn't be said of the others, who were in the pay of the Medici and looked at him with bored expressions, as though listening to the ravings of a lunatic.

'The butchery in the city was so appalling that Federico da Montefeltro almost refused the honours given him on his return from the war! Even the Pope condemned it as the basest and most shameful of massacres. I cannot see how Lorenzo de' Medici can be saved from excommunication – it is only a matter of time! The archbishop himself feels profound embarrassment over what happened.'

'Come, Francesco,' cried Gentile de' Becchi, 'don't lay it on so thick! I would remind you that the Archbishop of Florence is currently confined to Rome for his attack upon Lorenzo's life, so I wouldn't use him as a moral exemplar. We all know that you Pazzi hate the Medici because you feel they eclipse your prestige and your fortunes. And of course, none of us blames you for it! Each of us is free to believe what he wishes. But do not ask too much of your lucky star. Pope Sixtus is certainly more friendly than his predecessor and that is good news, but I doubt that the pontiff will excommunicate Lorenzo for bringing a rebel city under the Florentine aegis. Because, at the end of the day, that is what happened, you said so yourself. So let us discuss more serious matters.'

'But we all know that the real reason for Lorenzo's actions was a desire to take possession of the alum deposits discovered in Volterra—' insisted Pazzi.

'And what of it?' snapped Becchi. 'If Florence becomes richer and stronger, do we not all stand to benefit? Since when has the richness of our city been a problem? Personal profit and self-interest have become the rule, so why should someone be stigmatized for acting in the interests of the community?'

Those words did nothing to calm the mood – on the contrary, they sounded almost like a provocation. Francesco de' Pazzi's eyes grew red with rage. With his black doublet studded with pearls and his long dark beard, he made a powerful impression. He belonged to one of the most powerful families in Florence and would defend his honour at any cost; and he would not let himself be insulted in front of everyone, much less by that half-baked politician. If he could have, he would have strangled him right here with his own two hands.

'How dare you, Becchi? What the hell are you babbling about? You should mind what you say and how you say it! You think yourself strong because of your friendship with Lorenzo de' Medici, but that doesn't make you untouchable!'

'So now you threaten me, Francesco? And do you really think that I am afraid of you?'

Gentile de' Becchi's words simply fanned the flames of the argument, and the hot-tempered Francesco de' Pazzi looked as though he were about to physically attack him.

It was Pier Soderini who tried to calm the waters. Soderini had an elegant way about him, and his voice, steady and charming, was capable of soothing even the most violent disagreements.

'Come, sirs, let us not waste our days on this matter. What my friend Francesco says is true: Florence has disgraced itself by burning Volterra and butchering its inhabitants. And, as much as it may vex them to hear it, our good Gentile de' Becchi, Lorenzo de' Medici and with him Federico da Montefeltro bear some of the blame. On the other hand, it is equally true that, by rebelling, Volterra could have set a dangerous precedent and encouraged similar revolts from other vassal cities. Lorenzo de' Medici did well to block its nascent ambitions and thus to underline Florence's importance as a republic and its independence from Rome and Milan. What we all hope now is that the war ends and peace returns as a result of this extraordinary show of force which, for all its faults, will at least serve to discourage further disorder.'

Pier Soderini paused, almost as though gauging the effects of his words. A fine orator and possessed of lively intelligence, he was no lover of the Medici, but he understood perfectly when it was the time for action and when it was the time for words.

And in that moment, attacking Lorenzo's actions was the wrong move because, at the end of the day, Florence had emerged victorious – even though it had done so thanks to a gang of mercenaries.

But Lorenzo couldn't be blamed for that. It was better to keep quiet and plot in silence, when the others would not be expecting it. Revenge was a dish best served cold, and God alone knew how much rancour Francesco de' Pazzi and his supporters nurtured towards the family that lorded it over the city while at the same time flaunting an appearance of impartiality and restraint.

That being the case, the best thing to do was to keep quiet and wait to see how things turned out.

So when he saw Gentile de' Becchi and Niccolò Martelli nodding, Pier Soderini realized he had said the right thing.

He put his hand on de' Pazzi's wrist to prevent him from saying anything, and concluded:

'Francesco has pointed out – with some anger, it must be said – an inarguable fact. But all of us feel that a show of force, no matter how disproportionate, is always welcome when it serves to calm the spirits and remind others of our supremacy. But now, if you agree, I suggest returning to the question of the resources we intend to offer His Holiness the Pope for his crusade, in which Florence must play a leading role.'

As he finished his speech, Soderini glanced over at Francesco de' Pazzi who, for once, grasped his meaning and avoided starting up the argument once more.

Reassured by Soderini's words, Gentile de' Becchi,

Niccolò Martelli and all the other councillors affiliated with the Medici breathed a sigh of relief, glad that the debate had returned to less controversial matters.

Little did they know that the men in front of them considered the question anything but closed.

20

The Black Kite

Standing in the tall grass and using a leaf as a whistle, Leonardo let the summer sun caress his face. He too had heard the rumours about the massacre in Volterra. That wouldn't help Lorenzo, he thought. Not at all. He would have liked to be able to help him out, but something stopped him. He had promised himself that he would never speak to Lorenzo again. Perhaps it was just his stupid pride, but he had no intention of giving up one of his most prized treasures: the principle of sticking to his decisions.

Despite how much more bitter it made his loneliness.

He seemed to be almost incapable of making friends or finding lovers, and yet it had been Lucrezia herself who had told him that Lorenzo was distancing himself from them. Perhaps that distance between them was exactly what Lorenzo wanted, though. Was not it a way to protect them? Leonardo hadn't really thought about it at first. Lorenzo had insisted so much on their remaining friends, and Leonardo had sensed he was sincere, but when they had each made their decision, it had seemed to him that he was happier this way.

Or perhaps relieved was a better word.

It was if the siege of Volterra had been providential, preventing their friendship from becoming a source of danger for him and for Lucrezia.

He knew that some time ago Lucrezia had gone to see Lorenzo and that he had made love to her for the whole night but that after realizing his mistake he had sent her away, despite the intensity of his feelings for her. It was as if Lorenzo wanted to lock himself up, isolating himself with his power and his loyalty to his only true lady and mistress: Florence.

Of course, he still wrote poems dedicated to Lucrezia, and despite all his good intentions, he would never be able to remove her from his mind and heart.

Leonardo had no idea what the relationship between Lorenzo and Clarice was like. He knew their marriage was no romance, but he did not doubt that his friend was trying to do his best.

Lately, Lorenzo seemed determined to be faithful to his family and his city, and that kind of integrity was exactly what Leonardo was seeking too – even though he did not have a city to defend, or a woman to love, or a bride to honour. In one sense, he had nothing; but in another, he had everything.

Freedom and love of knowledge were more than enough, and were also the only two sentiments he intended protecting in his life.

He thought back to the previous night. Once again, he had dreamed of the kite.

He had imagined that he was a child again and that he was swinging in his cradle when a kite had come to him. It had circled in the sky and then glided into his room through the open window.

It was a majestic bird with bronze-coloured feathers. It had perched on the edge of the cradle and, to his surprise, it had put its tail feathers into his mouth, flapping them and swirling them around between his lips.

It was a strange and disquieting dream, but Leonardo had not been afraid either then or later.

Perhaps the vision had something to do with his uncle Francesco, with whom he had always enjoyed strolling through fields and woods. It was Francesco who had first told him about the kite's forked tail and how that extraordinary bird could ride the air currents and reach the most incredible heights, taking advantage of the wind when it climbed and gliding on the breeze when it descended. It had been that crazy unkempt uncle who had given him his love of nature and of all the wonders of creation.

They almost always went down to the river together

and then back to the forest to observe the metamorphoses of the insects and the composition of the brown clods of earth. He used to wonder how it was possible that a delicate blade of grass managed, with the first, tenuous warmth of spring, to pierce the dark earth, still coated with frost.

And then, one day, that simple but wonderful life had been interrupted. His father Piero had convinced his grandfather to take him to Florence.

Grandfather Antonio had put his hands on his cheeks and raised his face to him.

'You'll see Florence, my boy! You'll see the world!'

Leonardo didn't understand what his grandfather meant, but his father and Uncle Francesco were smiling at him; therefore, even if reluctantly, he had smiled too. He already knew that he would be nostalgic for the carefree days he had spent with his uncle, but he also realized that time was over. In confirmation of this sensation, that night he had dreamed of the kite, which flew onto his bed and tried to open his mouth with its forked tail.

The next morning, Leonardo had left for Florence and after a journey that he would not have called short, nor yet long, had arrived in that incredible city.

As those memories, so deeply imprinted, ran through his mind, Leonardo raised his eyes to the sky.

He heard the loud whistling of a black kite.

21

Plots

Girolamo Riario was awaiting his uncle.

He had in mind a project that, if properly planned, could be of some use in expanding his hegemony by weakening Florence and strengthening Rome.

He had talked about it at length with Ludovico Ricci and had concluded that not only did it have a concrete chance of success, but that it would also be the first move in a complex plot which would allow them to rid themselves of Lorenzo de' Medici.

As he waited, he examined his surroundings.

He stood on the third floor of Castel Sant'Angelo in the study where his uncle liked to lock himself away to read and think up his plans. It was a cramped little room which was accessed via a secret passage operated by a masterpiece of engineering: the little door hidden in the wall revealed its presence only after being activated via a painting hung in the large room next door.

He looked at the dark mahogany desk cluttered with papers and scrolls, inkwells and pens. The pontifical seal and wax for fastening his missives. The small bust of his uncle in white marble by Mino da Fiesole. The frescoes on the walls depicting the Judgement of God, painted by Ghirlandaio: these were only some of the minor masterpieces with which the Pope had begun to celebrate his own and his family's glory, gradually crowding Rome with new works, the most ambitious of which was the construction of the Ponte Sisto in his own honour.

Francesco della Rovere made no secret of his wish to see Rome flourish again through his patronage – funded, of course, with the taxes and prebends that filled the pontifical coffers. He had gone to great lengths to justify the construction of the new bridge which would bear his name, citing as a reason that he was tired of seeing the faithful crowding Ponte Sant'Angelo as they tried to get to the left shore of the Tiber and San Pietro.

But Girolamo cared little about the motives behind the profusion of public works and monuments because at that moment he was there for a specific reason.

As captain of the papal army he had seen his power increase greatly, but now he desired his own estates – his own seigniory, so to speak – and he wanted it not too far from Florence so he could keep an eye on Lorenzo de' Medici, whom he hoped soon to see swept away. But to succeed, it was absolutely imperative he obtain an investiture and concession of land from the Pope.

While he was reflecting upon this, the door opened with a click and the pontiff himself entered.

Francesco della Rovere was a man of considerable height: as thin and resilient as a reed, he had aristocratic features, pronounced cheekbones and penetrating, intelligent eyes. He had refined his already remarkable talents through obsessive studying, and over the years had taught philosophy in prestigious universities such as Venice and Padua. He knew his nephew better than anyone else – and he was aware of both his lust for power and propensity for impulsivity. He gave him a searching look. He was well aware that Girolamo never did anything without a reason, and this made him absolutely predictable: Sixtus IV could read his behaviour as easily as he could read one of his books.

'My beloved nephew...' he began.

Girolamo approached him, kneeling and kissing Sixtus's ring.

'Come,' said the pontiff, 'you are my nephew – we can do without some of the formalities, surely?'

'You are still the Pope and I owe you the devotion of the faithful, the obedience of the captain of the papal army and the gratitude of your nephew.'

Francesco della Rovere nodded: the answer had pleased him. His nephew was perhaps not the finest of strategists or the most elegant of speakers, but he certainly knew what to say and when to say it, and that already made him the dearest of all the relatives he showered with honours and titles – for Francesco had immediately realized that the papacy would be the means of making his family one of the most powerful in history.

'So, my beloved nephew,' the Pope said benevolently, 'what news do you bring me? Good, I hope, as I am about to send Cardinal Carafa off on one of the most formidable crusades ever seen in the Holy Land and my mood is so buoyant that I could not bear to have some skirmish between nobles spoil it!'

Girolamo Riario noted the implied admonition in his uncle's words. He brushed a rebellious lock of long brown hair from his face, smoothed his moustaches and gave voice to what had long been on his mind.

'Your holiness, I hope my words will not vex you, but as you will soon see, they are aimed at finding the solution to a problem rather than creating one.'

'May the Lord be praised,' said Sixtus IV with a mischievous smile, having already guessed what it was Girolamo wished to speak to him about.

'May he always be praised. You will certainly remember how Lorenzo de' Medici sacked Volterra, slaying the inhabitants at the hands of Federico da Montefeltro.'

'One of the most awful deeds of these dark years, dear nephew.'

'Yes,' said Girolamo, 'and all to get possession of an alum mine so as to enrich their already considerable coffers. But this is beside the point. What I wish to discuss with you is the pressing need to find someone willing to keep in check Florence and a man who, unless he is stopped, could seriously embarrass the Duchy of Modena and the Republic of Siena, frustrating irreparably the Papal States' legitimate aspirations to enlarge its borders.'

'In other words?' asked the Pope with a frown.

'In other words, your holiness, Lorenzo de' Medici represents an obstacle to your power. Volterra was a vassal city, of course, but what might happen if Lorenzo decides he is not content with his borders? That's why I have conceived a plan that could rid you of this potential enemy at a stroke. I think I can state with confidence that you have no particular esteem for this family of modest woolmen which, over the years, has convinced itself it can do as it likes.'

'Precisely. And yet I cannot publicly encourage your hatred of the Medici because the fact remains that they are powerful and have influential friends.'

This time it was Girolamo who nodded.

'Naturally, your holiness, and that is why I took care to reflect before formulating the proposal I am about to make: to guarantee your grace a guard dog at the gates of your state so that, if the Medici should venture to enlarge their sphere of influence, your dog can give the alarm and even take them on, if needs be. And that guard dog, your grace, is me – your humble, faithful nephew and the captain of the papal army, standing here in front of you.'

The Pope stifled a laugh. Was his nephew really so devoted as to call himself a guard dog of the Papal States? Francesco was impressed: fidelity was not a virtue to be underestimated and was all the more rare in times like those, when even kinship and blood ties seemed regulated by the laws of self-interest. 'And what would you like in exchange for this valuable service?' he asked.

'I ask for the lordship of Imola, your grace. It is a small terrain, strategically located at the northern border of the Florentine Republic. From its castles we can effectively monitor what Lorenzo de' Medici is plotting, especially since one of my most trusted men has confirmed to me the Pazzi family's intention of sooner or later putting an end to Lorenzo's hegemony.'

Was that all? thought Francesco della Rovere. *In exchange for one of the smallest seigniories could I really have this most faithful watchdog guarding Lorenzo de' Medici?*

It sounded too good to be true.

Of course, giving him Imola might generate some rumbles of protest, and perhaps even criticism, but after all, was he or was he not the Pope? Who would dare to oppose his decision? Francesco Maria Sforza, the Duke of Milan? Of course not, if the lordship were adequately paid for: that land belonged to him but he would gladly give it up for a reasonable price. He was a pragmatic man and his Duchy was costly to maintain, so the Pope was certain he would be happy to have some money in hand.

It was the Pazzi family that worried him. He tried to understand exactly what his nephew was planning.

'My beloved nephew, I will gladly grant you the lordship of Imola and, indeed, you do well to ask me for it, because it seems to me a very small reward for the job you have decided to undertake. I will act soon; you have my word. But what I don't quite understand is the role the Pazzi will play in all this. I know Francesco and I confess that I do not trust his temper. Tell me that you do not have some obscure plot in mind, because in that case I could not in any way defend you.'

'Far be it from me to even think of such a thing,' Girolamo assured him. 'What I intend to do is form an alliance with the Pazzi so that Florence itself removes Lorenzo and his brother Giuliano, as was the case with Cosimo and his brother Lorenzo.'

'You do remember how it ended that time, don't you?' asked the Pope.

'Yes. But this time things will go differently.'

'Very well, then,' said his uncle, his lips spreading into a smile. 'Prepare to ride to Imola. I promise you it will soon be yours.'

Francesco bowed. 'My infinite thanks for not denying me this privilege.'

'Nonsense,' concluded the pontiff. 'You are right when you say that there's no limit to Lorenzo de' Medici's arrogance, and knowing that you are guarding against him trying to expand his possessions to our detriment is of great comfort to me.'

So saying, the Pope held out his hand to the nephew as a sign of farewell. The interview was over.

Francesco kissed the ring again; then, thanking his uncle one last time, he took his leave.

22

The Seed of Doubt

The reins of the city were slipping from his hand.

Lorenzo felt that a wound had been opened in Volterra and unless it was treated it would fester and infect the entire world with its unhealthy humours. But how to do it?

For a moment, he glimpsed his reflection in a silver tray.

A tired man looked back at him.

Alone.

Without friends.

Without confidants.

For months now, his wife had been locked away in prayer, avoiding him whenever she could. His mother was seriously ill.

Even Giuliano had distanced himself from him after what had happened in Volterra.

He looked at the sun-bathed garden of the villa in Careggi and thought of his grandfather Cosimo, of when he had waited for him at the foot of the stairs to play together among the bushes.

How he missed him!

His mind went back to a few days before, when he had berated Federico da Montefeltro for failing to keep his war hounds in check and allowing Volterra to be torn apart, despite the orders he had been given in the courtyard of the Palazzo Medici.

Federico had listened to him in silence and then murmured three words: 'You cannot imagine.'

Lorenzo had tried to make him talk, but to no avail. Montefeltro had closed himself up inside an impenetrable silence as if what he had seen had so upset him it had stolen his power of speech.

When he left, Lorenzo realized he had made a new enemy.

His readings of the *Corpus Hermeticum* of Hermes Trismegistus and the *Platonic Theology* which Marsilio Ficino had dedicated to him had been of no avail.

Indeed, they set him before his own inadequacy, because in his desperate attempt to protect Florence and his family, he had failed first of all as a human being: he had worried too much about the earthly journey which was unrelated to the soul and the power of ideas. Yet did ideas not underlie peace and prosperity? Were not ideas the concepts that presided over the unity of a land and an equitable distribution of wealth?

And what did he want, ultimately, if not a secure city state that could nurture the arts and celebrate the splendours of *humanitas*, mankind's love of unadorned knowledge?

He had always considered art and knowledge as tools to broaden horizons – not only his own but also those of his fellow citizens – and seen the aim of personal wealth as the creation of beauty and profit for one's community: this was its highest aspiration. And this was possible thanks to the achievements of his father Piero and his grandfather Cosimo, the first financiers of the construction of the sumptuous dome of Santa Maria del Fiore and of the episcopal council that had laid the foundations for a reunification of the Christian and Greek Churches.

Why, then, must he always come up against rebellions and conspiracies?

Why, every time he tried to build something, did others think only to destroy his vision?

He inhaled the scent of lavender and wisteria and let himself be lulled by the beauty of what he saw.

But it was not enough. He went downstairs and walked into the large garden, hoping that the sight of nature might for a moment drive away the thoughts that, like a pack of hounds, robbed him of sleep and lucidity.

He had wanted to take a clear line in his conduct, but now he was beginning to doubt that he had succeeded. And, on the other hand, could his decisions ever possibly satisfy everyone?

Florence loved him; of that at least he was certain. And he loved Florence with all of his being.

Yet he felt he had lost the affections of people who were important to him. He had driven them away. Had he truly done it to protect them, or was it just a story he kept repeating in a vain attempt to absolve himself?

He missed Leonardo, and he missed Lucrezia.

And there was no solution to that torment.

Clarice looked in the mirror.

Looking back at her was a woman with long, flame-coloured hair. Her blue eyes, once so bright, were now clouded, as though mist had made them watery and faded.

She realized that her face was even thinner than usual. She no longer had any appetite, and although she had no intention of letting herself die of starvation, she was losing interest in anything life could offer her.

She lived a recluse's existence at the bottom of the family hierarchy. She had pushed away Lorenzo, who had recently stopped visiting her, and had taken refuge in prayer and reading.

How long ago that argument about Lucrezia now seemed. Clarice knew he had not stopped seeing her, and that, despite his pleasantries, her husband did not love her at all. And even when he had promised her that he would do everything possible to stay away from his lover, Clarice had sensed the lack of conviction in his words, as if it were just some trifling matter to be dismissed with a wave of his hand.

But in spite of everything, his lack of attention had profoundly wounded her.

From that moment and forever more.

She saw the purple shadows under her eyes which made her look as though she were being consumed by some unknown disease. Yet she suffered from no pain in her body. It was her soul that was breaking and that she needed to mend. And there was no hope of that. She had neither the right needle nor the right thread – those could only have been created by a loving heart. Her willpower and her hopes were so weak that all she could do was turn the evil she wanted to commit upon himself. And since, apart from her gauntness, there were no visible consequences of her malady, she had decided to carve the marks of her shame into her own flesh.

As she stood staring into the looking glass, she took a magnificent dagger with a gold wolf's-head handle and a sharp, gleaming blade from the shelf.

She placed it on her alabaster skin just above her breast, and, after taking a deep breath, cut the white flesh until she saw it bleed. The cut was deep enough to bleed abundantly, a crimson arc from which ruby-coloured droplets dripped down, soaking her delicate white nightgown.

Entranced, Clarice gazed at the perfection of the two colours then saw, as though for the first time, the web of scars criss-crossing her chest.

What did it matter? Would anyone ever notice it? She had been doing it for months.

She covered her breast and wore black clothes with collars that went up to her chin.

Even in summer.

How many times before had she given herself over to the pleasure of that subtle pain, which reminded her, once again, of her inability to satisfy her husband and the Medici family?

She had sworn to herself that she would not give in. Never.

That she would not have other men.

That she would not rebel against that state of affairs.

She swore it for her father, who had wanted this marriage because it tied them to one of the most powerful families of the day.

She did not want to disappoint him.

And she did not want to give Lucrezia Tornabuoni or Lorenzo the satisfaction either. She would endure, despising herself all the while for not being strong enough to kill him. Because there were times when she truly fantasized about the possibility of taking his life for having destroyed hers.

What a joke it would be if the man so many wanted dead was found with his throat cut by the woman who should have honoured him more than any other!

She smiled at the thought – but there was bitterness in her smile.

The knife made a sinister sound as she placed it back down on the small silver tray. From a drawer she pulled out a handkerchief and wiped the blood from her hands.

It took a while to get them clean, but she didn't care. It would inculcate the memory of her inadequacy into her even more effectively.

Soon it would be time for vespers and she would go to the chapel. She would feel the hard wood against her knees and would mortify her person once again, letting herself be lulled by God's mercy. And in God's mercy, she would drown in joy.

OCTOBER 1473

23

Enemies and Allies

Gentile de' Becchi rode without pause. The fields, shiny with rain, and the muddy roads made his journey even more arduous but there was no time to waste: he had to warn Lorenzo and Giuliano, who had gone to Careggi after the commitments of the last few weeks.

They would be there discussing laisses and stanzas with Marsilio Ficino and the other intellectuals of the Neoplatonic Academy, but Gentile must warn them as soon as possible of the terrible news that threatened to undermine their hegemony with the violence of a hammer blow.

It didn't take an expert in conspiracies to work out what was happening.

Exhausted, he arrived in view of the villa and soon afterwards passed the guards at the gate and entrusted his horse to the servants with orders to give it shelter and a generous bucket of fodder.

When he entered, he asked to be received immediately by Lorenzo and Giuliano and soon found himself facing the two Medici brothers. The elder of the two was dressed soberly as always – he rarely indulged in fashionable clothes – while Giuliano sported a magnificent indigo doublet with exquisite silver and gold stitching.

Lorenzo embraced him warmly, as did his brother. Gentile felt deep affection for both of them and it was precisely for this reason that he could not wait a moment longer.

'Girolamo Riario is the new lord of Imola,' he said. 'And you know perfectly well what that means.'

'That that dandy will now be preparing to cause us some headaches,' said Lorenzo. He reflected for a moment. 'What I wonder is where he found the money. As far as I was aware, he was thirty thousand ducats short of being able to buy it from Galeazzo Maria Sforza.'

'Can't you guess?' asked Gentile de' Becchi.

Lorenzo looked at him, his intelligent gaze reading the thoughts of his interlocutor with disarming ease. He sighed.

'Of course. His uncle. The Pope.'

But that was only part of the story.

'And from the Pazzi,' added Gentile de' Becchi.

Lorenzo put a hand to his forehead.

'Of course, the Pazzi. Who never miss a chance to vex us.'

Gentile nodded.

'But what can he do from Imola?' asked Giuliano with a hint of ill-concealed disquiet.

'After appointing Pietro Riario as Archbishop of Florence, the pontiff now aims to have one of his war hounds to the north. Is Girolamo not the Captain General of the Church?'

'Exactly,' confirmed Becchi.

'Really?' asked Giuliano incredulously.

'Yes, brother – so now Sixtus can keep an eye on us from inside *and* outside Florence. You did well to come right away, Gentile. Your loyalty and friendship honour us.'

'It would never have occurred to me to do otherwise. But if I may continue, I'm afraid that the issue will not stop here.'

Lorenzo raised an eyebrow and gestured to Becchi to continue.

'You see, my lords, what I really fear is that, having received money from the Pazzi for the purchase of Imola, the Pope's next move will be to oust the Medici from the Apostolic Chamber.'

'What do you mean?' said an incredulous Giuliano. 'You know perfectly well that's not possible; the Medici have been in charge of administering the finances of the papacy for a hundred years. He certainly won't dare break such a tradition.'

'Unfortunately, Giuliano, I'm afraid Gentile is right,' said Lorenzo. 'Sixtus IV is the Pope, and if he were to decide that the bank which currently administers the Apostolic Chamber is unsuited to the Papal States, he has the authority and power to entrust the task to another. The Pazzi have acted with admirable timing and cunning. Now I understand how much trouble this will cause us.' Lorenzo looked worried. 'What do you recommend we do, Gentile? Should we fear this Riario so much that we have to deal with him? Should we worry that after Imola he plans on expanding his territories and threatening other cities to the north?'

'In truth, my lord, I have no idea. As you know, many say that Riario is a madman and bloodthirsty to boot. If he were to make joint cause with other enemies of ours, he might turn out to be a fearsome adversary. His star is on the rise, and there seems to be no limit to his ambition. He can count on the pontifical army, and seems to be close to marrying Caterina Sforza.'

Lorenzo's annoyance almost got the better of him, but he managed to repress it.

'Is that so?'

'Therefore I would try to get as much information about him as possible,' Becchi continued.

'We have to do more than that.'

'What do you mean, Lorenzo?' asked Giuliano.

'We can't let Sixtus take the initiative. We must start forging alliances with states that have traditionally been friendly towards us so that in the event of an offensive, we can immediately count on support from those on the other side of Imola. That way, if our good Girolamo Riario tries to harm Florence, he will soon find himself caught between two fires.'

'Do you mean Milan and Venice?' asked Becchi.

'Of Venice I have little doubt, but are you certain that Galeazzo Maria Sforza will fight against his future son-in-law?' asked Giuliano.

'Marriages mean little; no one knows that better than me,' said Lorenzo, not without some bitterness. 'I am confident about Galeazzo Maria – the friendship between our families has deep roots.'

'True,' said Becchi, 'it was your grandfather who allowed Francesco Sforza to conquer Milan. Without Cosimo de' Medici he would have remained a soldier of fortune.'

'We will make sure to remind Galeazzo Maria of that. But we can wait no longer,' continued Lorenzo. 'We must move now, so we are ready. And of course we must do it with subtlety and discretion. But there is another question here which I think is important.'

'What?' asked Becchi, as surprised as ever to see how quickly Lorenzo took the necessary decisions and countermeasures. The man possessed extraordinary pragmatism combined with incredible political intuition and a willingness to use the tools of power. Yet he was always able to stop himself a moment before going beyond the limit.

'I've been hearing from many different sources that the people of Florence are unhappy with the way they say I have shaped the Republic. In short, they say that I have stripped its institutions of meaning and power. Now, I have no intention of claiming that I have not made some changes which are in our interest, but I'd like to counteract these rumours, using agitators on one hand and facts on the other.'

'The many feasts you hold and your friendship with Botticelli do not help either, in truth,' said Becchi.

'It is not Botticelli who irks the people – they adore him. Though I can see how traditionalist families and the Church might not. But I have already lost Leonardo and I do not intend to renounce the friendship of a painter like Botticelli. He will remain my protégé. No, my friend, there's another issue: I intend to open our palazzo up not only to intellectuals and artists, but also to the less well off and to the common people. I will try to give them advice and protection. And money, of course. My grandfather Cosimo always told me that with the people and the plebeians behind us we could never lose. He told me that right here, in the garden of this magnificent villa, when he was playing with me.'

'I remember you back when I was obstinately trying to teach you to read and count. I can see the two of you together.' And so saying, the man who once had been Lorenzo's preceptor struggled to hold back his emotions.

'And I am infinitely grateful for your obstinacy, for I would have lost the better part of myself had I not listened to you. In any case, we must inaugurate this new custom. The Palazzo Medici must always have its doors open not only to artists and intellectuals but also to the common people, because it is through them that we will consolidate our support.'

'We will choose days when men and women from all walks of life can visit us and tell us about the difficulties they face in their daily lives,' said Giuliano. 'And we will help them, even giving them money if necessary.'

'Well said, brother,' said Lorenzo. 'By welcoming them into our home and by funding feasts that the common people can attend, we will persuade those families who consider us too arrogant and too rich to think less harshly of us, and through our supporters we will have more chance of influencing the decisions of the High Council and the Council of the Hundred.'

'And by consolidating our support and strengthening our alliances, the Medici will not be unprepared for whatever papal moves lie in store,' concluded Becchi.

'I couldn't have said it better myself,' said Lorenzo, allowing himself a smile.

He did not fear Sixtus IV and he had every intention of showing him what he was capable of. If the Pope was the spiritual guide then he would do everything he could to put up against him a secular power inspired by art, reason and intellect.

'It is decided, then,' concluded Lorenzo, 'the time has come to meet Venice and Milan. We will make a pact with the doge Nicolò Marcello and with Galeazzo Maria Sforza, but we must hurry. I will write to them tomorrow on our return to Florence to establish the times and manner of the agreements. I envision an anti-papal league which can protect us from the interference of the pontiff.'

It was just a matter of time. Lorenzo knew that sooner or later he would have to undertake some bitter negotiations and raise his voice, and would most likely find himself at odds with the power of Rome. But he and his brother did not lack resources, and he felt that it would not be impossible for them, if they were both cautious and clever, to establish themselves as a Republic which the others would have to take seriously.

The people were the key, and always had been. And he was a Medici.

He would not betray his origins.

24

The Hunt on Horseback

The dogs growled, impatient to hurl themselves at their prey. They had scented the male and couldn't wait to chase him.

'Loose the hounds!' shouted Girolamo, standing in the stirrups, his short dark-green cape flapping in the cold air as he gave the order.

The kennel-hands, who held at least half a dozen Bleu d'Auvergne pointers and Hungarian greyhounds each on leashes, quickly set about freeing them. As soon as they were loose, the dogs leapt forward, barking as if they were possessed. Fast and powerful, they bolted off with an elegance as composed as it was lethal: they would find the boar and wear him down by forcing him to run for miles.

The horn rang out and Girolamo immediately spurred his horse on into a gallop. Behind him came Francesco de' Pazzi, Ludovico Ricci and the nobles of his court at Imola.

The others had difficulty keeping up with Riario, who seemed to be in the grip of some kind of madness. There was such passion in him that he never wanted to let the honour and satisfaction of victory escape him. He must be the first to find the boar and plant a spear in its chest.

The estate around his property was made up of a dense tangle of pine and fir woods: a solid mass of green punctuated by the gold of the larches even in winter.

Girolamo could smell the fear. The pack of hounds was drawing closer, and the fleeing beast screeched and snorted in pain as it ran. Soon Girolamo saw a Bleu d'Auvergne with its belly torn open and its steaming entrails draped over the pine needles.

He had to be careful: the beast was treacherous and would not let itself be so easily taken. All the better, he thought. It would be more enjoyable.

He spurred on his mount in a mad rush through the branches.

With what breath remained in his lungs, he blew a change of direction on the hunting horn as he hurtled like a thunderbolt through the thick of the forest. The kennel-hands freed a fresh set of Bleu d'Auvergne pointers and Hungarian greyhounds to support and replace the others.

Soon, Girolamo would order them to unleash the fierce molossers, which would weaken the beast with well-timed attacks so as to soften it up for his spear.

As hard as they spurred on their mounts, Francesco de' Pazzi and Ludovico Ricci struggled to keep up with Riario. Ludovico, in particular, was certain that he had lost him, and worried as he thought back to his mother's admonitions. Girolamo had invited her to his castle in Imola, as he had wanted to meet her in person. He had heard of her proverbial beauty and found it was true that, although no longer young, she still possessed extraordinary charm: enough to bewitch any man.

Since she was no longer as confident on horseback as she had been in her youth, she had asked not to join the hunt, however, and was now awaiting them at the castle.

Naturally, she had not failed to point out to Ludovico how important that hunt was, especially given how enthusiastically Girolamo Riario spoke of it. He did so with a passion that was ardent to say the least, and when he spoke of prey and spears, his eyes sparkled with a pleasure that bordered on fanaticism. And judging by how Ludovico seemed to have lost track of him, that did indeed seem to be the case. Girolamo signalled his location with blasts on his horn of an intensity and frequency that not even Orlando would have been able to match when he had found himself overwhelmed by the hosts of Ganelon of Mainz.

Ludovico smiled as he considered the man's weaknesses. Girolamo Riario ardently desired to prove his courage and cunning, despite being bitterly aware that he was inadequately supplied with both. But such was his stubbornness in refusing to accept his failings that he often managed to overcome that obstacle. But while he was not courageous, he was certainly spirited, and even though no one would have considered him cunning, all could agree that he was capable of flashes of guile.

In any case, compared to Francesco de' Pazzi he was a refined strategist. The latter was no fool, far from it, but he had a violent and bloody temperament and seemed unable to control himself.

Ludovico was not afraid of him, but he certainly didn't trust him. In Francesco's eyes there was a disturbing perverseness and an unhealthy joy that made one thing clear: once he began to attack, none could predict when he would stop.

Ludovico continued to spur on his palfrey, being careful to avoid low branches or falling off his horse.

The barking of the dogs grew closer.

He heard an inhuman cry and, as he emerged into a clearing, saw something that for a moment took his breath away.

'Give me a spear, now!' thundered Girolamo Riario.

He was on his horse in front of the boar. The beast had a short bristly coat and its long tusks were covered with scarlet. Around it, their bellies torn open, at least four dogs lay on their sides like abandoned toys.

One of the molossers managed to bite the boar hard, and the animal was bleeding and grunting in a way that made the blood freeze in Ludovico's veins. It was still able to move, though, and managed to injure the hound with a well-aimed blow from its long tusks. The molosser began to howl pitifully.

'Come on, come on, give me a spear, now!' shouted Riario.

A kennel-hand passed him one. For a moment Girolamo seemed to carefully consider the distance; then he looked the beast in the eye and threw.

The spear struck the beast full in the chest. It shrieked one last time and fell to the ground.

Not even then did the wounded molosser which had managed to bite the creature relinquish its grip.

When he saw that the beast had fallen, Girolamo dismounted. He went over to the boar and, extracting a long hunting knife, plunged it into the animal's belly. Then, with his free hand, he stroked the molosser's head.

'Bravo, Spingarda, bravo – you never let it go, did you?'

The dog whimpered, and as its master stroked its head it finally released the boar's flesh from the deadly grasp of its teeth. The creature's chest was covered with blood; its fate was sealed. At the thought of how loyally the hound had served him, Girolamo could not hold back his tears.

And it was precisely at that moment that it happened.

The dogs began to wail nervously. Had they scented something?

The dark form of a creature flashed through the bushes: an imposing mass, covered with short bristles.

The terrible grunt that followed left no doubt.

The boar burst out of the bushes like a cannonball, heading straight for Girolamo Riario.

The lord of Imola stood frozen, staring at it and knowing that he had made a fatal mistake.

25

The Prey

When he saw what was about to happen, Ludovico didn't hesitate.

He spurred his horse over to the nearest kennel-hand and grabbed the spear from his hand. His panic at the scene taking place before him had loosened the man's grip, and he let it go with surprising ease.

Ludovico took a firm grip on the spear, stood up in the stirrups and raised it above his head.

In his hand Girolamo Riario held his hunting knife, which was dripping with blood from the belly of the dead beast. His eyes were wide open and he seemed paralysed with fear.

At incredible speed for its size, the second boar lowered its head and charged him.

At that moment, with a shout, Ludovico threw the spear. It flew through the air with a whistle, the blade flashing, and stuck deeply into the flank of the animal, which gave a monstrous grunt of pain.

But though the boar slowed, it did not stop its charge.

The spear must have weakened its fury, though, since the speed of its strides decreased, making its impact with Girolamo's legs less devastating. The animal slammed into him with all its enormous weight, sending Riario sprawling to the ground under the momentum of its rage, which had now become agony.

In the meantime, Francesco de' Pazzi had dismounted and unsheathed a dagger with a shining blade and flung himself upon the animal, stabbing its flank and belly.

But by now the boar was dead: the spear Ludovico had thrown had penetrated deep into its side.

With the help of his servants, Girolamo Riario got back to his feet and shot a grateful look at the protégé who had saved his life.

Then he went over to Francesco de' Pazzi who, blind with fury, was still attacking the carcass of the dead animal, stabbing his long knife into the torn flesh and pulling it out covered in blood, again and again. His long black hair was plastered to his head with the humours and entrails of the dead boar and his eyes glinted with absurd ferocity.

'That's enough, my friend,' whispered Girolamo, as though he were talking to a capricious child or a madman. Both of which Francesco perhaps was. 'That's enough. Don't you see that he's dead now?' And so saying, he brought his hand over Francesco's, who still clutched the handle of the knife with a stubbornness not unlike that of the molosser.

As soon as he felt the hand of the lord of Imola on his own, Francesco stopped.

He looked around him and his demented eyes, glowing with madness, froze the blood of the kennel-hands, the servants and of Riario himself.

Only Ludovico maintained his calm.

Now he understood perfectly what kind of person he was dealing with. He would need to keep it in mind.

The room was magnificent and the table laid carefully with silver trays and Neapolitan porcelain.

The high coffered ceilings with their gold friezes, the fabulous tapestries on the walls, the finely carved furniture: Girolamo Riario had spared no expense to furnish his stern, warlike castle near Imola. Thanks to his uncle's support, he had settled there as the local lord and had immediately begun squeezing the city's populace and the peasants with taxes of all kinds, filling his coffers with money and the halls of his gloomy residence with splendid furnishings and decorations.

But despite her advancing age, Laura Ricci was still the most surprising of all the lights which shone in that salon.

Something of the suffering she had endured over the course of her life had been given back to her in the form of beauty. An eternal loveliness, so to speak. It seemed almost as though pain had given her youthful beauty a sensual grace usually peculiar to animals – as though the imperfections of maturity had conferred upon her a more profound and lascivious charm. And the deeper the pain sank within her, becoming resentment and regret, the more that feeling like a blade in the guts cloaked her with an inexplicable allure.

Although she was well over fifty, and must in fact have been closer to sixty, her eyes still flashed with a wild light which distracted from the deep wrinkles that scored that beautiful face with its amber complexion. The white streaks left ostentatiously in her black hair communicated an unsettling yet irresistible restlessness. And then there was her clothing: the black dress and the *gamurra* of the same colour, the diamonds shimmering like splinters on her breast, the silver stitching of the fabric, and her bosom – still pert and seductive – pressing against her neckline.

None of the guests could take their eyes off her.

There was nothing rational about it, simply formidable charisma on one side and on the other an inability to fight against the iron will that was capable of influencing the intentions of the men at the table.

'Today, your son saved my life, my beautiful lady of Norcia.'

Riario's voice betrayed the emotion he felt about the daring way he had been torn from the clutches of death, an emotion heightened by the aura of restless magnificence that seemed to hover around the face and bosom of Laura Ricci.

The woman was silent, merely nodding. Riario looked surprised.

'Does that leave you indifferent?' he asked with a hint of irritation.

Laura waited another moment before answering. It was amusing to see how ineptly the man handled being kept waiting.

Eventually she spoke.

'Not at all, my lord,' she said laconically. 'I already knew of it.'

But those few words were not enough for the lord of Imola.

'Really?' he asked incredulously, raising an eyebrow. 'And how, if I might ask?'

'I read it in the cards.'

'In the cards?' asked Francesco de' Pazzi.

'In the tarot,' continued Laura.

This merely confused him, as the Florentine nobleman now had even less idea what she was talking about. He knew of only one kind of cards, and they contained no information about fortunate escapes.

As though reading his mind, Laura came to his rescue with an explanation.

'This is not a game, my lord, but rather a pack of very special cards that, if studied and read properly, can suggest events which will happen in the near future.'

Francesco de' Pazzi was stunned. 'Ah,' he said, pretending to understand.

Laura smiled benevolently, but did not elaborate.

'So you are a fortune teller, my dear lady,' said Girolamo Riario contemptuously.

'I am a reader of the tarot,' said Laura. 'I preach no future, I limit myself to reading the signs contained in the cards and matching them with the life of the person to whom they refer. I simply observe and tell what I read. I am no charlatan, and I attempt to dupe no one. It is up to those who listen to me to decide whether to believe what I see or not. But what is certain is that I saw the attack of the second beast that almost killed you in the cards this very morning.'

'If that is true, you could at least have warned me!' answered Riario. 'You would have spared me a great fright.'

'You had already left. And in any case, did my son not save your life?'

'There you are damnably right,' agreed the lord of Imola. 'Had it not been for his presence of mind, that boar would have first broken my legs and then ripped open my stomach. It was huge, and very angry. I owe everything to your son and I will be able to refuse him no favours. You may ask me for anything, Ludovico.'

So saying, Girolamo drained the red wine from his goblet, and the cup-bearer hurried to refill it immediately.

'To tell the truth,' said Ludovico, who had remained silent for a moment, 'the only thing I ask of you, and which would really give me satisfaction, is to serve you, my lord.'

'What a wonderful answer, my boy. I confess that I see in you the son that I never had. And after meeting your mother, I am, if it is possible, even more enthusiastic.'

Laura granted him a smile.

Francesco de' Pazzi, meanwhile, was bewildered by this exchange of compliments and courtesies, so after pouring himself a drink and taking a bite of cold pigeon pie, decided it was time to make his voice heard.

Despite his manners being far removed from the courtliness of the others at the table, he tried to formulate his proposal as subtly as possible. He cleared his throat as though it might bring the discussion back to the principal topic of their meeting.

'My good sir. My lady Laura. Young Ludovico. I enjoyed the hunt this morning and am enjoying this rich dinner tonight. But let me come to the reason for our meeting. I hope you will not think me too direct. We know how it is our intention, for various reasons, to, let us say, *eliminate* the Medici from Florence, freeing the city from a family of leeches that is monopolising all resources in the name of their prestige and lust for power. Just to make clear my real intentions: I can already say that for my part I would be more than willing to cut off the head of Lorenzo and his brother so as to free us once and for all of that pair of snakes.'

Girolamo Riario burst out laughing so uncontrollably that he spilled his wine, drenching his beard. When he noticed that Francesco de' Pazzi not only did not understand the reason for his amusement but was on the verge of becoming offended and, most likely, letting all hell loose, he had the good manners to explain.

'Good Lord, my noble friend, that is certainly plain speaking, is it not? I confess that your idea appeals to me, but I must agree with my advisers that it would be unwise in political terms. A cold-blooded murder could provoke a war, and that would not be a desirable outcome. What use will all our plotting have been if we reduce Florence to ashes?'

'What do you suggest, then?' retorted the annoyed Florentine. The conversation had already gone on too long for his tastes.

'Exile,' said Laura. Girolamo Riario nodded.

'And how can you be so certain that exile is the best solution for the Medici?' asked Francesco de' Pazzi.

Laura's eyes glittered.

'This is a very good question, Messer de' Pazzi. But let me say, my good sir, that I have seen things you could not even imagine. I was there when Cosimo and Lorenzo de' Medici were exiled from the city of Florence following accusations of high treason. At the time, I was under the protection of Rinaldo degli Albizzi.'

'And therefore,' observed Francesco, 'you will remember perfectly how it ended.'

'I understand your meaning: that exile was the wrong choice because the Medici returned stronger than before and freed themselves of Rinaldo.'

'Precisely.'

'That is true. But the exile did not produce the desired results because under Rinaldo's aegis, the city was hungry and exploited. Florence did not like Rinaldo at all – rather it both hated him and was afraid of him. You cannot govern Florence that way. The city needs not to be tamed, but seduced.'

'I confess that I do not understand: what is so different this time that justifies trying again a tactic that has already proved unsuccessful?'

Laura was leading the conversation with impressive ease and Girolamo found himself hanging on her every word. *That* was who the young Ludovico resembled – his mother, of course.

'I will proceed by degrees. Do you believe that your family can take responsibility for leading an alliance with the adversaries of the Medici so that, using a diversion, we can all strike Lorenzo together? In other words: do you think that the Pazzi, and in particular your uncle Jacopo – as well as yourself, of course – would be on our side?' asked Laura.

'You would not ask that if you knew how much money we have lent to Pope Sixtus to ensure—'

Francesco stopped himself. It would have been vulgar to bring up the fact that his family had lent the pontiff thirty thousand ducats to allow Girolamo Riario to buy the lordship of Imola. But by leaving that sentence hanging, he had managed to make it clear how deep the ties between his family and the papacy were without offending Riario openly.

On balance, he had spoken well. He could hardly have done it better even if he had considered his words beforehand.

'We all know what you mean and we are grateful for your... discretion. After all, it was the Pope who gave you the administration of the pontifical finances, so I imagine that discretion and gratitude are a duty. The reason I ask this is because it was divisions that caused Albizzi's defeat. He was abandoned by his allies, and that is a mistake we cannot afford to make. And bearing in mind that Guglielmo de' Pazzi and Bianca de' Medici are husband and wife, well, you can see why the question arises, can you not?'

Francesco nodded, as did Girolamo, who was grateful to this extraordinary woman for sparing him an outburst of wrath. Ludovico looked at his mother with admiration.

'The question is pertinent, I agree,' said Francesco. 'However, I can assure you immediately that our family is united and recognizes only one enemy.'

'That is what I hoped to hear you say. Very well. Now, each of us has a good reason for wanting the downfall of the Medici, but I would like to be sure that our motives are strong and will not waver in the face of any reversal of fortune. We can only prevail over the Medici if we can attack Lorenzo and his brother from both inside and outside the city. Which is why I believe that excommunication would be of great help at this time.'

Laura looked at Girolamo Riario.

'Do you know of anyone with the power to do such a thing, my lord?' she said.

26

Strange Paintings

'Messer Leonardo, would you do me the honour of looking me in the face while I speak to you?'

Lucrezia was furious with him and with herself. She felt that Lorenzo needed them both but had no way of leaving the dark place where the exercise of power seemed to have trapped him.

She had gone to see Leonardo at his workshop, but as soon as he had opened the door the place had sent a shiver down her spine: she had realized immediately that the painter she had known had disappeared and in his place there was now only a half-crazed man with dirty hair and a long beard who barely washed and seemed to have lost himself in a tempest of indecent and frightening drawings.

Gone were the blues and greens, the clear, airy lines: they had vanished into a past that Leonardo seemed to want to deny altogether. In that large, dimly lit, grotto-like room, male bodies in a whole range of positions assailed her. Sketches of bodies, arms, hands and legs covered the walls like the carvings of some mad sculptor.

Laura looked at him. She wanted answers.

'And why should I?' he said in a whisper, as though he were in another world – one which was probably as incomprehensible to her as it would have been to every other person on earth.

'So that you can listen to me instead of drowning in this ocean of indescribable drawings!'

Leonardo laughed weakly, as though he could not believe what he had heard.

'And why do you think them indescribable, my lady?'

'Never mind,' continued Lucrezia, still barely able to believe her eyes. 'I did not come here to talk about naked men and similar obscenities.'

Leonardo glared at her. At that point, yes, she had managed to gain his attention – and also, perhaps, his scorn.

He shook his head; then he spoke in the same soft tone of voice that Lucrezia remembered from the day he had painted her portrait.

'Lucrezia,' he said, 'before you tell me about Lorenzo, let me tell you one thing, or rather two. The first, which is of minor importance, concerns the nature of these drawings.' Leonardo gestured to some of them, which showed naked men with visible musculature. Of these, at least two showed a male model whose skin seemed to have been removed as though he were an onion. The sheets were full of annotations and numbers. Lucrezia did not understand, but Leonardo seemed to want to explain.

'They depict the human body, Lucrezia. The way each of us is made. I am studying, as hard as I can, the machine that represents each man and woman, since they are the perfect harmonic form. And, in a sense, inexplicable. How can I paint a man or a woman without knowing the proportions of the body? It would be as if a soldier had no notion of fencing, or a woolman of carding. I do it also because I believe that by knowing the organs and forms that oversee the functioning of our body we can, over time, overcome its limits. Mine is not love for the obscene but for knowledge. I am forced to lock myself up in cemeteries and hospitals to study corpses since no one seems to understand the importance of such analysis. And yet it should be the basis of all study, because it is to man, first of all, and to woman, that we must look if we want to give our time meaning.'

Lucrezia looked at him without fully understanding what he meant. She wanted to ask questions, but she was afraid: Leonardo looked practically possessed. His hair was as long and dirty as hawsers which had spent too long trailing in the water. He was in a pitiful state.

But Leonardo did not allow himself to be distracted. His thoughts were on matters that she could not perhaps even see, and he seemed to be standing in some imaginary bell tower, looking at the world from above with his dreamy gaze, able to grasp the imponderable in the most hidden shadows of life.

'The second point concerns Lorenzo. I know how much you love him and how much he loves you. Precisely for this reason you must stay away from one another. In this, he is much wiser than me. In fact, I suspect that our quarrel, so sudden, so violent, was planned by him for the sole purpose of keeping me away from him and, in so doing, protecting me. What he did not understand then, and perhaps does not even now, is that I do not need protection. But you do.'

Lucrezia's beautiful face burned with annoyance.

'You men are such fools! What does protection mean? Do you have any idea what a woman in love is capable of? No, Leonardo, because you are as incapable of love as Lorenzo is. The pair of you are convinced that you need no one except yourselves, but all your achievements, your treasured knowledge, mean *nothing* unless you have someone with whom to share the satisfactions they give you. And I am tired of being told what's best for me! *I* know what's best for me, and believe me when I tell you that in no way does that mean loneliness or regret for a lost love!'

Leonardo looked at her bitterly. 'How much wisdom there is in you... I realize it now. I don't agree with what you say, at least not at all of it, but I cannot claim that it isn't logical. And, of course, on one point you are perfectly right, Lucrezia: only you know what is best for yourself.'

Then he fell silent. He waited, as though trying hard to find the right words.

'I apologize for my arrogance,' he said. 'Please believe that I absolutely did not mean to offend you. I simply sense that, in his way, Lorenzo feels that by doing this he is showing that he loves you even more. I would not expect you to agree, of course, but if what you have told me is true, then perhaps it would be more prudent to hide it in the deepest folds of your heart, Lucrezia. Lorenzo is much loved, but the hosts of his enemies are vast, and constantly growing. Do you really want to weaken him by distracting him with your love? So that in thinking of you, he exposes his flank to the opponents who are trying to destroy him?'

On hearing those words, Lucrezia felt a sharp pain inside her – a wound which felt much deeper because it was so unexpected and sudden. She would not have believed that Leonardo could talk to her like that.

It almost seemed that not only did he care nothing for her, but that he had no interest in any human being. How cruel had he been to tell her such a thing, knowing what she felt for the man who had once been his good friend?

On the other hand she felt that, as insane, violent and ruthless as his words were, there was a grain of truth in them. And that truth hurt her badly – so badly that she would never have believed she could be so humiliated by her own failings.

What if the only result of her demanding to be loved and to be able to see Lorenzo was to cloud his lucidity and obscure his view of the blade used to cut short his life? Had she ever thought about that?

Lorenzo was worried for her and had tried to protect her, to prevent her from becoming a target for his enemies. But what did she do for him, apart from demanding to see him like a capricious little girl? Or like a lover unable to make do with herself?

She burst into tears, because she felt that her selfishness was more miserable than Leonardo's words, and the more she cried, the more she recognized the bitter taste of truth. And a solution made its way into her mind, and then conquered her heart.

Seeing her so distraught, Leonardo embraced her, feeling as though he were holding a helpless little bird close to him. Lucrezia's face and body were beautiful, of course, but her heart was even more so. There was the intense, magnificent grace which Leonardo had sensed when he had tried to paint her portrait and capture her glow, as bright as that of a comet.

He felt her heart beating wildly, as if it were about to burst out of her breast at any moment.

He kissed her face, her burning cheeks, her exposed throat and her long black eyelashes, and wiped the tears from her lips.

Lucrezia returned his kisses, but before their affection could turn into passion, Leonardo stopped.

'I can't do it,' he said.

'Why?' she asked with a hint of disbelief.

'Because you don't want me. You want Lorenzo, and I am not him. And even if I wanted you, I could never betray a friend.'

Lucrezia shook her head bitterly, making her black curls sway.

'It's not true! I like you, Leonardo. There is a sweetness and a sensitivity in you that no other man will ever have. But perhaps...' Lucrezia asked hesitantly, 'it is you who does not like me?'

'That's beside the point.' There was a strange anger in Leonardo's tone. 'Leave now. You would have done better not to have come at all.'

'But why?' asked Lucrezia uncomprehendingly.

'Get out! Did you not hear me?' And this time Leonardo shouted. His sudden anger shocked her, and Lucrezia felt her tears falling even more rapidly than before.

'Perhaps you're right,' she said, 'I should never have come at all.

FEBRUARY 1474

27

Against the Pope

Galeazzo Maria Sforza was a tall, robust man, and his considerable size was surpassed only by the extraordinary energy that he exhibited in every action: his way of walking, his handshake, his laughter, and even his conversation. All who met him could sense the incredible life force within him; it was as though his veins ran with fire instead of blood. His long dark hair, his brown eyes, his regular face with its steady gaze: he was a self-confident man who had fought alongside Louis XI of France against Charles the Bold, Duke of Burgundy, and, barricaded in the abbey of Novalesa near Susa, had held off Amadeus IX of Savoy's men for weeks on end. Until his mother, Bianca Maria Visconti, had convinced the Piedmontese gentleman to desist, under threat of retaliation by the French sovereign, at which point Amadeus had given up. Upon his return to Milan, Galeazzo Maria had been welcomed as a hero.

Lorenzo greeted him with great respect. He knew how rightly esteemed he was, not to mention that he represented the Duchy of Milan, an essential ally in his approaching battle with the Pope.

Doge Nicolò Marcello was of a completely different type: tall and thin and no longer in his prime, his white hair tucked beneath his *corno*, the pointed headgear indicative of his rank, held in place by a band embroidered with gold and set with precious stones as large as hazelnuts. His tired eyes and sharp nose spoke of a man who had lived for a very long time and who had found himself leading Venice when he probably would have preferred not to. Nevertheless, his hospitality had been exquisite, and Lorenzo was still trying to come to terms with the splendour of the Palazzo Ducale, which was even greater than the marvels of the Palazzo della Signoria in Florence.

Between the magnificent tall bookcases in finely carved wood, the ceiling ornamented with gold leaves, the large fireplace – in which a roaring fire burned – decorated with friezes and adorned with *putti* riding dolphins, the imposing coat of arms of the great lion of St Mark, the myriad of manuscripts and volumes with which the shelves were stuffed and the paintings of Giovanni Bellini and the mahogany writing desks, Lorenzo did not know where to look. The doge's apartments were a marvel. The library in which he found himself in that moment left him speechless. After having contacted the doge, Lorenzo had accepted the subsequent invitation from the supreme authority of the Most Serene Republic in order to agree a pact with Milan and Venice which would give them mutual protection from the ambitions of Pope Sixtus IV.

And now he was face to face with both, attempting to forge an alliance that could, perhaps, overthrow the pontifical superpower.

It was Nicolò Marcello who spoke first. Like his interlocutors, he sat on a wooden bench, intricately carved and inlaid with gold, the embroidery of his red toga with its white ermine collar sparkling in the light.

'My very welcome guests,' he said, 'I thank you for accepting my invitation and for your solicitude and courtesy. You know very well the reason why we have decided to meet: the Pope is taking advantage of his influence to assign lordships and titles to relatives and friends. Not only that: when his intolerable nepotism is pointed out, he reacts with denials and threats of war. Even as we speak, he is proposing his niece in marriage to Ferdinand, King of Naples, in the hope of obtaining his support.'

Lorenzo nodded, impressed by Nicolò Marcello's pragmatism and his lucid presentation of the facts.

'Excellency, it is an honour to be here. Not only do I agree with what you say, but I would add that, lately,

Sixtus has been trying to broaden his sphere of influence and, in this regard, has assigned to his nephew Girolamo Riario the lordship of Imola, so as to play guard dog at the gates of Florence. It seems all too clear to me that such a move is aimed at taking control of Romagna in the hope of isolating Florence and eventually bringing it under his own dominion, perhaps by handing the government of the Republic to his beloved nephew. It is quite clear that such a manoeuvre would be nothing less than a prelude to an attempt at expansion that could reach the Venetian mainland. Now, I know very well that my little Republic is a small thing compared to your great estates, and yet I believe that its integrity and independence are of great use to you.'

This time it was Nicolò Marcello who nodded.

'Your humility does you honour, my friend, but both I and the Duke of Milan know perfectly well that you hold the balance of power in the current political situation. And deservedly, I would add. Your role is vital because, in part for geographical reasons, you are the first power in a position to absorb the impact of any possible papal expansion. So do not be modest with us.'

Galeazzo Maria coughed. He had listened to both and now he wanted to make the voice of Milan heard.

Nicolò Marcello gestured to him to speak.

'Excellent and magnificent gentlemen, what you say is so true that I myself had to promise my daughter Caterina to Girolamo Riario, otherwise neither he nor his uncle would give me respite. What I wish to make clear immediately is that such an act in no way means I condone or support the Pope's conduct.'

'You would not be here, otherwise,' said the doge.

'Naturally. And, in fact, I also believe that the time has come for us to make a pact which guarantees mutual support, so that whenever one of our cities is unjustly attacked, the other two can intervene promptly. If we reflect for a moment, we will soon realize that Milan, Venice and Florence are strategically placed, because they are capable of guarding the north-west, the north-east and the south. An alliance is therefore not only logical but also full of potential, and might usher in a consolidation which would bring Ferrara, Siena, Genoa and many other cities under our aegis. At the same time, we would be in a perfect position to face the expansionist aims of Pope Sixtus IV and his greedy nephews.'

'So if I understand it correctly, Milan and Venice would be ready to support Florence in the event of an attack?' said Lorenzo. In light of what was happening in Rome, he needed to know.

'Certainly,' replied the doge, 'especially because Florence would do the same for us. What I want to ask you, my friends, is this: how much is Sixtus supporting your internal enemies? Forgive my lack of tact, but I have heard that he has been making approaches to the Pazzi in Florence, while Nicola Capponi has long thundered against the Duke of Milan from the Latin chair of Milan University, accusing him of being a tyrant and urging his students to kill him... And so I would like to ask you if I have been misinformed.'

'Your excellency,' said Galeazzo Maria Sforza, 'we know how efficient your network of spies is, and once again you have been informed perfectly. What you are saying is so true, in fact, that I am shortly going to arrange for Nicola Capponi to be investigated and imprisoned for high treason towards the Duchy, so as to eliminate the problem at its root.'

'The sooner you do, the better it will be for you, believe me. Here in Venice, the Ten – our criminal magistracy – have the specific task of removing all those who endanger, in whatever way, the established order of the Most Serene Republic. Of course, if you were ever to repeat these words of mine, know that I would deny them immediately,' said the doge with an amused smile.

'I would never allow myself to do anything of the kind,' said Galeazzo Maria.

'And you, Magnificent Lorenzo? What of the Pazzi?'

'Your excellency, your question is a legitimate and indeed necessary one in the light of the alliance we are about to make. What can I say?' He shrugged. 'I think it's clear that Sixtus is supporting the Pazzi family after they gave him the money to buy the lordship of Imola from the Duke of Milan last year.'

Galeazzo Maria raised an eyebrow and at the same time both his hands. 'It was not my intention to do you harm,' he said, as though to head off any possible criticism.

'I am not accusing you in any way,' Lorenzo went on, 'and I know very well that you had no intention of causing difficulties for my city. It is Riario who is the problem. His loyalty to his uncle the pontiff is impressive, though natural, given that it is the pontiff who is behind his fortune. But I digress... The point is that the Pazzi are certainly strengthening their position.

'Excellency,' he continued, turning to Nicolò Marcello, 'it is impossible to separate internal threats from external ones – they are inextricably linked.'

'I can see that very well,' confirmed the doge, who had found Lorenzo's reply slightly less than reassuring.

'And on the other hand,' continued Lorenzo, 'I do not think the Pazzi would ever dare take action from within the city. Their interests lead them elsewhere.'

'To Rome,' said Galeazzo Maria.

'Precisely,' agreed Lorenzo. 'Since the Pazzi became the administrators of the Apostolic Chamber, Francesco especially is more often to be found in the Eternal City than in Florence.'

'The treasure of the pontiff... which is of immense proportions,' commented the doge, with a hint of concern. 'Francesco's administration is responsible for the management of Tolfa's alum mine, which is one of the greatest sources of wealth known to man. Do you not fear such adversaries? It seems clear how dangerous the Pazzi are. There is no soldier, cardinal or politician who cannot be bought when one has such means.' Nicolò Marcello still seemed little comforted by Medici's words.

'Nobody would claim otherwise,' said Lorenzo, 'and yet I still do not think the threat to Florence will actually come from within. If Francesco's uncle Jacopo de' Pazzi tried to turn the people against us, he would end up with a handful of nothing. For some time now, I have welcomed the common people into my palazzo, giving them an audience and, together with my brother Giuliano, attempting to find solutions to their problems. We have worked at this in the pursuit of the common good – in fact our activities in this area have recently been doubled. Our relationships with the nobility are also good and while it is true that not all of us are friends, it is equally true that we boast powerful allies, not to mention our historical agreement with the Orsini family of Rome.'

'Very well, gentlemen, I thank you for your frankness. As you know, Venice is currently enjoying a period of relative calm.'

'It seems to me that the situation in Albania is not exactly idyllic,' observed the Duke of Milan.

'We have many enemies, and I do not deny that our admirals are facing not a few difficulties in those seas,' confirmed the doge without losing his composure, 'but, for various reasons, our internal situation is much less chaotic than yours. In light of what we have said, I therefore believe that the conditions for drawing up a document of understanding have been fulfilled. Provided, however, that you put your internal affairs in order. So let us say that Venice gives you its trust, confident that you will know how to manage the part for which you are responsible – that of your own territory. As far as possible external aggressions are concerned, we are in agreement. In fact, if you consider it a good idea, I could ask my most trusted lawyers to draft – in concert with yours, of course – an agreement. Nothing too formal or pedantic, simply a few words to outline this alliance. And in the meantime, I am happy to welcome you to Venice. I am sure you will find it not without charm.'

'By Bacchus, I'm sure of that!' said Galeazzo Maria Sforza, rising from the bench upon which he had been uncomfortably perched. 'I am keen to admire the lagoon from Piazza San Marco. As, I imagine, are you?' he said, turning to Lorenzo.

Lorenzo the Magnificent nodded. Of course he would allow himself a few days to admire Venice, but at the same time he would make sure that his lawyers were vigilant and careful in drafting the document. He trusted his new allies, but he did not want to make the mistake of underestimating their cunning. Which, in the case of the Venetians, was legendary.

While he was immersed in these thoughts, the doge too stood up and gave them their leave.

After the formal farewells were concluded, Lorenzo left the Palazzo Ducale reasonably certain that he had agreed on the terms of a good alliance for Florence.

APRIL 1476

28

The Accusation

They had come for him on a cool rainy night.

He had been at Andrea del Verrocchio's workshop. They had put manacles on his wrists and legs and led him to the Palazzo del Podestà. His head bowed, Leonardo had walked in silence behind the squadron of guards.

He had not eaten for days. For months now, he had been overcome with a sense of profound disillusionment.

On the one hand, he could not face painting, with the precision and rigour that required, and on the other, he feared his obsession with the proportions and the harmony of the human body had overthrown his reason. He had found himself living like some creature of the night, frequenting the gloomy halls of the hospitals, observing corpses whenever he could and rejoicing like a lunatic whenever he was able to get his hands on a dead man's body. It happened rarely enough, though, so in order to obtain one in good condition he had not hesitated to scour the battlefields, rummaging among the corpses like a vulture.

And he had been afraid.

Because a thirst was consuming him: every time he explored the hidden treasures, the red and purple organs housed in the belly and breast of that fleshy suit of armour, he felt an unspeakable joy.

He carefully recorded measurements and characteristics and each day filled sheets of parchment with calculations and reflections, covering them with his mirror writing so that no one could steal his discoveries.

Of course, often he was forced to settle for the carcasses of pigs or frogs. It was not the same thing, but he had to do it somehow.

He also had a couple of boys who, for a few coins, agreed to pose naked for him, letting him study and draw them. The exterior of the human body was as important as the interior.

There were times when he knew that all this would have offended the sensibilities of any who saw what he was doing. They would have considered it obscene, and yet the need to discover and understand erased those doubts, and Leonardo waited with feverish impatience for the moment when he could lay his hands once more on a man's body or the carcass of an animal.

It did not surprise him at all, therefore, that the guards had come to get him. He had no idea of the charge for which he was being led to the Palazzo del Podestà, but he knew very well they had ample choice.

The captain of the guards handed him over to the jailers, who led him in chains to a cold, narrow cell. They kicked him as they threw him inside, and one of them spat on him, calling him a disgusting sodomite.

He ended up lying on the cold stone while the door slammed shut behind him with a bang.

Ludovico Ricci rubbed his hands. Finally, after racking their brains to agree upon a strategy, Girolamo Riario and Francesco de' Pazzi had decided to act.

They had concluded that the first thing to do was to try and cast Lorenzo in a bad light – and striking at those he cared for was a way of provoking him out into the open.

Ludovico knew that the lord of Florence held Leonardo, the young artist from Vinci, in great esteem and was deeply fond of him. He was aware of the fact that the two had for some reason decided to go their separate ways but was equally convinced that their friendship remained, and that if Leonardo were in danger, Lorenzo would do anything to help him.

Absorbed in these thoughts, he entered the Red Dove tavern and almost immediately saw Francesco de' Pazzi seated at a table. His coal-black beard wet with its juices, he was tucking into a colossal pork shank. When he raised his mouth from his meal, revealing yellow teeth intent on chewing the dense red flesh, Ludovico almost retched. The man was disgusting, in some ways the closest thing to a beast that he'd ever met. He was not uncultivated, nor was he a fool, but he indulged his appetites and vices so brazenly that the sight of him when he was engaged in such activities was intolerable.

He almost seemed to do it deliberately to provoke.

With a certain apprehension, Ludovico took a seat in front of him.

Francesco de' Pazzi belched and wiped his beard and lips, which were covered with grease and leftover food, with the back of one hand as well as the magnificent sleeve of his velvet doublet; then he grabbed a clay jug and poured himself a glass of red wine. He greeted Ludovico with an absent-minded gesture.

The lady of the house came over to the table.

'May I bring you something, my lord?'

Ludovico was not particularly hungry, so he considered for a moment.

'Could you bring me some fresh fruit?'

The innkeeper nodded and disappeared.

Francesco de' Pazzi looked at him as he might at a lunatic.

'Just fruit and nothing else?' he asked. 'You'll end up

disappearing, my lad! You are already as scrawny as a skeleton. Good God, eat something more nutritious!'

Ludovico shrugged. 'I will leave that task to you. For me, fruit will be enough.'

Francesco de' Pazzi shook his head.

'Do as you please; it's not my problem. So,' he said, tearing off another large hunk of roast meat, 'what news do you bring me?'

While the innkeeper reappeared with a knife and a plate full of fruit, Ludovico began his story.

'Well, while we decide whether it is necessary to eliminate Lorenzo, I have set up a trap in order to discredit him in the eyes of the populace. I think it is wise to make him unpopular and weaken the support he has built up through his victories over Florence's vassal cities – Prato and Volterra – the feasts and spectacles he offers, all those works of art commissioned and financed by the city, and above all the feverish way he curries the favour of prominent members of wealthy society and, more importantly, of large swathes of the plebs and the ordinary people.'

Francesco de' Pazzi shook his head again.

'You do realize we're just wasting time, don't you? I am of the belief that we should exterminate the Medici, by which I mean all of them, none excluded, starting with the two brothers. Do not forget that even if Lorenzo were exiled, that would still leave Giuliano, and the whole family and its supporters would rally around him. Therefore they must both be struck in a way that prevents them from getting up again. Snakes must be crushed, there is no other solution!'

Ludovico nodded while he peeled a bright green pear. He knew he had to play along with Francesco, especially as he actually agreed with him, but several times over the last year Girolamo Riario had advised him not to come up with a definitive solution. Ludovico had the feeling that this request was influenced by the Pope who, though hating the Medici, could not justify a conspiracy which had their murder as its ultimate goal.

'I am aware of this, my lord, and let me be clear, I agree with you completely. Perhaps I would not have done a couple of years ago, but I too now believe that their death is the most logical solution to all our problems. But on the other hand, we know perfectly well that a plan expressly supported by the Pope and the captain of his papal army has much more chance of success. So—'

'As I recall, your mother was of the same opinion. Am I wrong?'

Ludovico nodded. 'I do not deny it. However, if you will permit me, I will come to the point. Assuming that there is between Lorenzo de' Medici and Leonardo da Vinci—'

'The painter?' interrupted Francesco de' Pazzi.

'Yes,' replied Ludovico, a flash of annoyance in his

eyes. He hated being interrupted, especially twice in a row.

But Francesco de' Pazzi cared little about this diabolical brat whose only merit was being the protégé of the lord of Imola and the son of a handsome slut who was getting on in years, and so he found it amusing to cut him off like that. The boy didn't have a drop of nobility in his blood, let alone an aristocratic lineage like Francesco's own. His courage was as inferior as his bloodline, and if he dared complain, he would find his throat cut.

But Ludovico was shrewd enough to say nothing.

'As I was saying...' he resumed, 'starting from the assumption that there is a deep friendship between Lorenzo de' Medici and Leonardo da Vinci, and that therefore the first would be willing to do anything to protect the second from the most disgraceful accusations, I encouraged one of our men to make an anonymous complaint to the Night Guards of the crime of sodomy against Leonardo da Vinci and a very young boy who on some occasions poses naked for him.'

'And would you be so kind as to explain to me where all this is supposed to lead us?'

'Patience, my lord. I am convinced that Lorenzo will manage to free Leonardo, but in doing so he will put himself under suspicion of aiding a sodomite, which would finally give the Pope the opportunity to threaten the Medici with excommunication. If you add to this that Lorenzo would also have the Archbishop of Florence and the Archbishop of Pisa, who has long shared our sympathies, against him, you will agree that he would emerge from it deeply compromised. And if Leonardo were to be condemned, Lorenzo would be so distraught at his friend's death that he would be a much easier target. As you can see, one way or the other we win.'

'Your confidence in such a bizarre plan seems excessive, but if Riario believes that it can be useful for our purpose, I can only give my endorsement.'

'Riario and his uncle, do not forget,' Ludovico reminded him. 'I realize that the plan is a complex one, but from what I have heard, the lord of Imola believes that this charge against Leonardo might confirm Lorenzo's reputation as a champion of vice. All can see how his follies with the Neoplatonic Academy, his passion for the outrageous paintings of Botticelli, his endless feasts with their secular themes, and his love affair with Lucrezia Donati are nothing more than the foundations of a vision of the world completely unmoored from spirituality and religion. And if we add to that a friendship with an artist who has been accused of sodomy... well, all the forces of religion could be unleashed against him. And believe me, my lord, in the long run this accusation will produce the consequences we are hoping for.'

'And what of Giuliano, his brother?'

'He too would be overwhelmed by infamy. Riario, and through him the Pope, intends to make the Medici the very symbol of vice and fornication, of infidelity and opportunism, of betrayal and disregard of any form of faith. By exiling Lorenzo outside the flock of God-fearing men, he might ultimately widen the boundaries of his own state and hand over the keys of the most important cities to his allies. And to you, those of Florence.'

'That's all I want. So be it, then!' concluded Francesco de' Pazzi in a gloomy tone. 'Let's see what happens. I still have my doubts about the success of this project, but there's nothing to stop us from opting for a more extreme solution should it fail.'

And with those words, Francesco tore off another piece of meat from the bone, his greasy teeth flashing yellow beneath his black beard and his dark eyes glinting with a cruel and malevolent light.

The die was cast.

29

The Interview

As soon as he'd heard about Leonardo's arrest, Lorenzo had raced to the Palazzo del Podestà. He didn't know what he was going to say, but one thing was certain: he would do everything in his power to clear his friend of the heinous accusation against him.

It was dawn, and Florence was awakening under a sky as pale as a shroud. He'd wanted to avoid taking the carriage, as his visit risked causing a stir, and he had informed a man there he trusted who would discreetly lead him to the cell where Leonardo was locked up: the less clamour there was, the easier it would be for him to direct the judgment of the magistracy.

He proceeded, therefore, at a good pace. The nocturnal humours were drying in the morning air, and the smell of the streets was intense and pungent.

Stray dogs snarled softly as they contended for bones. Despite his efforts to embellish and adorn the city with commissions, despite the provision that a few years earlier had ordered the butchers' shops to be transferred to the Ponte Vecchio, freeing the streets of foul-smelling meat and animal carcasses, Florence remained in some ways a gigantic rabbit warren – a smokey maze of mud and blood overlooked by beautiful palazzos and basilicas in a bizarre contrast that, upon closer inspection, was surprisingly cruel.

Breathlessly, he arrived in front of Santa Maria del Fiore and the vast mass of Filippo Brunelleschi's dome, which loomed over the city. After all these years, Lorenzo was still amazed at how the incredible red structure, invisible from the streets of the city, seemed to appear suddenly out of nowhere – almost as if Brunelleschi had wanted to make it even more breathtaking. And indeed, Lorenzo once again felt his breath halt in his throat when he saw before him the gigantic dome, which almost looked like a sky within the sky. There was in it all the wonder of the inexplicable and supernatural, as if art were the only language capable of communicating the grace of God and making visible his greatness.

Running past the cathedral, he turned into Via del Proconsolo, leaving the small square of Santa Maria del Campo behind him, and soon found himself approaching the Palazzo del Podestà.

At the entrance he was greeted by a guard who, with a simple gesture of understanding and without uttering a word, led him to the prisons. They crossed the courtyard, dominated by the great crenellated tower of the Volognana.

Soon afterwards, Lorenzo was walking along a narrow corridor, the torches along the wall giving off blood-red light.

After passing a series of cells, the guard stopped in front of the last one. He put the key into the lock and opened the heavy iron door. Lorenzo entered.

'I'm out here if you need me, my lord,' the guard muttered under his breath.

'I won't,' Lorenzo replied. He heard a clatter of locks and the door closed behind him.

He let his eyes grow accustomed to the dim light of that malodorous cell and saw a man sitting on a bed, his long, thin blond hair covering his face and a threadbare tunic adhering like a second skin to his lean body. The long beard gave that face, whose subtle and well-shaped features Lorenzo recognized, something of the aura of a prophet.

Without raising his eyes from the floor of beaten earth, Leonardo greeted him. The bitterness in the voice was as profound as the weariness that seemed to permeate his soul even more than his body. Everything that had happened over the previous few years came to a head in that moment: the quarrel over the war in

Volterra, the accusations, the broken friendship and the long-distance dialogue they had maintained, with the obligations of power on the one side and the search for an understanding of things on the other.

So when he spoke, it was with an intensity that not even he would have thought possible, the infinite disappointment of those tormented years audible in his voice.

'Once again,' he said, 'you come to me. Despite everything I said to you in the past, even though it was I who abandoned you. I am ashamed of myself, in a way. Yet I know that my actions reflected what I felt. And my convictions, despite the many errors I have made over these years, have not changed. I still believe that a city should not be conquered because it has a right to its freedom. And that freedom must be defended, even with weapons. But whoever attacks the freedom of others commits a crime. So in light of all this, I must ask you: what have you come here to do?'

'I came because I could not have done otherwise. I cannot abandon a friend in trouble.' Lorenzo's words came from the heart. He was tired of always thinking before he spoke: he wanted to act without worrying about the consequences for once.

'You are the greatest artist this city has ever had, and yet you insist on living in this way!' he went on.

'Which way?'

'Like a recluse. It seems almost that life is of no interest to you, that people are nothing but distractions from some larger design whose details you wish to know. But by hiding away from everyone, you wound others and, worse, wound yourself.'

'It is very strange to hear you say things like this.'

Lorenzo shook his head.

'I know what you are implying, but it's not me that we're talking about now. The charge against you is extremely serious. I still need to understand what evidence they have in hand, but if the Officers of the Night were to consider you guilty of sodomy, the sentence would be terrible. As your friend, I would never forgive myself if I didn't do everything possible to have the charges dropped!'

'Nobody asked for your help.' Despite the firmness of his words, Leonardo's tone did not change. 'And anyway – has it not occurred to you that it might be true?' And so saying he raised his head, his pale eyes meeting Lorenzo's almost challengingly. There was something strange about his gaze, a sort of calm that made Lorenzo uncomfortable.

'I don't care! It is not for me to judge what or who you like. Do you really think me so small-minded? But despite that, sodomy is still a crime in this city, and until proven otherwise, if there is no concrete proof there is no reason for you to stay in this filthy cell.'

'So? What are you going to do?'

'Can't you guess?'

Leonardo stared at him for a long time. Lorenzo did not look away. He knew that this man was his friend, he recognized his magnetism, the aura that allowed him to swiftly convince any interlocutor of the value of his opinion. Yet at that moment, Leonardo seemed absent. Perhaps in recent times he had become so used to observing life, animals, nature, colours, lights and shadows that he had forgotten how to listen to men's hearts.

'I've wanted to talk to you for years,' Lorenzo went on. 'For years I've dreamed of being your friend again. Can we not return to the way things once were? Or even better than that, because neither of us is today the man he used to be, and together we could do much greater things. I don't care if we have enemies; I don't care if they plot against us. I'm sick of having to think! Of having to worry that our friendship might benefit my adversaries. And I can't believe you harbour a grudge against me, not after all these years.'

'You are right, in fact, my friend. But you see the state we are in. You, forced to fight even ghosts, and I in a cell, accused of a crime of which I might even be guilty.'

'Not for long, you have my word on it.'

'I believe you. And what will we do then?'

'For starters, we'll get you out of here. And then you'll get back to work.'

'For you?'

'You've never worked for me. For Florence.'

'For Florence...' Leonardo seemed to reflect. 'And why should I? What has Florence ever done for me?'

'True enough! Then in that case, you will do it for yourself. Do you think I don't know that you rarely finish the things that you start? Have you ever thought that it would be nice for once to become impassioned about something and carry it through? A piece of art, Leonardo, I ask you for a piece of art! And then I will help you to leave Florence.'

Leonardo remained silent for a long time, seemingly weighing the implications of what he had heard.

'I do not hate this city,' he said eventually. 'I owe a great deal to Andrea del Verrocchio and I owe a great deal to you. And also... to Lucrezia.'

'Lucrezia...?' murmured Lorenzo.

'She loves you so. She is the most beautiful woman I've ever met, and there is something about her that completely enchants me. It's not her lips or her gaze, though. I think it's... her *courage*. But I cannot say whether you deserve to be loved by a woman like her.'

Lorenzo seemed to reflect for a moment.

'I think I agree,' he concluded in a melancholy voice. 'But this is not the time to talk about her.'

'Of course, it never is.'

Lorenzo seemed not to have heard this – or, more likely, preferred not to do so.

'Come,' he said, 'time is short, my friend, and we

must act. I have an idea. Let me get to work and you'll see: you'll be out of here sooner than you expect.'

And so saying, Lorenzo banged the large iron ring on the door.

After a few moments the key was put into the lock and turned with a creak.

'Hold on, my friend,' said Lorenzo.

As he always did, Leonardo looked at him with clear and sincere eyes.

'Be careful. I have the impression that what you are about to do will have consequences for you. And I thank you for honouring me with your friendship.'

Lorenzo smiled at him and then the door closed and Leonardo was alone.

30

The Officers of the Night

Lorenzo knew the Magistrature of the Office of the Night well.

It couldn't exactly be called his creation, but anyone claiming it was an invention of the Medici aimed at repressing sodomitical behaviour after the failures of secular and ecclesiastical institutions to do so wouldn't have been too far from the truth.

For this reason he was optimistic that he had a good chance of ensuring that the accusation against Leonardo was dropped. His father and his grandfather before him hadn't hesitated to use that same magistrature, created *ad hoc* for sexual crimes, as an effective tool against their personal political enemies, as well as a deterrent capable of forcing the uncertain morality of the citizens, both nobles and plebeians, back within the limits of decency.

In fact, the Magistrature of the Office of the Night had influenced public opinion, ensuring the gradual demotion of sodomy from capital to serious crime: deserving certainly to be punished by emasculation, but never by the death by fire which had previously been the norm.

The anonymous accusations against Leonardo had been deposited in the Mouths of Truth scattered around Florence, but lacked hard evidence. It was therefore with some optimism that Lorenzo left the prison in the early morning and went to see the Chief of the Office of the Night, Filippo Pitti.

He didn't have far to go, as Pitti's offices were in a room in the Palazzo del Podestà – more precisely, inside the Volognana tower.

Lorenzo knew for certain that at that time of day there was a good chance that Filippo would be alone. He nurtured an obsessive dedication for his work and spent almost all of his time in that office. When he was not there, he was certainly out on some investigation.

After knocking and announcing himself, Lorenzo entered.

Filippo sat at a table of dark oak, submerged in papers, documents and seals. As soon as he saw Lorenzo he got to his feet and came over to greet him. He wore the black toga with gold embroidery which was the uniform of his magistracy.

His eyes were tired and in all likelihood he hadn't slept in days. His sharp face hinted at a firmness and a rare rigour of thought which made him the perfect man for that task.

Medici and Pitti were not exactly on excellent terms, but Filippo always demonstrated a clear autonomy of judgement and behaviour. He was a well-balanced man of great intellectual honesty and Lorenzo did not doubt him. Lorenzo squeezed his hand.

'I did not expect to see you in this office, Messer Lorenzo,' he said, returning his grip. 'May I ask you the reason for such an honour?'

The magistrate's question was perfectly legitimate, and Lorenzo realized immediately that it would be pointless to attempt artifice or tricks.

'Messer Filippo, I have been informed of the arrest of Leonardo da Vinci on an accusation of sodomy. I hardly need to state that not only do I believe him to be innocent, but would like to see the evidence supporting such an accusation.'

The magistrate's blue eyes flashed. Lorenzo's request, and the manner in which it had been proffered, was extremely unusual. Worse: it sounded more like a command than a simple question.

Lorenzo sensed Pitti's reaction. 'If, of course, that is possible,' he hastened to add.

Filippo seemed to consider it and the hard lines of his face softened for a moment.

Then he spoke.

'My dear Lorenzo, I understand your interest and I confess that the news was a surprise to me too. I must say, though, that your asking me about the case in this way is completely irregular.' Filippo paused as though searching for the appropriate words. 'Knowing of your esteem for the young artist, though, I understand the reasons for your anger. What I can tell you is that at the moment the complaint is anonymous but does seem to be well documented. We found it in the Mouth of Truth of the Palazzo della Signoria. Moreover, it does not involve only Leonardo, as one might reasonably expect, and therefore I cannot exclude *a priori* the possibility of the alleged crime.'

Lorenzo sighed. The matter was far more complex than he had expected.

She felt him above her.

His hoarse voice hissed insults at her, and yet she loved the rough, savage way he had of taking her. It was as though she was possessed. Anna welcomed him with all of herself, as if she were nothing but a piece of meat. She felt her lord's strong, throbbing member, as taut as a hellhound, while it penetrated her to her core, and in her eyes there was nothing more beautiful than being taken – and humiliated – by Girolamo Riario, the lord of Imola.

In this way, she had become his favourite.

And Girolamo wanted her. Sometimes he had her with other girls, but more frequently by herself.

Considering what awaited her at home, she was more than happy to be mistreated by him. As mad and obsessive as his sexual vigour was, it was much better than what life had reserved for her thus far.

Once again, she thrust her backside towards him. She loved inviting him like that, and she knew it pleased him. Even a simple woman like her could understand what his preferences were. Indeed, it was precisely for that reason he liked her so much. Because she was one of the common people and her body, with its large breasts, sweet, brown eyes, long hazel hair and soft, broad flanks, possessed an irrepressible beauty.

Girolamo loved sodomizing her, pushing her face into the cushions and mounting her with an unspeakable rage. And she indulged him – in fact she openly invited him to penetrate her and demean her with all the rage of which he was capable. It was a cheap price to pay for a room of her own and three meals a day.

She lived like a queen and all she had to do was open her legs. She could scarcely believe her luck. And so she was always ready, grateful and happy.

She knew it wouldn't last forever, but as long as her good fortune continued, she would live as she would never have dreamed possible. And so, as soon as he slid out of her, she turned around and took his member in her mouth. It was hot and wet and dripping with humours.

Girolamo came with a cry and then collapsed on the bed, while she remained on all fours, her knees red from the hard wood of the floor.

She smiled.

All she had to do was do exactly what he wanted. Nothing else.

31

Prisoner

Clarice looked up. She had been on her knees on the wooden plank for longer than she could remember. Yet she knew she had no other choice.

She looked up at the journey of the Magi. She knew that fresco so well she could have described it with her eyes shut. And she thought about how much hypocrisy it contained.

She saw the three kings, each with his own gift to offer the child: gold, frankincense and myrrh. She kept her eyes on the youngest of the three who headed the procession. Caspar sat upright upon a horse of dazzling white, his hair a cascade of blond curls. He wore a crown, a gold band surmounted by a blue chaperon and decorated with gilded emblems and adorned with precious stones and strings of pearls. That proud look, the robe of white brocade that gave the dominant colour to the frescoed wall: everything about it left the observer dazzled, and Clarice could not look away.

Despite her anger, despite her frustration, despite the sense of isolation that her life gave her daily, she could not ignore the splendour of the fresco.

Benozzo Gozzoli had surpassed himself: the use of lapis lazuli powder for the blue background, the glittering lacquers, the gold shining in the inlays and glistening in the dim and red light of the candles, all the infinite imagination was of such magnificence that it left you speechless.

She looked at Caspar's parade and it was at that point that, as always, she was overcome with nausea. The Medici had been arrogant enough to have themselves portrayed as following him: Cosimo was the old man riding the mule, Piero his son was on his white steed, just like Caspar, and, in the thick of dignitaries there was Lorenzo, much more handsome than he was in real life.

As she clasped her hands together, Clarice gave a bitter smile: God, how she hated him! And that poison, that pain that filled her, was the child of her desperate need to love him – even though Lorenzo now ignored her: politely and kindly, of course, but she no longer meant anything to him. He much preferred spending his free time with artists and intellectuals.

She did not even know if he still saw Lucrezia Donati. The ladies of her retinue who usually managed to procure news for her had been struggling to obtain any information recently. Yet in her heart, Clarice knew the answer to that question which tormented her every day.

Of course he does, cried a harsh voice, *there's no doubt about it!* That woman had bewitched Lorenzo's heart once and for all, and although he was completely absorbed in the task of governing Florence while offering the citizens the illusion of respecting republican institutions, he certainly had to be finding ways to see her.

For some time now, Clarice had been so alone that she had begun to channel her isolation into fervent expiation: she mortified her flesh. Under her robes, the endless pattern of blood-encrusted cuts on her chest had grown even thicker.

With that repressed, excruciating pain, Clarice gave herself pleasure, for suffering was the alloy which shaped her life. And in that desolate existence she inhabited, the blade, the self-inflicted wounds and the punishment of her body all merged in mystical ecstasy.

She could all too easily bring to mind the image of those sessions when she had carved her milk-white flesh with the dagger while the fingers of her left hand touched the swollen red lips of her vulva, penetrating it and pleasuring herself.

It had never occurred to her to seek a lover to take the place of her husband, because, in spite of everything, she could not get Lorenzo out of her thoughts.

When they had last been together, he had been almost apologetic while he had taken her.

She had not objected, because her bitterness and loneliness had twisted and tamed her, turned her into the shadow of the woman she had been. She had kept him inside her until he had come, flooding her with his seed.

And once again she had fallen pregnant. Because, in spite of the arrogant words Lucrezia Tornabuoni had once addressed to her to justify her son's failings – intimating that Clarice should never question his faithfulness – she had managed to produce healthy offspring.

Lucrezia, her eldest daughter, was a beautiful little girl with blond hair and pale skin, her cheeks always ready to blush. She was now six years old and was judicious and intelligent. Piero, the second, was becoming as strong as a little ox, while Maddalena and Contessa Beatrice were both very sweet. Giovanni had been born the year before, and at that moment, his irresistible puppy-like charm made him her favourite.

Of course, the children gave her joy – they had saved her from the thoughts of suicide she had long nurtured.

But they were not enough: she felt as though she had been belittled as a woman, and Lorenzo's spurning of her was something she could never accept.

She sighed, raised her eyes once more and saw Balthazar: his dark skin, his eight-pointed crown, his green robe studded with gold embroidery whose colour dictated that of the entire southern wall of the chapel, and the bushes of white and red roses and cypresses lined up against the intense shades of the background.

Clarice felt tears streak down her cheeks.

She thought about when Lorenzo looked at her gravely, worried that she might open her mouth and reveal all of her inadequacies in front of Marsilio Ficino, Pico della Mirandola, Poliziano, Nicola Cusano or that crowd of intellectuals who were nothing but a mass of sycophants. Parasites, encouraging Lorenzo to write sonnets dedicated to that whore Lucrezia Donati!

She felt salt on her skin and there was a growing knot in her throat that felt as if it were about to choke her, like some gigantic iron sphere put there by an invisible tormentor.

She looked up for the third time into the eye of Melchior, the eldest of the Magi and in some respects the symbol of the approaching end of the earthly sojourn. With those three figures, so symbolic and so precise, the mind of the painter had marked out the seasons of life, and each time Clarice looked at them she saw the ruthless flow of her existence.

She had been young once, and now she was about to enter maturity. She was not yet old, of course, but the years had slipped away one after the other and as she reflected she realized how she had wasted her life condemning herself to a seclusion which had given her no joy except that of her children.

How she wished she needed nothing except herself! Her inability to make that true was the more painful because had it been the case, she would at least have been able to enjoy what the Medici offered her: prestige and wealth. Instead, that stubborn desire to please her husband and her foolish pride had ruined any hope of satisfaction.

She had become obsessed with wanting to punish Lucrezia Donati, yet she feared her husband's reaction. She knew perfectly well that she was in the right, but Lorenzo would not fail to make her pay for it if he found out that she had plotted against his lover.

But then, what did she have to lose?

And what joy it would give her to know that Lucrezia was finally suffering as she did, at least in part! Because in part would be more than enough – the woman had taken everything and had left her with nothing!

Clarice looked at Melchior again. She stared at the procession with its red-clad entourage and, through the tears that now blurred her vision, the scarlet seemed to spread over the painting, becoming so intense that it resembled an ocean of blood.

Every fibre of Clarice's being trembled at that sight. It seemed to her that this vision announced something terrible. Horrified by what it seemed to be foretelling, she lowered her gaze, hoping to push away the dark and ominous feeling that was hammering at her heart.

32

The Trial

Presided over by Filippo Pitti, the Officers of the Night sat on wooden benches. Pitti gestured for the guard to introduce the first defendant who would also be heard as a witness in the case.

Jacopo Saltarelli entered. He was an effeminate young goldsmith who gave the impression of having nothing to fear: his expression was defiant, almost disdainful, and his chained hands were clenched into fists. He wore a ragged tunic which must once have been white but which was now stained and grey with dust.

He was led to the witness stand. Seated in a wooden chair before him was Leonardo, his chin touching his chest and his long hair falling forward and making it impossible to see his face.

The trial would take place behind closed doors, even though Lorenzo had obtained the right to be present together with some of the city's elders.

'Messer Jacopo Saltarelli,' began Filippo Pitti, 'you are accused of the crime of sodomy and of taking part in various sordid acts for the pleasure of those who requested such wickedness. I would ask you if you recognize any of them here before you.'

A cold silence filled the room. Lorenzo held his breath.

Jacopo Saltarelli raised his head. His eyes became less firm when he heard those words. He seemed hesitant and for a moment fiddled with a fold of his threadbare robe.

Eventually, he gave a silly smile, full of allusive wickedness.

'Yes,' he said laconically.

'Could you be more precise, Messer Saltarelli,' asked Filippo Pitti. 'Could you point to the person?'

With a fiery stare, Saltarelli almost lasciviously stretched out his arm and pointed to Leonardo.

'Him,' he said. 'He wanted me to undress and then he... took me.'

'Do you therefore recognize the man with whom you committed unspeakable deeds?'

Saltarelli nodded.

'Could you tell us what you did?'

Lorenzo looked at Leonardo. He had raised his head and his gaze was as cold and distant as if the trial concerned someone else.

'Three weeks ago, I was in this man's workshop.'

'Do you mean Andrea del Verrocchio's workshop?'

'No,' answered Saltarelli, 'I was in his personal workshop, in Oltrarno. That man has protectors and can afford his own workshop, my lord.'

'What do you mean?' asked Filippo Pitti suspiciously.

'Precisely what I said.'

'Oh no, you cannot simply come out with a statement like that and imagine that that is an end to it – speak!'

Jacopo Saltarelli snorted. He looked as though he realized he had said too much.

'Well, I've only heard rumours.'

'And what did they say?'

'That Leonardo is well liked, my lord. And that his friends include even Lorenzo de' Medici.'

There was a chorus of surprised voices from those attending the trial. Lorenzo wanted to intervene, but remained silent so as not to make the situation worse.

'And do you have evidence to support what you say?' asked Filippo Pitti. His voice was flat and betrayed no emotion.

Saltarelli hesitated. He seemed to be debating if it was worth sticking his neck out any further than he already had.

Francesco de' Pazzi, who was also among those who had been permitted to attend the trial, now had a nice arrow for his bow and was already hard at work using it – his deep voice boomed.

'Silence!' said Filippo Pitti. 'Jacopo Saltarelli, do you have proof of your statement? I ask you not because a possible friendship between Messer Leonardo da Vinci and Lorenzo de' Medici would be a crime but because you must get used to telling us facts which you are able to prove. I repeat: do you have proof of what you say?'

'No, my lord, it's just rumours.'

Filippo Pitti nodded.

'As I thought. I confess that I have the feeling that almost all of your affirmations are fantasies.'

At those words, Lorenzo breathed a sigh of relief. That meant that Filippo Pitti had pressed Saltarelli only to demonstrate his way of doing things. If his statements were unproven, it was reasonable to conclude that Leonardo's sodomy too might be the fruit of Saltarelli's imagination. And since it had been unsigned, Saltarelli might also have been the author of the complaint. The man had fostered the germ of suspicion in the room, though: suspicion that he was a friend of Leonardo, a possible sodomite. Suspicion that he encouraged such practices. He looked over at Francesco de' Pazzi and knew what he would be able to do with a suspicion of that kind. Through his rabble-rousers he would inflate it into something enormous, regardless of the outcome of the trial.

'In any case, let us return to the matter at hand,' said Filippo Pitti. 'You say that three weeks ago you were in the workshop of Messer da Vinci.'

'Yes, my lord,' confirmed Saltarelli.

'Go on,' Filippo encouraged him.

'Well, I was completely naked and had been lying there for several hours. I was tired. I hadn't eaten and it was late at night. So I asked Messer Leonardo if I could take a break. But he told me to carry on. I insisted that I felt absolutely exhausted.' Saltarelli stopped for a moment, as though remembering events which had caused him great suffering.

'And at that point what happened?' asked Filippo Pitti.

'Leonardo took me violently,' answered Saltarelli. 'He pushed me up against the table and penetrated me until he was satisfied.'

Filippo Pitti raised an eyebrow.

'That's all? All of a sudden, this man decides to put you against a table and sodomize you?'

'Yes my lord. That's what happened, whether you believe it or not.'

Filippo Pitti didn't seem to be listening, however, and instead raised his hands in surrender. 'I said nothing, Messer Saltarelli... And that is all?'

Saltarelli nodded.

Filippo Pitti turned to the guard. 'Take him out and bring in the next witness,' he said.

Lorenzo was stunned to see Lucrezia enter the hall.

What the hell was she doing at Leonardo's trial? Was she really a witness? And what would she say? His mind was bursting with questions.

Lucrezia wore a beautiful periwinkle-coloured gown, its embroidered sleeves decorated with pearls which adorned her beautiful arms. Her gaze was steady and her dark eyes determined.

At the sight of her, more than one of those attending the trial sighed, hoping that one day she would grace their bed, if only for a moment.

Leonardo did not seem surprised. He sat there staring ahead of him with an almost absent expression on his face.

Filippo Pitti greeted her and gestured for her to take her place on the witness stand, then he summarized the facts of the trial.

'My lady Lucrezia Donati, I thank you for being here today. I know you asked to be deposed as a witness as soon as you learned that Messer Leonardo da Vinci had been accused of the crime of active sodomy against the young Jacopo Saltarelli. According to what the court has heard, three weeks ago, the latter went to the workshop of Messer da Vinci in order to pose for him and stayed there after vespers for almost the whole night. After a few hours, Messer Leonardo forced Messer Jacopo to undergo unspeakable acts. These are the facts on the basis of the reconstruction offered by Saltarelli himself. Messer da Vinci, for his part, remains in silence. What I ask of you is this: what can you say to disavow these accusations?'

'I will tell you right away, my lord.' Lucrezia's voice was strong and well modulated. For a moment she stared at Lorenzo, a defiant look on her face. 'What Jacopo Saltarelli says is false.'

This time Filippo Pitti started with surprise.

'Really?' he said. 'And how can you say that with such certainty?'

'Because I did not see him in Leonardo da Vinci's workshop that evening.'

'And how can you be so sure?'

'Because I was there at that hour. And I was alone.'

At the sound of those words, a chorus of astonished voices rose from the audience.

33

The Testimony

'That night I went to see Messer Leonardo to talk to him. For reasons that are irrelevant here, I was distraught. I remember that he was tired. He was trying as always to understand the secrets of the human body: its proportions, harmonies and contours. Those who do not know Messer da Vinci will not understand, but he is a perfectionist and carries out his studies in the most rigorous and careful way. He was dissatisfied with his inability to transfer what he saw on paper or canvas into paintings. As I said, I was distraught for personal reasons. What I remember is that we gave each other courage.'

Filippo Pitti had listened carefully to those words.

'Could you be more precise, my lady Lucrezia?'

'I do not remember how it started, but at a certain

point I was in his arms and he was in mine. You can imagine the rest.'

'How long did you remain thus?'

'Until the morning.' And while she said those words, Lucrezia glanced at Lorenzo. It was only for a moment, but it was enough to see how angry he was. His emotion would have been invisible to most but to her, who knew him so well, it was obvious how furious he was: there was that long wrinkle down the middle of his forehead that appeared when he was about to explode.

Lucrezia did not allow herself the luxury of a smile but inside she rejoiced.

Filippo Pitti continued.

'And I imagine,' he said, 'that in all that time you never saw Jacopo Saltarelli.'

'I did not.'

'Very well, my lady Lucrezia. We thank you for your words and your time. I can imagine how much they have cost you. You have no idea how important your statement today has been and how much pointless work it has spared us. If you wish, you may withdraw, with the grateful thanks of this court.'

Lucrezia gave a respectful nod, and then was led to the exit.

Lorenzo looked at Leonardo. His friend's gaze had not changed one bit – it was as cold and absent as it had been at the beginning.

Meanwhile, Filippo Pitti was consulting with the

other magistrates. It seemed that this last testimony had dispelled their doubts.

'Gentlemen,' he said firmly, 'in light of what we have heard today, I believe I can conclude the following without the need for any debate. On behalf of the Officers of the Night, the judiciary which I have the honour to chair, I conclude the following: the complaint of the crime of sodomy presented against Messer Leonardo da Vinci was anonymous. The only evidence to support it was represented by the statement of Jacopo Saltarelli, a young goldsmith, who claims to have been involved in the practice of passive sodomy three weeks ago.'

The other Officers of the Night nodded in agreement with Filippo Pitti's reconstruction.

'And on the other side,' continued the magistrate, 'is a woman who, at the cost of her honour and dignity, comes here to testify that she was with Messer Leonardo da Vinci the same night for occasional relations with him. She is neither his lover nor his wife, and she is not involved with him in any way. She stands to gain nothing from her actions – she only stands to lose. And her testimony does not appear in any way flawed and possesses all the characteristics of being the truth. Therefore, in light of the above, given the anonymity of the complaint and milady Lucrezia Donati's disinterested declaration, I believe, as president of the Officers of the Night, that I must absolve Leonardo da Vinci from any accusation of sodomy and dismiss the case immediately.'

The volume of the audience's voices suddenly increased.

Francesco de' Pazzi shook his head and others whispered in disbelief, perhaps more surprised by Lucrezia Donati's statement than by everything else. They knew of her passion for Lorenzo de' Medici, but her testimony had completely turned the tables. In their eyes, the picture had became even more sordid and now bordered on depravity. Lucrezia Donati made love both with Medici and with the young painter, whom many still suspected of sodomy, since the dismissal would certainly not quiet the gossip.

Those whispers and slanders were like drops of poison in Lorenzo's ears.

Leonardo was free, and for that Lorenzo was pleased. But at what price! Lucrezia had lied to him and so had Leonardo. The artist had been careful not to tell him anything about that night with Lucrezia. Of course, she did not belong to him, but Leonardo knew about his feelings for her. If Leonardo had confessed to him that he had had a moment of weakness, he might have been able to understand, but he could never have imagined having to find out about it like this.

He felt betrayed. Especially because, when he looked at Leonardo, he saw that the man was behaving as though the business was none of his concern. As usual. Despite not having refused his help when he had rushed to visit him in his cell in the Palazzo del Podestà the previous day and then asked the president of the Night Officers for clemency.

But Filippo Pitti had not finished yet. 'On the basis of the above, I therefore order that Messer Leonardo da Vinci be immediately released. Captain, please attend to it,' he concluded, turning to the leader of the city guards. Without adding anything else, the Officers of the Night rose from their benches and, over the hum of the comments of the gentlemen who filled the courtroom, departed.

Consumed by anger, Lorenzo remained seated, his hands clenched tightly into fists. He had to know, he thought.

Or he would lose his mind.

34

Rage and Conspiracy

The blow had landed before he had even realized it was coming. He had been so busy trying to get to Leonardo that he hadn't noticed someone was coming at him from behind.

He felt hot blood gush from his split lip and lost his balance, stumbling and crashing painfully down on to the ground. With his right hand he reached for the crossbow at his belt, but then he remembered that he hadn't brought it with him. He hadn't thought he'd need it at a trial.

The pain radiated outwards from his lip to his jaw, and from there to his whole head. He found himself on his elbows as he tried to get to his feet.

Francesco de' Pazzi towered over him.

'You filthy bastard! Friend of whores and sodomites! You are destroying this city, dragging it down into the circles of hell – reducing it to a place devoted to orgies and gluttony! But know this: I will not allow it!'

Lorenzo spat out a mouthful of blood and stood up.

'Pah! You are nothing but a slanderer, Francesco. And don't fool yourself that your threats frighten me. The people are with me, and so are the plebs and most of the nobles. You have no chance against me.'

He wiped his lips with the back of his hand, savouring the blood as though trying to imprint the affront and the lies he had just discovered upon his memory, and then spat again.

'Watch yourself, Lorenzo! Thinking yourself above the Republic and everyone in it may cost you dear one day!'

'That is indeed a bizarre accusation coming from one who lent Riario money to allow him to purchase of the lordship of Imola so as to be given the administration of the pontifical finances as well as the favour of the Pope.'

'And you hate it, don't you?'

'Not as much as you will hate what will happen to you!'

'Am I supposed to be afraid?'

'Do as you like,' answered Lorenzo in a dull voice.

'I believe that this city is tired of you and your arrogance.'

'They have already tried to remove us from Florence in the past. I don't need to remind you how that all ended. We returned and became stronger than before. And do you know why?'

It was Francesco's turn to spit with anger. The ball of saliva spattered Lorenzo's toes.

'I don't care.'

'Because we *are* Florence.'

'You're nothing but an arrogant idiot. But your presumption will cost you. You will be defeated – utterly.'

'I am eager to see this defeat you promise. Because all I see now is a conceited swaggerer uttering empty threats.'

'It is only a matter of time,' said Francesco de' Pazzi. 'After all, I have already got close to you without you even realizing. Or did you actually believe that the attack on Lucrezia Donati was a coincidence? If you did then you are even more stupid than I thought.'

Lorenzo flushed with rage. 'How dare you?' he shouted. 'You'll see what happens to you if you touch even a single hair on Lucrezia's head!'

He was completely out of control, but Francesco de' Pazzi was already stalking away, leaving him standing there in the alleyway with a split lip.

Girolamo Riario looked Francesco Salviati, the Archbishop of Pisa, in the eyes.

His uncle, the Pope, had described Salviati as a man who might be useful against the Medici, and, in fact, the mention of their name alone had been enough to provoke incandescent fury.

Red blotches had appeared on his face and, his voice trembling with rage, Francesco Salviati had spat out a stream of invective about Lorenzo and Giuliano because only two years ago they had done everything possible to prevent his candidacy to the Florentine archbishopric, for which Rinaldo Orsini had been preferred.

And they had succeeded. Not even the Pope had managed to change the course of events.

'Death,' said Francesco Salviati, as though praying, 'death is the only solution for those two accursed wretches.'

'These are very strange words indeed to hear spoken by a man of faith like you, excellency,' observed Riario provokingly, as a test of the intensity of his intentions.

'You wouldn't say that if you knew how cruelly Lorenzo and Giuliano pursue their goals, and with how much arrogance they work for their own advantage. But apart from that, the real reason lies in a desire to free Florence. I believe the city is tired of their feasts, of the obscene and licentious art that Lorenzo encourages, the orgies and banquets, of his proven infidelity to his wife Clarice Orsini, of the shameful way in which he reformed the Florentine Republic and made it his own kingdom! When he was twenty, the nobles dubbed him "the Magnificent", and begged him to take the destiny of the city in his hands, but I think they now regret that bitterly – partly because, to be frank, I struggle to see the magnificence of his deeds.'

Francesco Salviati's words poured out like a river bursting its banks and Girolamo Riario concluded that, once again, his uncle had been right. It was then that he decided to plant the seed of the conspiracy and inform the archbishop of his intentions.

'What if I told you that what you say is so true that men and women of good will are joining forces to overthrow this political order? If I were to inform you of the fact that there is a grand Florentine family which cannot wait to take power to restore the city's ancient freedoms? If I told you that the Pope himself had to fight the Medici to be able to award me, his nephew, with the lordship of Imola?'

Girolamo let that last statement hang in the air while Francesco Salviati rubbed his chin with the back of his hand and listened with increasing interest, a perfidious light growing brighter in his eyes.

'I would say that I would be eager to be part of such an undertaking. Tell me how I can serve this cause and I will join you and those who want to stop the Medici, because, believe me, the time has come! In fact, we are late.'

'We must have patience, excellency. The preparations need to be made carefully, but I am hopeful of being ready in a few months' time. Though our desire to see them fall is strong, we must not make the mistake of underestimating them. They are well protected, and above all we cannot risk making martyrs of them.'

'That would be an unforgivable mistake,' agreed the archbishop.

'It would,' replied Girolamo Riario, 'and for that reason we must proceed with caution, fomenting dissent and using agitators to fan the flames to create a climate of hate against the Medici so that it will be Florence itself which wants an end to them. We cannot take the risk of repeating what happened with Cosimo the Elder.'

Francesco Salviati nodded and pushed back his perfumed chestnut locks. There was an ostentatious elegance about him that he had not managed to give up despite the sobriety which the faith and especially his role as shepherd of a flock imposed upon him.

'And who might this Florentine family which is so historically averse to the Medici be? Because only one comes to mind, and what they have undergone over the years would justify any desire for revenge.'

'Can you not guess the name for yourself?'

'The Pazzi? I can only imagine that it must be them. Lorenzo de' Medici prevented them from holding any political office and if it had not been for your uncle giving them the administration of the finances of the Apostolic Chamber, they would have fallen on hard times.'

Girolamo Riario nodded. 'Precisely. Nothing escapes you, excellency. Let me add, however, that, despite what one might imagine, the Pazzi are on the rise, both in terms of their popularity and in terms of their wealth. Being treasurers of the pontifical assets means they administer the Tolfa alum mines, which produce immense wealth. The loss of those mines was a devastating blow to the Medici, who had administered them for a hundred years. This is why the Pazzi will help us to strike at Lorenzo's family from inside the city. And at the same time, I will guarantee an attack from outside.'

'Really? Do you think you can find others outside Florence who want to put an end to Lorenzo? Because, thanks to his ruthlessness, I have the impression that it would be very difficult to find anyone who is not either his friend or too frightened of him to risk raising his sword against them. Milan and Galeazzo Maria Sforza? They certainly would not. Venice? Nor they! On the contrary, I have heard that he has recently taken the precaution of signing an anti-papal alliance.'

'You are very well informed, excellency.'

Francesco Salviati sighed. 'One does what one can. It is impossible to remain on two feet in such trying times unless one is a couple of moves ahead of the others.'

'A wise habit,' said Girolamo Riario, not without a hint of admiration. 'In any case, not all of them are allies of Florence, and that is without counting those who may be today but might not be tomorrow. After all, I will soon be marrying Caterina Sforza...'

'And please accept my heartfelt congratulations on the happy event,' the archbishop hurriedly cut in in affected, courtly tones.

'Though I of course welcome your good wishes, allow me to say that my mentioning it had less to do with marriages and kinship than it did with guarantees of support. I would remind you that my uncle recently obtained the friendship of Ferdinand, King of Naples, waiving the annual tribute he owed to the Papal States and allowing his nephew, Leonardo della Rovere, to marry Ferdinand's natural daughter. Not to mention that he conferred upon Federico d'Urbino the title of duke and then had his daughter engaged to Giovanni della Rovere, assigning to him the Vicariate of Sinigaglia and Mondavio. In short, if Florence trembles, Rome will not stand by watching. Indeed, in this regard, I can guarantee that the new captain of the papal army, Giovan Battista da Montesecco, will take our side. As you can see, the situation in which we find ourselves is already well advanced and it is now a matter of getting Florence on to our side.'

'As I said,' concluded Archbishop Salviati, 'I intend to participate in this undertaking, and I rejoice that you have been so busy. So let the games begin, and may good fortune reward us.'

Girolamo Riario smiled: the web was growing thicker and the day when Florence would finally be freed from the plague of the Medici was drawing closer. 'It surely will, excellency,' he concluded with a hint of satisfaction. 'It surely will.'

35

Forgiveness Must Be Earned

Lucrezia knew to whom the carriage belonged, and she knew perfectly well where it was taking her. Far from Florence, along country roads that led to a secluded farmhouse hidden in a beech forest where, that bright and green April, nature was more alive than ever.

But pain consumed her heart because she knew she was travelling towards a confrontation. She tidied her hair. When those men had come to get her, she had realized immediately that it made no sense to resist unless she wished to spend the rest of her life wallowing in her pain.

She knew that she had been right to say what she had a few days earlier: for many reasons, not least because she had saved a genius. Regardless of whatever else happened, that alone was worth every letter, every punishment, even if it meant living in solitude forever, scorned as a wanton.

She no longer cared.

And in a certain sense, that indifference which now began to fill her like a fog was her strength, since there was nothing for which she need attempt to justify herself: how many times had she asked for only a little attention – for a gesture or a caress – only to be denied it for the most spurious reasons?

She had felt used and put aside. Perhaps even loved, of course, and with an intense passion, but only for a brief time, or for moments which then disappeared, only to return after seemingly endless silences, hopes and prayers.

She was tired and disappointed, and now that she had done what she had done, she realized that she should have acted sooner.

The road rose among the beech trees, their boughs covered in new green leaves. The colours of the forest sped past the carriage windows accompanied by the creaking of the wheels as the horses with their shiny manes trotted along the path, their hooves hammering on the ground: it might have been the beginning of a fairy tale, but Lucrezia knew it would end in anger, resentment and torment. That was what life had always given her, and the beauty it had conceded her had always turned against her. Her future goal, she decided, would be to age and fade like the colour of a forgotten dress.

At that moment the carriage stopped. Someone opened the door and a long-haired man with a thin moustache helped her down and led her to the farm's entrance. Without knocking, he opened the door wide and showed her into a room that Lucrezia knew well: the large fireplace was cold now, the beautiful armchairs empty, and the silence cut through her like a gelid, rusty blade. There was a feeling of intense abandonment there – a deep and profound melancholy that seemed to envelop the place.

His arms folded, he was standing at the centre of the room, waiting. With that sunken face and those jutting cheekbones and dull eyes, he looked like the ghost of himself.

Lorenzo stood staring at her without speaking. She stared back.

Perhaps that was what they both sought: to share silence. They were good at that.

They felt the growing tension, a poison between them that had been fed over the years by mutual betrayals, disregarded promises, denied kisses and unspoken words. They were drowning there in front of one another in that sea of rancour.

No longer able to bear the silence, Lorenzo spoke.

'Do you remember what I said to you a long time ago? That if the love between us failed, it would be entirely our fault?'

She had no desire to make it easy for him, but on that point at least she could only agree.

'You were right, even if that made it no less bitter.'

Her words inflamed his anger.

'It was you who betrayed me.'

'You have no idea how wrong you are!' she cried.

'Really?'

'Yes, really!'

'So I only imagined the words I heard at the trial, then?'

'No you did not,' she said, so emphatically so that it would stay with Lorenzo forever. She wanted to hurt him. For once in her life, she wanted to be the one to hurt him.

A bitter smile appeared on his lips and he bent his head to the side.

'So why deny it?'

'Deny what?'

'That you betrayed me.'

'You're a fool.' She laughed.

'You find this amusing?'

'After all your indifference, finally seeing you in difficulty amuses me, yes. Because, you see, if what happened had not happened, you would never have brought me here – you would not even have spoken to me.'

'What do you mean?'

'You heard me.'

Lorenzo sighed.

'And by the looks of things, I did well to keep you away.'

'Think what you want. Can I go now? I doubt that my presence here is of any help. To either of us.

'No you cannot,' he said in a voice suddenly blazing with anger. 'I want you to confess!'

'Confess what?'

'Everything... everything you did that night!'

'Ah, so you're interested in knowing about me now, are you?' Her voice dripped disdain, and she was surprised by the strange pleasure it gave her to vent the frustrations she had been forced to suppress all those years. 'Now that you think I betrayed you! But before, when I still loved you, you didn't care if I were alive or dead!'

'That's not true!'

'It *is*! I cannot believe I fell in love with a coward like you!'

'Speak!'

'What will you do if I don't? Hang me?'

'Don't talk nonsense.'

'All you know how to do is demand, you think only of yourself—'

'I want to know...'

'What?'

'... the truth!'

'Do you want to know the truth? *Really*? Here it is, then! I've never loved Leonardo. Nor did I lie with him. I had gone to his studio to talk about you, hoping that he could help me! Because you weren't there, you've *never* been there for me for the last four years. Four long, wretched years. So when I discovered that Leonardo had been accused of sodomy, I thought of a way to save him, because he has always been so good to everyone, myself included, and he has never had the help of anyone in return.'

'He had mine!'

'Ah, yours! But your help has to be paid for – and dearly at that!'

Lorenzo moved even closer to her.

'Am I supposed believe a woman who lied to me so artfully? Why didn't you tell me what you were planning to do?'

The sound of the slap hitting his cheek was as sharp as a whiplash.

In that moment, Lucrezia hated him.

Lorenzo felt his face burning. With shame.

'I told you that nothing happened. I didn't have time to explain. I did it to save him. I used the memories of a night three years earlier, as I told you! I lied! I thought that any magistrate would be more likely to believe a woman who sacrificed her honour on the altar of justice than a dissolute young goldsmith.'

Lorenzo remained silent. The slap had reawakened him from the obsession that had been lurking within him until that moment. The meaning of her words began to sink in.

'You mean that you lied to save him?'

'That is what I said.'

'And you have never slept with him?'

Lucrezia shook her head in denial. 'That is what disappoints me most – that you are worried only about yourself. You don't care about me.'

'That's not true! If I didn't, I wouldn't have brought you here! I know I was wrong to push you away, but after what happened to you that day you were ambushed, when it was only a miracle that prevented the worst, I feared that continuing to see you would only put you in danger!'

'But you didn't hesitate to do it now, did you?' There was more bitterness than anger in Lucrezia's words.

'You are unfair. Of course I was jealous. But because I love you, I wish you could be mine alone and I know that it cannot be. I know too that I have disappointed you and lost your love. And I deserve it. But I have changed so much... and then when I heard what you said...'

'Stop,' she said. 'You're only making things worse.'

'At least now I know the truth... and what a fool I've been.'

'I don't wish to see you any more.'

'Lucrezia... I understand. But I swear, I'll make you change your mind.'

'Try it, if you really care.'

'I will, you can be sure of it.'

She turned away.

'I want to go home, if you do not mind.'

'I wish you would stay,' he said.

'I am sorry,' replied Lucrezia, 'but forgiveness must be earned.'

DECEMBER 1476

36

The Fall

The snow whirled down, covering Milan in a blanket of white. It was St Stephen's Day.

Clad in long boots and a cloak with a fur collar so thick that he looked like a bear, Galeazzo Maria Sforza climbed out of his carriage. His sword hung by his side and its scabbard, encrusted with gold and gems, rattled as the duke walked towards the cathedral doors. That morning he felt particularly well. He paused for a moment outside the cathedral before entering and took a deep breath of the cold air.

The day was bathed in winter sun: filtered by the pearl-coloured sky its faint rays resembled liquid silver.

Galeazzo Maria reached the great doors of the cathedral, the soles of his boots crunching on the thick white mantle of fallen snow that glistened all around.

Creaking out a lament as they swung on their hinges, the doors were opened to him.

Before the duke was the magnificent view of the crowded cathedral: the imposing naves, the multi-coloured windows and the vast hanging candelabras blazing with dozens of white candles.

Suddenly, the glowing scene was flushed with red.

He felt an unexpected pain in his side, almost as though an animal had bitten him, and others came ruthless after it, rending his flesh. It felt as though their icy teeth were tearing into his belly and neck, ripping his body apart. His blood gushed out and he fell to his knees under the hail of blows from the daggers that stabbed at him. Before him, he recognized Giovanni Andrea Lampugnani, staring at him through eyes red with madness.

The faithful who crowded the pews began to cry out, their chilling shouts of horror echoing around the carnival of death taking place before their eyes.

Galeazzo Maria gasped and his hands clawed at the air in a desperate attempt to stop the vile and ruthless attack. But in vain. He fell forward on to his face as the snow continued to descend, blowing through the open cathedral doors on gusts of icy wind.

The duke's guards threw themselves on the three assailants, one of them stabbing Giovanni Andrea Lampugnani with a halberd. The blade tore open his belly, shattering his ribcage and almost impaling him on the weapon's shaft. The guard had charged with such enthusiasm that the tip of his weapon banged up against one of the columns of the cathedral.

He saw the life draining from the conspirator's eyes.

Still shouting with panic, the crowd of the faithful flooded into the aisles, some managing to get out while the guards chased the other two attackers through the doors.

The ambassadors of Ferrara and Mantua, who had arrived that day to pay homage and hand over gifts from their lords to Galeazzo Maria Sforza, stood there speechless, their hands clasped, staring at the dead body of the duke slumped in the middle of the central nave. The red lake that was spreading out beneath him seemed to devour the surrounding space.

The bishop made the sign of the cross while, in vain, he tried to restore calm. Milan sank suddenly into chaos.

But in that scene of horror and shame, while the stones of the cathedral soaked up the blood of its lord and master, at least one of the many there desperately pounding their chests in grief rejoiced in his heart for what he had seen.

Ludovico Ricci smiled because he knew that event would forever change history. The Medici had lost a powerful ally, and their hope of strengthening their position outside Florence became that much weaker. And that was in the interest of Rome and Sixtus IV, and therefore of Girolamo Riario and all of the rest of them.

Indeed, the assassination of Galeazzo Maria seemed a good omen for what the Florentine conspirators had in mind.

37

The Law

'Don't you understand, we are weak! First there was all the fuss with Leonardo and Lucrezia because of that accusation! I am glad that he was acquitted, but the voices of those who call us unbelievers, whoremongers and friends to sodomites have been raised against us for too long now.' Giuliano's voice was almost hysterical. 'Not to mention that the death of Galeazzo Maria Sforza was a disaster, especially at a time like this.'

Lorenzo knew that his brother was right, but he couldn't bear it when Giuliano let himself go like that and put the onus for remaining calm and finding a solution or any alternative on to him. And it wasn't the first time – indeed, it happened repeatedly.

'The league will fall apart!' Giuliano continued. 'And Rome will expand its sphere of influence. There's no limit to the Pope's ambition!'

'That need not necessarily happen,' said Lorenzo. 'Venice is still with us, and I am hopeful that, in spite of this horrible blow to the Duchy, the situation may finally return to being favourable to us.'

'How? In what way?'

'I don't know yet. If I had a solution I would hardly be here listening to you despairing without making any attempt to control yourself, would I?' snapped Lorenzo, this time unable to hold back his irritation.

'But if our alliance with Milan is going to weaken now Sforza's dead, we ought to strengthen our position in Florence.' Giuliano was trying to remain calm, but failed to hold back the question on his lips. 'Do you have any ideas?'

'For some time I have been considering a law that would benefit us: a way to defend ourselves and remain strong while preventing our adversaries from increasing their assets.'

'I don't think I understand.'

'I'll try to be less cryptic then,' said Lorenzo, getting up from his chair. 'We know perfectly well that, thanks to the institution of marriage, vast fortunes can be introduced into a family upon the death of the father-in-law. In this regard I would like to tell you a short story. It will take me some time, so please make yourself comfortable.'

Lorenzo was looking at his brother but in reality seemed to be talking to himself. He paused for a moment and then began.

'At one time, a man named Vitaliano Borromeo was the Visconti's treasurer in Milan. Thanks to the duke's favour, he was able to strengthen his banking activity and opened new branches in Bruges and London. And there was more. So skilful was he at intertwining his own affairs with those of the ducal court that he granted unprecedented financial support to Filippo Maria Visconti. In return he obtained other properties, fiefdoms and privileges, thus laying the foundations for a vast patrimony. In addition to large estates on Lake Maggiore, about forty years ago he acquired the castle and the village of Arona with the parish church, Cannobio, Lesa and the Vergante region, Mergozzo and Vogogna – the fourteenth-century castle there, attributed to Giovanni Visconti, which he subsequently extended, Val Vigezzo, Borgo Ticino and Gattico. Finally he obtained the title of count for the fiefdom of Arona and authorization to equip the fortress with imposing fortifications.'

Lorenzo paused again, as though catching his breath after that impressive list of properties and lands. He went over to the fireplace and poked at the fire. Giuliano waited.

'But the fortunes of the Borromeo family continued to rise with Vitaliano's son, Filippo, who was still lending money to the Visconti and then to the Sforza. Francesco Sforza himself enfeoffed a series of other lands and donated them to Borromeo, who accumulated such vast wealth that apparently, on his death, the sum of twenty-four million gold florins was shared between his sons...'

'*Million?*' asked Giuliano incredulously.

Lorenzo nodded. 'Precisely. But let me continue. Of his children, the one who concerns us is Giovanni, whose only descendant was the beautiful Beatrice. Now, do you remember to whom she is promised in wedlock?'

'Giovanni de' Pazzi,' said Giuliano. For a moment he didn't follow his brother's train of thought, then suddenly it struck him. 'Wait, you mean that...'

'The day Giovanni Borromeo accidentally passes away, who do you think will inherit his father's fortune?'

'Beatrice.'

'And then?'

'Giovanni...'

'... de' Pazzi,' said Lorenzo. 'So here is what I propose to do. We cannot wait, not after what happened to Galeazzo Maria Sforza. We need to pass a law immediately that prevents the Pazzi from getting their hands on the Borromeos' property. And I have already thought of the way, to tell the truth.'

'Which is?'

'It must be forbidden for husbands to inherit their wives' property through marriage. It is the only way we will be able to prevent the Pazzi from legitimately obtaining the wealth of Beatrice Borromeo. I don't need to tell you the trouble such wealth could cause us. Even our own wealth is not remotely comparable to that of the Borromeos and if, through some reckless oversight, we should let it pass, we would certainly be signing our own death sentence. The Pazzi already control the Tolfa alum mine as administrators of the Apostolic Chamber. We can't allow them to get their hands on this too.'

Giuliano walked over to the large windows of the salon and looked outside.

The winter afternoon was fading into a gloomy evening. This Christmas promised to be a dark one for his family, but fortunately his brother was watching over them. Lorenzo was always vigilant, and his talent for anticipating his opponent's moves was as extraordinary as his indisputable political skill.

'How will you go about it?' asked Giuliano.

'We must act quickly and have that law approved. The sooner we succeed the better, because then it won't look as if we're plotting against our enemies. We will say that it is a law aimed at safeguarding the *ratio* of family branches, so that what belongs to one does not become mixed with that of another. But what matters now is speed. We'll enact a law that, in the absence of brothers, deprives female daughters of their inheritance and passes it directly to any male cousins. That way we will prevent the already considerable patrimony of the Pazzi from increasing.'

'But can we get away with it?'

'Giuliano, this isn't a question of asking for permission,' sighed Lorenzo. 'We must do as I say, or believe me, the House of Medici risks extinction.'

38

Omens

The sword was not particularly heavy, but after the first few swings it felt as if it were made of lead. Ludovico was dripping with sweat, the drops beading his forehead and falling into his eyes. He shook his head and wiped his face with the back of his glove in an attempt to dry them as best he could.

That fact seemed to amuse his lord and teacher, Girolamo Riario, who continued to provoke and taunt him. His superiority in the duel was such that the entire exercise felt completely pointless to Ludovico.

He parried a couple of slashes and then took a swing at his opponent. The resulting thrust was so feeble that Girolamo had no difficulty sidestepping it and striking him on the shoulders with his sword, sending him crashing to the stone floor of the armoury.

Ludovico looked up at the wooden racks of halberds above him.

The lord of Imola, meanwhile, burst out laughing.

'The road is still long, dear boy! You have much to learn.'

With difficulty, Ludovico stood up. His arms were heavy and when he fell he had bruised his shoulder, which now ached.

He tried to put his guard up, but as soon as he raised his sword Girolamo attacked him with an upward swing and Ludovico realized that his sword was about to fly out of his hands. With immense effort he managed not to lose his grip, but as he struggled to get back into position, somehow managing to keep hold of his weapon, he felt the tip of Girolamo's sword against his throat.

A cruel smile on his face, the lord of Imola studied him.

'You need to be faster,' he said, while Ludovico blushed with shame. 'And you must become more robust. You're too thin and your legs are as skinny as a stork's. Tomorrow we will start again,' he concluded.

As they put away their swords, two servants approached, each of them handing one of the swordsmen a scented towel with which to dry off his sweat. Girolamo didn't even touch his, while Ludovico dried himself carefully, losing himself for a moment in the aromas of roses.

He felt as though he had been born again.

'So, the plan involving Messer Leonardo proved to be completely ineffective, hmm? I confess that I had expected it to be more fruitful. Destiny decided, though, that someone would help us by killing Sforza. Of course, they all imagine that I am grieved, since I am to marry his daughter Caterina, but to be honest, I don't give a damn.' And in confirmation of his words, Girolamo guffawed heartily.

Ludovico let the gentleman of Imola enjoy his joke, and then he spoke.

'In any case,' he remarked, 'it did have some effect upon the Medici: I have heard that Lorenzo's relations with the beautiful Lucrezia Donati are no longer so good since she confessed that she'd been to bed with that half-sodomite Leonardo da Vinci. So perhaps we have at least managed to unnerve Lorenzo the Magnificent. Now that the Milanese alliance has failed him, the road finally appears open to us. Not to mention that voices on various sides are criticizing him for having encouraged the licentiousness of Florentine customs.'

'That is certainly good news. And now the Archbishop of Pisa is on our side too. I have personally ensured that Giovan Battista da Montesecco is willing to lead the papal troops against Florence and that Federico da Montefeltro, Duke of Urbino, will do his part. As for the Pazzi, well, they hate the Medici so much that I am struggling to keep Francesco from acting now and sending all our plans up in smoke. We must call a meeting in order to establish how and when it should be done, because in light of recent events and the sodomy scandal, even my uncle is now in favour of the Medici's death.'

'So however unsuccessful it was, the trial did obtain a result,' pointed out Ludovico, not without some satisfaction.

'Of course it did, you little devil. The question is such a scabrous one that the Pope almost jumped out of his chair when he heard about it.'

'The ideal thing would be if he ordered them excommunicated.'

'Unfortunately, as you pointed out, the trial didn't end with a conviction, so there is no real chance of that happening. Even the Pope has his hands tied.'

Ludovico sighed.

'Don't despair,' continued Girolamo Riario. 'The net is about to close and, all things considered, you did a good job; I am pleased with you. Now, run to your mother. She asked me to send you to her as soon as I had finished trying to teach you the rudiments of duelling. Tell her that you are improving a little at a time, and that since she came to live here, to my great joy, fortune finally seems to be favouring our side.'

Ludovico knocked and heard his mother's voice telling him to come in. Girolamo Riario had given her a sizeable wing of his castle to use, and Laura had set up a large living room in it. She had so stuffed it with extravagant and bizarre furnishings that it now resembled the study of a fortune teller or witch, adorned with pentacles and arcane symbols, relics and strange grimoires, coloured bottles and dusty jars, the use of many of which was completely unknown to him. Ludovico couldn't understand why she insisted on surrounding herself with all those objects, but his mother was so important to him that he willingly accepted her eccentricities.

With her purple-stained fingers, Laura was turning the yellowed pages of an old witches' grimoire. She owned several, all seemingly very ancient, and spent much of her time reading them. When she wasn't consulting those gloomy tomes with their disturbing illustrations, she was reading the tarot.

Despite these curious habit of hers, though, his mother was everything to him, and, like an obedient child, he always recounted the events of the day to her.

'How did it go?' she asked, without looking up from the page.

'Riario says that I am improving a little at a time.'

Laura looked up. 'I didn't ask you to tell me what he *said*. I asked you to tell me how it *went*.'

Ludovico's puff of annoyance earned him a glare from his mother.

'Oh very *well* – I need to become faster and more robust,' said Ludovico. 'I am too light, according to him, and my thin legs don't help. The truth is that he is always ahead of me, as if he knows exactly what I am about to do, and that I can parry his blows only feebly. You know what I'm like; I've never had much talent for physical activities. I still have a great deal to learn.'

'Then we will have to remedy these deficiencies of yours!' said Laura, putting down the book.

She went over to him and stared at him with her large black eyes.

To Ludovico they looked like wells, deep enough for one to drown in. They always had that effect on him, and he feared that he might lose himself if he stared into them for too long.

This occasion was no exception.

Suddenly, before he realized what was happening, his mother had untied his leather breeches. He stood there immobile, frozen.

'Relax,' she whispered. 'Now we will make a man of you. And by the end of this day you will have taken me so many times that your legs will certainly have begun to strengthen.'

NOVEMBER 1477

39

Palazzo Plots

Light flooded into the salon through the beautiful mullioned windows decorated with the three half-moons which were the family's coat of arms, turning to gold the dust that danced in the luminous festoons.

The contrast of the friezes and vines which adorned the upper levels with the solid, sober ashlar-work of the ground floor made the Palazzo Pazzi the most elegant in all of Florence. It therefore seemed even stranger that it was lending itself to the conception of a dark and ruthless plan.

In the salon, Jacopo de' Pazzi could find no rest. In his heart, he felt that a bitter fruit was maturing which would bring them no good. He always reproached his nephew Francesco for neglecting Florence and spending too much time in Rome making friends who put strange ideas in his head. Such as, for example, this Girolamo Riario who now stood before him dressed, like Francesco, completely in black and with a manner so arrogant, so contemptuous, that it was as if he considered himself lord of the world. He was, moreover, the favourite nephew of the Pope, to whom the Pazzi certainly owed a great deal. Perhaps too much, thought Jacopo.

While he was absorbed in these gloomy thoughts, Archbishop Francesco Salviati helped himself to a cup of red wine, sipped it with great gusto and broke the silence.

'Excellent wine,' he began. 'Now, I understand that today we find ourselves guests in this marvellous palazzo in order to decide how to solve the question of the Medici...'

'Great God!' cried Messer Jacopo. 'Must we shout it to the four winds? I beg you, excellency, a minimum of discretion!'

'Very well, very well,' replied the archbishop. 'In any case, whatever the project is called, that's what we are here to speak about!'

'Yes,' said Francesco. 'My dear uncle, I know your aversion to the plan we are hatching, but you will certainly agree that the Medici have done everything to fan the flames of our resentment: first they prevented the names of our best men from being picked so that the interests of the Pazzi were never represented in the city's government. Then, as if this were not enough, they prevented my brother Giovanni, your nephew, from acquiring the assets he legitimately ought to have inherited from his wife Beatrice. Now I ask you, is not that an affront? What more must we suffer before we finally rebel against the abuses of a family that behaves as if we are its servants and forces us to remain in the shadows? Because, in all sincerity, I tell you, I no longer intend to stand by and watch what is rightfully mine taken from me!'

Old Messer Jacopo shook his head. His nephew had always been a troublemaker, but at the same time, he wasn't totally wrong. It was no lie that Lorenzo had behaved shamefully by passing a law for the sole purpose of harming the Pazzi. That had certainly not been a fair and praiseworthy way of doing things.

'Francesco,' he said, 'I can't disagree with what you say. But killing the two brothers is a serious business and I wonder if there is not a different way of solving the problem. Bear in mind that Guglielmo – who is also your brother – is married to Bianca de' Medici, and that we are therefore in some way relatives. Perhaps we could come up with a way to have them exiled...'

'Once I would have agreed with you. Your nephew will confirm that in the past I fought to avoid such an *extreme* solution. But today? After all that has happened? Well, I no longer think that exile is the answer.' Girolamo Riario's voice was like a lash upon

Messer Jacopo's ears. 'This city has already tried that once, and we all know how that ended. I believe that today Lorenzo de' Medici does whatever he wants in Florence. He is a skilled politician, as he has shown all too well by excluding you from any office or position, and he is a friend of the people and the plebs whose unconditional support he has guaranteed with his filthy festivities, and even some noble families have taken his side. But this is a fact that has put morality and decorum at risk. Of this, my uncle the Pope has no doubt and if he has not yet managed to excommunicate Lorenzo, it is only a matter of time. We all know of his infidelity, of his lascivious, unhealthy love for Lucrezia Donati, of his friendship with Leonardo da Vinci, an artist suspected of sodomy, and of his appreciation for the licentious art of Sandro Botticelli. So what are we waiting for? For Florence to become synonymous with orgies and ill repute?'

Jacopo de' Pazzi sighed. 'This too is true; I can't deny it. And it is certain that much could be done for Florence with the Medici out of the way.'

'Have you forgotten what he did in Prato, and especially in Volterra?' said the Archbishop of Pisa. 'He let Federico da Montefeltro exterminate the unarmed population. The inhabitants of that unfortunate city still weep for the blood spilled and the violence done them. Do you have scruples about eliminating such a man? I say this to you: Lorenzo and his brother Giuliano are the curse of this city and the sooner we get rid of them, the better it will be for everyone.'

Francesco Salviati had spoken so enthusiastically that the patriarch of the Pazzi seemed finally to resolve to give his support to their heinous project. The archbishop's words had contained all the truth he was seeking: apart from their political jockeying to remain in power, their questionable morals and their annoying exhibitions of pomp, what had most struck him had been the reminder of the cruelty with which Lorenzo had allowed the vassal cities of Florence to be devastated. With those words, Francesco Salviati had provided him with a valid motive, perhaps the best motive possible, to give his backing to what they were planning to do.

'Very well,' he said. 'There are many reasons for what we are going to do, but this is the most just of all of them, because those shameful acts deprived the entire city of its dignity. So I therefore ask you: do you have a plan?'

Girolamo Riario smiled, and was so moved that he shook hands with his pupil, Ludovico, who was also present that day. Old Jacopo was giving them his blessing and that meant the project had an excellent chance of succeeding, since Jacopo enjoyed a prestige and authority in Florence that would certainly convince a large part of the city's aristocracy to support their conspiracy.

'In fact,' Riario said, 'we do. Would you like to explain it to him, Francesco?'

Jacopo's nephew did not need asking twice.

'Well, dear uncle, first of all the names: Giovan Battista da Montesecco, one of the captains of the papal troops, who will lead a contingent to the gates of Florence; then there are Stefano and Bernardo Bandini, Jacopo di Poggio Bracciolini and Antonio Maffei, a priest of Volterra, who wants revenge for his city. The plan is simple. Archbishop Francesco Salviati will arrive in Florence from Pisa in the company of Montesecco, the Pope's captain, together with the young cardinal Raffaello Riario, another of Pope Sixtus's beloved nephews, and will come to pay you a visit, noble uncle. To reassure the Medici, we will say that the cardinal has come from Rome to Florence to complete his studies and that he will be staying here simply by chance. In fact, you will accommodate him in the Montughi villa, outside the city. From what I know of them, Lorenzo and Giuliano will learn of this immediately and will wish to invite them to their home, as is their habit. And that could be the perfect opportunity.'

'Of course,' Girolamo continued for him, 'my cousin Raffaello Riario will be in the dark about it all, so that his words will be even more convincing, precisely because they will be sincere. When Lorenzo invites my young cousin to one of his villas, the archbishop and the captain, along with a small armed escort, will accompany him and, at the banquet, will murder Lorenzo and Giuliano. Because I am sure that you will agree, Messer Jacopo, that both brothers must be eliminated.'

Jacopo nodded. At least on that point, he agreed. If it had to be done, then neither of the brothers could survive. But the plan still did not completely convince him.

'You are sure of the loyalty of all these people to the cause? I would not want any of them to pull out at the last moment.'

'They are trustworthy men, scrupulously chosen,' Girolamo Riario said.

'And you, sir?' asked Messer Jacopo. 'Will you take part?'

'I would like to immensely,' said the lord of Imola with a grin on his face, 'but I fear that will not be possible.'

'Ah.'

'But do not be afraid, Messer Pazzi, in my place there will be this noble young man, my pupil Messer Ludovico Ricci, the son of the lady of Norcia.'

Sensing his uncle was about to protest, Francesco intervened. 'I have seen him at work, my dear uncle, and I can assure you that he is a young man of many qualities – a boy of great intelligence who is capable of acting at the right moment.'

'Really?' said Messer Jacopo, his tone making it clear how little faith he placed in his nephew's words. 'Let us truly hope so, my boy, because at the moment all I see is a young man with a crafty face. I do not criticize you for that, my lad,' he said, turning to Ludovico. 'What I mean is that this looks like a rather paltry crew – all the more so because the person who is its leader is the first to remove himself from the company.'

'That's not it at all,' said Girolamo, who was beginning to lose patience. 'I simply cannot afford to be seen by the Medici. My uncle is the Pope, and since I became lord of Imola against their will, my presence would be suspect. In short, it would be a hindrance rather than an advantage. But as I told you, I will leave this noble task to one of those dearest to me – Ludovico, who will in all respects be my emissary.'

'So be it, then,' said Messer Jacopo, 'you seem to have come up with a detailed plan, and it is true that there are many motives for such an act. In any case, make sure you are discreet; it is hard to keep a secret in this city, and we absolutely cannot allow ourselves to be found out. I think we should disperse now – it's better that no one sees us together, so forgive me if I don't invite you to stay longer.'

'You are dismissing us, then?' asked Girolamo Riario rather coldly.

'Precisely,' replied Messer Jacopo in the same tone, because he did not much like the lord of Imola, just as he did not particularly like the rest of the company.

Upon hearing those words, each of the guests took his leave.

40

The Farm Girl

As he walked across the Ponte Vecchio, Leonardo inhaled the odours that were blowing in the cold air. The smell of butchered meat was especially intense as he passed the shops of the butchers which, red with blood, jutted out over the water. On the ground, the crusts of frozen snow, defiled by the remains of the carcasses, slowly melted, and flowed in dark rivulets into the Arno River below. There were the colours and aromas of vegetables: the ashlar white of the cauliflowers, the brown of the potatoes and the dark purple of the beetroots, with their sweet scent as intense as that of the fennel. The greengrocers loudly sang the praises of their products and Leonardo watched with pleasure the swirl of shapes and colours that made that crowded place throb with life.

After being acquitted of the sodomy charge, he had returned to the workshop of Andrea del Verrocchio, who had welcomed him with a big smile, happy that everything had turned out for the best. Leonardo knew that he owed everything to Lucrezia – if it hadn't been for her, he would probably have been sent to prison. That act of generosity had moved him, even though he knew that it concealed a desire to hurt Lorenzo. And to judge from the rumours, it must have succeeded.

As for him, he had kept his mouth shut.

He had learned that, in those cases, the best thing to do was to disappear, and that was what he had done. He had stopped conducting his studies into the human body – or rather, had interrupted them – and had devoted himself body and soul to painting. Not that the results had been particularly wonderful since, thanks to the impossibility of conducting further detailed anatomical studies, the inadequacy of his style both disappointed and annoyed him, but he had to make a virtue of necessity. He had applied himself with even greater vigour than usual, and the commitment had paid off because Andrea had left to him and to his friend Lorenzo di Credi, who was another of the maestro's pupils, the task of completing the altarpiece which would adorn the cathedral of Pistoia.

Leonardo was working with particular dedication on the face of Mary, blessed by the angel Gabriel, while she gently reclined her head and crossed her arms over her chest in acceptance. Her expression was causing him headaches, as he wanted to preserve her grace and submissive goodness without losing any of the regality of the pose. Lorenzo di Credi had been teasing him about it all morning and now he was racking his brain to find a solution.

That was why he had decided to go out for a while.

His best ideas often came to him while he was walking across the Ponte Vecchio, and he was certain that it was from real life that he needed to take inspiration.

While he was absorbed in his thoughts, his eyes glimpsed among the people crowding around the vegetables stalls a flash of light: hair the colour of red gold lit for a moment by the pale sun. It was a girl with beautiful shoulders carrying an empty basket. She must be a peasant, thought Leonardo, who had come to the market to sell her goods. As he watched her move through the people thronging the bridge, Leonardo followed her, hoping not to be seen while trying at the same time to glimpse her face.

He saw in that face a purity he had never before witnessed.

Feeling almost like a thief, he hurriedly sketched what he could: there was so much sweetness in that face, with its pale blue eyes and almost frightened candour. The cold air had given a slight redness to her skin, which was otherwise as white as snow.

When she turned her head, Leonardo sketched at incredible speed, knowing that she would never be more perfect than in that moment. Her eyes were almost closed, her lashes long and soft, but her hair did not hide her face, whose features were the very essence of tenderness and femininity.

Clarice stared at Leonardo furtively. She was fascinated by him. People said he lived with his head completely in the clouds, lost in his studies of art, and to see him now, nobody would have doubted it. He was so busy looking at that beautiful girl and sketching her simple but wonderful features that it was a miracle he did not stumble into one of the vegetable stalls. The drawing must be magnificent, though, she was sure of it. At first she had almost been suspicious and had been on the verge of warning the young peasant in some way, but then she realized that this strange artist, with his long blond hair, had no intention of harming her.

The memory that it was from Leonardo her husband had commissioned the portrait of Lucrezia Donati broke her mood for a moment, but she did not want to ruin that little stolen moment: the unknowing model and the surreptitious painter who, in turn, did not know he was being spied upon.

She felt alive and, for once, happy. Even if there was something strange and forbidden about what she saw.

There was so little joy in her life, though, that even a moment like this was as precious as it was unique.

Far from the Palazzo Medici, there among the shops of the Ponte Vecchio, Clarice could at least find some diversion. She was fascinated by the colours and the cries and the people and all the bottled-up energy that seemed ready to explode at any moment.

Even more incredible was seeing, unseen, how a man could capture forever the simple beauty of a woman in the confusion of the market. There was poetry and grace in the scene she was observing.

Clarice decided that she would preserve it as one of the few beautiful things she would keep always with her.

She smiled.

Then she overtook Leonardo and turned towards home.

APRIL 1478

41

The Wait

Jacopo de' Pazzi was worried that everything would go wrong. He could feel it in his soul.

His fear was that yesterday's events would repeat themselves and that one of the two most important people would be missing at the Easter Mass: Giuliano de' Medici.

Santa Maria del Fiore was packed with believers, the pews nearest the altar filled with the nobles and the wealthy and the rest filled with the common people and the plebs. The pungent odour of the incense, the perfumes of the garlands of flowers, the splendour of the robes of the men and women of the most powerful families in Florence – everything was in its place. Even the young cardinal, Raffaello Riario, oblivious of everything, was right where he was supposed to be, by the main altar, officiating at the rite.

But Giuliano was not there.

And he had also been absent on the occasion of the feast organized by Lorenzo for the young Riario at the villa in Fiesole the day before. He had sent word that he was unwell.

The fact had proved to be not without consequences. Jacopo and Francesco had been forced to find a solution. They, and not Girolamo Riario, who was back home and safe within the walls of his castle in Imola.

While the conspirators were racking their brains about how to finally take their revenge, Riario's protégé – the diabolical Ludovico Ricci – had come up with an effective stratagem: suggesting that the young cardinal ask Lorenzo to accompany him to the solemn Mass on Easter Sunday at which he himself would officiate in Santa Maria del Fiore.

It was an authentic stroke of genius, and would allow the Pazzi and the other conspirators to kill the two brothers during the service. But at that point Giovan Battista da Montesecco, the captain of the papal troops who had been assigned the task of personally assassinating Lorenzo, had refused to participate, saying that he could never shed blood in a church.

In reality, Jacopo sensed that the captain of the papal army had been considering extricating himself from the conspiracy for a while now and that this had provided him with the perfect pretext for doing so. But regardless of that, the Pazzi could not do without a murderer capable of eliminating Lorenzo.

His nephew Francesco had hurriedly changed the plans. In consultation with Francesco Salviati, he had identified two priests, Stefano da Bagnone and Antonio Maffei, the latter of whom was already part of the plot, and to them was given the task of cutting Lorenzo's throat.

And that was why he, Francesco, Bernardo Bandini, Ludovico Ricci and the two priests in question were in the cathedral that morning.

Together with Raffaello Riario, Francesco Salviati had met Lorenzo in the churchyard of the cathedral, wishing him a happy Easter and commenting on Giuliano's absence.

When they had entered the church, the wait had become even more unnerving. There was indeed a risk that the younger Medici brother would not show his face that day either, which was why Jacopo's nephew Francesco and Bernardo Bandini were now heading towards the exit: their plan was to go to the Palazzo Medici and convince Giuliano to attend the Mass.

Jacopo de' Pazzi was in a cold sweat. His thoughts went to Niccolò da Tolentino, encamped in great secrecy outside Florence with an army of two thousand soldiers and awaiting a signal, upon which he and his men would rush into the city and take the Palazzo della Signoria to the cry of 'People and freedom'. In the meantime, Francesco Salviati was to have taken control of the palace from the inside and put the guards and the Gonfaloniere of Justice out of action.

But despite the fact that they had managed, *in extremis*, to assemble a new plan, the patriarch of the second most powerful family in Florence continued to despair. Time was passing and there was no sign at all of Giuliano.

Jacopo forced himself to appear calm or he knew he would give the game away. He had to behave normally, just as he always did on these occasions. He forced himself to smile at his nephews and shake people's hands, but the knowledge that everything was going wrong made him feel insecure. His nerves were shot and friends and acquaintances would soon realize that he was plotting something. He'd been a fool to ever agree to participate in this shoddily organized conspiracy.

While he was absorbed in his thoughts, he saw his right hand trembling visibly and grasped it with his left, hoping that no one had noticed. The rings he wore sparkled as brightly as if they contained some demonic essence, eager to unmask him in front of everyone.

He shook his head once again in a desperate attempt to free it of those absurdities, but monstrous voices filled his mind with inarticulate yet terrible sounds: he wanted to put his hands over his ears, but realized that it would be pointless, because the sounds came from inside his own mind.

He looked towards the altar, hoping that it would all soon be over.

He tried to convince himself that Francesco and Bernardo would be successful in their attempt to get Giuliano de' Medici to the church, but he struggled to believe it was possible.

He hoped that he was wrong.

He hoped that everything would go according to plan.

Almost running, Francesco de' Pazzi and Bernardo Bandini hastened towards the Palazzo Medici in Via Larga.

What had prevented Giuliano from being present at the Mass that morning remained a mystery, but Francesco knew that, whatever the reason, he would have to convince him to come to the cathedral. And that wouldn't be easy because, given their past history, Giuliano would be wary of him.

'You talk to him,' he said to his friend, 'he doesn't trust me.'

'And what am I supposed to say?' asked Bernardo, his voice uncertain. He was agitated and couldn't hide it.

'That Lorenzo has sent for him... that he needs him... tell him anything!'

'And do you think he'll listen to me?'

'He'd better,' said Francesco, his eyes glinting cruelly.

Bernardo began to tremble.

'I don't know if I can...' he stammered, breathless from the race to get to the Palazzo Medici in time. Francesco, who was ahead of him, stopped suddenly and shoved him hard against the wall of a building.

'Listen to me: I have no idea how you're going to do it and I don't care, but you'd better succeed, otherwise I will cut your throat too, do you understand?'

Francesco's eyes were almost popping out of their sockets and as he barked his orders, white foam sprayed his black beard.

Bernardo swallowed hard, feeling terror seizing his throat. He nodded weakly.

'All right,' he said softly, 'I'll find a way.'

'That's what I want to hear,' said Francesco. He gave a laugh that chilled Bernardo's blood and then let him go and patted him on the back.

They began to walk towards Via Larga and, once in sight of the Palazzo Medici, Francesco let Bernardo go in front, remaining as far behind him as possible.

They reached the door and knocked upon it until a servant came to open it.

'I'm Bernardo Bandini, I have come for Giuliano de' Medici. His brother Lorenzo sends me to tell him to join him immediately in the cathedral for the Easter Sunday Mass. He must be there. Can you give him my message?'

'Naturally, my lord,' replied the servant. 'And in the meantime, if you wish to wait for him—'

'We'll wait for him downstairs!' snapped Francesco.

'Very good.'

The servant led them inside and then climbed the stairs leading to the apartments on the first floor.

Bernardo and Francesco stood waiting in the middle of the courtyard.

42

Laura Ricci

She couldn't have missed it. Not that day.

Laura was savouring the climax of the vendetta she had been waiting for all those years. She had been nurturing her obsession for so long that she had almost forgotten when it had begun.

Her mind went back to when Rinaldo degli Albizzi had taken her with him, protecting her and providing her with a life that had at first seemed wonderful, before it had gradually taken on dark hues of resentment and broken-heartedness. And now? The Medici exterminated. Inside Santa Maria del Fiore. It was a splendid plan, and in perfect taste. How wonderful, she reflected, that their blood should be spilled right under Filippo Brunelleschi's dome – the dome that Lorenzo and Giuliano's grandfather Cosimo de' Medici had wanted at all costs. She had somehow managed to control her hatred, and this Sunday all those years of waiting would finally be rewarded.

Revenge itself. For Reinhardt Schwartz and for their murdered love. Justice did exist after all. She looked joyfully at the beautiful face of her son and her heart swelled with pride.

Sitting a few rows in front of her was Lorenzo de' Medici. Giuliano was still missing, but Laura felt certain that he would appear.

It amused her that Lorenzo didn't know who she was, and she was ecstatic at the thought of seeing the descendants of her sworn enemies die before her eyes. Especially because they were completely unaware of the role she had played in it all. Cosimo and his brother Lorenzo would turn in their graves, but the destinies of their grandchildren were now preordained.

She hoped Francesco de' Pazzi and Bernardo Bandini would succeed, and quickly. The Mass had already begun, and at this rate it would end before they got back.

They had chosen the *Ite, missa est*, the concluding words of the service, as the moment to begin the carnage, so there was still time, Laura told herself.

She took Ludovico's hand and squeezed it and he looked back at her, a smile illuminating his face. He venerated her and that fact gave her indescribable joy, because in the boundless love he had for her she found some consolation for the sufferings of her life. It was worth enduring sacrifice and pain, humiliation and violence to have a son like Ludovico. An indescribable feeling, something she had only felt long ago for Schwartz, bound them together.

He kissed her hand as if it were a relic and Laura shuddered. She would have liked to lick his lips then and there, and the thought of it sent her into ecstasies. She often had impure thoughts about Ludovico and implemented them whenever she could. And he, for his part, went along with her desires. He was a compliant lover, capable of ardour, certainly, but even more ready to comply with her every whim, no matter how insane and outrageous.

She smiled and struggled to hold back her laughter. It amused her greatly to be in a church. The others might consider it a temple, a sacred place, the cathedral of God, but it meant nothing to her – that superior being they were all praying to had never been interested in her, nor had he raised a finger to save her from the unspeakable, so why should she trouble herself over what he might have thought about her?

Later.

Later, she repeated to herself, she would celebrate her triumph properly.

But for now they must stay alert and ready. Ludovico was to help Francesco and Bernardo kill Lorenzo. He had a dagger hidden in his blue velvet jacket and he would use it, Laura was sure of it. His thirst for blood was easily the equal of her own.

He was her son, after all.

Giuliano descended the steep marble staircase that led to the courtyard. From above he saw Francesco de' Pazzi and Bernardo Bandini awaiting him. That morning he had donned a light-blue doublet and was not wearing his leather armour. He hadn't been well for the last few days. He had injured his leg and his side during a recent hunt: nothing too serious, but enough to make it hard to wear anything too rigid.

At the bottom of the stairs he greeted them both. He didn't trust Francesco de' Pazzi but the presence of Bernardo Bandini reassured him. Bandini wasn't exactly a friend, but he had enough regard for him to consider him a good acquaintance. It was Bernardo who spoke.

'My dear Giuliano, forgive us if we disturb you, but your brother Lorenzo sent us for you. The Easter Mass is being celebrated in Santa Maria del Fiore in honour of the young cardinal Raffaello Riario, so dear to all of us. Indeed, as you will certainly know, it is he who is officiating at the rite. Lorenzo asks you to hurry because, after delaying the beginning of the Mass in the hope you would arrive, he was forced to allow the new cardinal to begin.'

'Why didn't he come himself?'

'He couldn't leave,' Bandini replied promptly. 'Someone had to stay with the young cardinal.' After his earlier fears, he seemed to have rediscovered his tongue and, though no orator, was sufficiently courteous to sound convincing to Giuliano.

Francesco stood in silence, merely nodding. He seemed calm.

'Raffaello Riario would be very disappointed by your absence,' continued Bernardo. 'It is very important that you be there in person.'

What Bandini said was common sense and it was true that Lorenzo was very fond of the young cardinal – Giuliano couldn't not be there that morning; he had to show his face. Giuliano tried to reassure him. 'Don't worry, my friend,' he said at last, 'I'll come. I cannot go too fast, unfortunately, because of a stupid fall from a horse, but I will do my best to get to the cathedral as soon as possible.'

They set off and crossed the courtyard, leaving behind them the magnificent arches and columns that ran around it.

For a moment, Donatello's David, with his ambiguous gaze and that strange, almost immodest posture of his, seemed to stare at the mismatched group.

They emerged into the street, Bernardo walking next to Giuliano, a few steps behind Francesco.

Suddenly the young Medici seemed to stumble and Bandini supported him. 'Courage, my friend,' he said with a certain joviality, 'you wouldn't want to miss such an important event!' And he embraced him, making sure once more that Giuliano wasn't wearing any kind of protection or carrying with him a dagger.

Unknowing, Giuliano was grateful for his attention, and interpreted it as a gesture of affection.

Francesco de' Pazzi said nothing and kept to himself, not that Giuliano much wanted to enquire about his health. Though Lorenzo hated him, Giuliano had no particular grudge against old Jacopo's young nephew. He was not overly interested in politics, much preferring art, literature and beautiful women, and while he remembered that Lorenzo had approved the law that had prevented Francesco's brother Giovanni from getting his hands on the inheritance of his wife Beatrice Borromeo, it never occurred to him that he might attract the attention of the Pazzi.

43

Antonio Maffei

As soon as he saw them enter, Lorenzo stopped worrying. He would have been sad not to have seen his brother. The young cardinal was a delightful person, and it had been a pity that Giuliano hadn't been present for the meal the day before. Lorenzo knew that he had hurt himself slightly in a fall from a horse but he also had the impression that something else was distressing his brother. Sensing it might be a matter of the heart, he hadn't wanted to investigate, because he felt like the person least qualified to give advice on such matters.

When he had come into the cathedral he had seen Lucrezia, but as soon as she had laid eyes upon his face, she had turned away.

Was she still angry with him?

Giuliano stopped a few pews behind him, near where Gentile de' Becchi was sitting.

The faithful were receiving the body of Christ in the rite of communion.

For a moment Lorenzo let his gaze wander: when he was in Santa Maria del Fiore, his eyes needed, for a few moments at least, to drink in all the wonders that it housed.

It was a foolish pastime, but he allowed himself so few of them, and so rarely, that he did not want to give it up. Every time he entered the cathedral he was enchanted anew by the breathtaking height of the columns and the spans ending in the cross vaults. It was as if the architects had actually tried to join the heavens to the earth. The stained-glass windows, designed for the most part by Donatello and Lorenzo Ghiberti, coloured the rays of sunlight that filtered through them.

He sighed, awed by all that beauty and wonder, and his mind returned to a few hours before. When he had left home that morning, he had tried to take Clarice by the hand, but she had pulled away. He thought about how often it had happened lately, even in public. Everyone had seen it. But on the other hand, how could one blame her? He had neglected her for so long, and her resentment ran deeper than simple social pleasantries. He would have liked to make amends, but had no idea how to go about it, especially because just a few pews away sat the woman he actually loved and who now probably hated him too.

He wished he could turn back time. Live those last ten years differently and find himself there once again that Easter morning, but now surrounded by love. He had been so absorbed with politics and with trying to defend his family's position that he had lost all the affection he had once enjoyed. He was most bitter about the fact that none of the people around him – first and foremost Lucrezia and Leonardo – had understood his concerns.

He thought of what his friend had told him a long time ago: that power had deprived him of everything else. He was a lonely man and, over time, had come to accept it as the price he had to pay for ruling Florence. It had not been his decision – after his father's death, the city's elders had made it clear that it was his duty to govern. The truth was that he had never had a choice.

As he thought back over the years while the hymns filled the building, echoing through the vast spaces of the naves, he realized how much he'd had to cultivate the art of compromise and calculation, since it was numbers and nuances that fed the fragile balance of politics. And even though he had always known it was not what he wanted, he had devoted himself to it body and soul.

He had been doomed.

So here he was now this Easter Sunday: unfaithful husband, spurned lover, unreliable friend.

And there was no way to change the past. He hoped that God, if he actually existed, would have mercy on him.

Antonio Maffei had got as close to Lorenzo's pew as he could: de' Medici was protected by a circle of friends and guards who certainly would not let a stranger approach with impunity, but being a priest should work in his favour. He glanced over at his companion in this bloody Easter: Stefano da Bagnone. He didn't know him – Bagnone had only been chosen when Captain Giovan Battista da Montesecco had pulled out, but he didn't inspire confidence. His eyes were glassy and his hands so sweaty that he might as well have had the word 'murderer' inscribed upon his forehead. He kept raising his hand to his side where, under his tunic, he kept the dagger with which he was supposed to stab Lorenzo.

Maffei hoped that his fellow assassin would at least be cool-headed enough not to complicate things.

As far as he was concerned, Maffei could not wait to kill Lorenzo. He had been waiting for that moment for a long time. Too long – it had been six years now. Ever since his beloved Volterra had been turned into a bonfire and its inhabitants massacred by Federico da Montefeltro's soldiers. He still remembered that blood-soaked dawn: the streets of the city cluttered with corpses, the heads stuck on the ends of pikes, the women raped and left to die among the ruins.

Just the thought of it was still enough to make his stomach turn, and even though almost all the Florentines had blamed Montefeltro, he knew perfectly well that it was Lorenzo de' Medici who had ordered the extermination of the city. Whether he had done it intentionally or simply accepted its inevitability did not matter – as far as Maffei was concerned, it was the same thing. If Lorenzo had wanted, he could have mounted a horse and gone in person to prevent the massacre from happening, but he hadn't. He had remained within the walls of his city, completely uninterested in what was happening in Volterra.

The bastard!

So now Antonio Maffei felt ready. No, more than ready – eager! He would not hesitate. He mustn't underestimate the complexities of the situation, though. As relaxed as he felt at that moment, he had to be careful. He would have to strike hard and try to get his victim either in the neck or in his side. If the first blow was decisive, what followed would be easier, but hesitation or a bungled stab could be fatal.

The conspirators were counting upon the element of surprise but after their initial disorientation, the Medici's men would react. If they succeeded in quickly murdering both brothers, however, the shock would be great enough to allow the conspirators to get away and disappear into the crowd. In the meantime, Francesco Salviati and his men would move on the Palazzo della Signoria and, when the time came, mercenaries disguised as dignitaries and servants of the Archbishop of Pisa would attack the guards protecting the building and take control of it, and Niccolò da Tolentino's soldiers would enter through the Porta di San Gallo. The power of the Medici family would be overthrown.

The plan seemed solid enough to him. All they had to do was be cold and ruthless, and Antonio Maffei felt certain he was capable of that. He would not fail, not on the day he finally had the opportunity to avenge Volterra.

Just a little longer. And then it would all be over.

44

Ite, Missa Est

Raffaello Riario looked benevolently down at the faithful. His eyes searched the crowd and stopped at Lorenzo de' Medici, who had been so kind to him these last few days. With a simple nod, he expressed his gratitude.

Lorenzo returned his salute with an almost imperceptible gesture and smiled.

Raffaello began to read the final words of the mass.

At the very moment he was about to reach his brother, Giuliano felt something cold prick his chest. Before he had time to understand what it was, he found himself on his knees, his doublet soaked with red. In front of him stood Bernardo Bandini, grasping a dagger that was dripping with blood.

Something struck his back, sending him crashing face down on to the marble floor of the cathedral.

Francesco de' Pazzi had kicked him, and now he straddled him and, screaming like a lunatic, stabbed Giuliano again and again.

One. Two. Three. Four times.

With each blow, a scarlet festoon sprayed out while a black lake spread from under Giuliano's chest.

The younger Medici brother remained on the ground, unable to move. He gave an agonised gurgle and bloody bubbles formed on his lips.

Francesco de' Pazzi was like a wild animal, stabbing away with terrifying enthusiasm as he sunk the blade repeatedly into Giuliano's now butchered body. At the umpteenth blow, his dagger somehow took a strange trajectory and ended up in his own thigh, piercing first his hose and then his flesh. The murderer's blood mingled with that of the victim and Francesco screamed at the pain which was as acute as it was unexpected.

The air was full of the desperate cries of the faithful who now crowded the aisles.

His voice sounding barely human, Giuliano screamed.

'Have pity!' someone shouted, and a woman who had just risen from her pew fainted, collapsing to the floor.

Loud shouts rang out among the aisles.

*

Lorenzo had just left the pew where he had been sitting when he heard someone's strangled screams from behind him.

As he turned to see what was happening, he felt something scratch at his neck. Unable to understand what it had been, he raised his hand to his throat and realized that it was smeared with blood. And then, before him, he saw Francesco de' Pazzi wildly stabbing his brother's lifeless body in the middle of the nave.

'Giuliano!' he shouted with all the breath he had in his body. 'Giuliano!'

But his brother could not answer him. His lips twisted into a sneer that revealed his white teeth and his face smeared with blood, Francesco de' Pazzi looked up.

At that moment, another dagger whistled through the air. Somehow, almost miraculously, Lorenzo avoided the blade, throwing himself to one side and stumbling on the marble slabs of the floor. He reached for the dagger he carried with him, while his shoulder struck the marble.

'Becchi!' he cried, kicking out manically as he attempted desperately to get back to his feet. He grabbed a pew and pulled himself to his knees, and another knife whistled past a palm's distance from his face, the blade smashing into the wood, sending brown and white splinters flying into the air.

Lorenzo looked up and saw the frenzied eyes of a priest. He had no idea who the man was.

'Die, you bastard!' the priest shouted, swinging at him again with the dagger. Instinctively, Lorenzo crouched and heard the blade whistle through the air just above his head, then jumped forward, ramming the attacker with all the weight of his body. He heard the dry snap of a breaking bone as the priest crashed into a pew, dropping his dagger, which spun, clattering, across the marble floor.

'Lorenzo! *Lorenzo!*' shouted Gentile de' Becchi, dagger in hand. With him were two guards, their swords drawn and stained with blood. 'Get into the sacristy,' he shouted. 'Get into the *sacristy*!'

'Giuliano!' cried Lorenzo desperately. 'Where is Giuliano?'

And then he saw Lucrezia.

She was standing immobile, eyes staring and mouth open in a silent scream, leaning on a bench to avoid fainting.

Lorenzo raced towards her. From the corner of his eye he had seen Bernardo Bandini sneaking up on her, dagger in hand. But Lorenzo was quicker and when Bernardo swung at her throat, Lorenzo managed to block the blade just in time.

Bandini's rage and strength were such, however, that the weapon, though deflected from its original trajectory, slashed through the sleeve of Lorenzo's doublet, cutting deeply into his arm.

'Get into the sacristy, Lucrezia, hurry! They'll kill us all if we stay here!'

'Lorenzo!' she cried. 'You're hurt!'

'Go!' he shouted.

Gentile de' Becchi appeared, grabbed Lucrezia by the arm and dragged her away towards the sacristy. Lorenzo began to back away, his retreat protected by the guards in front of him, together with Francesco Nori, one of his trusted men. Suddenly, a young man clad in a red jerkin stabbed Nori in the chest, running him through with his blade.

The furious guards reacted by stabbing the young man from both sides, their two daggers sinking into his body. He had no chance of escape and collapsed to the ground, a bloody pool spreading out across the slabs of marble beneath him.

Lorenzo, Lucrezia, Becchi, Braccio Martelli and the other men faithful to the Medici had reached the sacristy, and they shut the doors behind them.

'Giuliano!' shouted Lorenzo, his voice breaking. '*Giuliano!*'

Weeping, Lucrezia embraced him. And then she saw the cut on his arm.

'Bandages!' she cried. 'Quickly, or he will bleed to death!'

While Braccio Martelli and his two men barricaded the door, piling everything they could find – chests, a cupboard, two tables and even chairs – against it,

Gentile de' Becchi, with great presence of mind, cut off a sleeve of his jacket.

'Use it as a bandage. But first clean the wound.'

Lucrezia found some fine linen garments in a chest and then took some water from a jug on one of the sacristy's tables. She dipped an embroidered stole from the chest in it, then cleaned the wound on his arm as well as the one on his neck, which was little more than a superficial cut, as best she could. Then she wrapped a white stole around his arm and tied it into place. It wasn't perfect but it would slow the bleeding for now.

Lorenzo was slumped against the wall.

'Giuliano,' he murmured. 'Giuliano.'

45

Palazzo della Signoria

His eyes were wild, his hair dishevelled by the wind, his face red with rage and his voice hoarse from the enthusiasm with which he had screamed 'People and freedom!' Astride his horse, Francesco Salviati looked like some lost soul; to see him in that state, consumed by rancour and fear, one might have mistaken him for one of the four Horsemen of the Apocalypse.

Few had responded to his cry along the way, but if nothing else he and his host of mercenaries from Perugia had managed to get to the gates of the Palazzo della Signoria unharmed.

Leaving their horses in the square, the men had entered the building, Salviati ordering some of them to guard the entrance while he went to speak with the

Gonfaloniere of Justice in order to take possession of the upper floors.

He climbed the stairs as if the devil were at his heels but soon realized that most of his men had stayed below: of the thirty men who were with him, only three or four had followed him up. Perhaps his orders had not been clear enough.

He decided not to think about it and carried on up to the first floor. Once there, he told a guard he wished to speak with the Gonfaloniere of Justice.

'Messer Petrucci is dining,' the man replied. He had long blond hair and an aquiline nose, and a mocking light flickered in his grey eyes. 'However,' he continued, 'whom should I announce?'

'Francesco Salviati, Archbishop of Pisa.'

'This is certainly a strange time to confer with the Gonfaloniere.'

'It's an emergency,' insisted Salviati, his voice trembling with fear and uncertainty.

The other sighed. 'Very well, I'll see what I can do. In the meantime, please wait for Messer Petrucci in there,' and he nodded towards a cosy, dimly lit study.

As the man walked away, Salviati entered the room and wondered what the hell he would say to the Gonfaloniere of Justice.

He and his men had imagined that they would be able to take over the building in no time at all, but they had underestimated the complexities of the situation. While the passing time eroded his few remaining certainties, he prayed that the other conspirators had done their parts.

After a while the Gonfaloniere entered. He was an imposing man with broad shoulders and a sincere expression who had once been captain of a squadron of mercenaries, and he was loyal to the Medici.

Hoping that he would sound convincing, Francesco Salviati gave him one of his best smiles.

'What good fortune that you are able to receive me, *messere*,' he began. 'I came to bring you a message...' But the words died in his throat, because his mellifluous tone did not seem to be having any effect.

The man in front of him appeared to be used to a different manner of dealings and his reaction to Salviati's affectations was the opposite of what he had intended. It almost seemed that he had profoundly irritated the man.

'Really, excellency? And of what nature? I will be frank, I have little time. I was eating, to tell the truth, so let us get straight to business.'

'The, ah, point... the point is... that I bring a message from the Pope.'

'From the *Pope*?' Cesare Petrucci was incredulous.

'Yes, His Holiness has... declared that Florence is no longer under the leadership of the Medici and...'

'I *beg* your pardon?'

Francesco Salviati swallowed. His words sounded uncertain even to him, so he could only imagine how tentative they sounded to the Gonfaloniere of Justice, whose next words confirmed Salviati's own fears.

'Let's speak plainly, excellency,' said Cesare Petrucci with a frown that was anything but friendly. 'I find it curious that the Archbishop of Pisa comes running, at this time of day, up the stairs of the Palazzo della Signoria to confer with me without having made prior arrangements. I am here and I am all ears, but you had better explain yourself!'

Things were going from bad to worse, thought Salviati. What should he do? He had been so busy thinking about organizing the conspiracy with Girolamo Riario and Francesco de' Pazzi that he had completely overlooked the part for which he was responsible, and now he was paying dearly for his inexperience. He had walked right into the trap.

Somewhere outside the study, there was a strange jangling sound. Salviati hoped that it was someone coming to back him up. Where the hell were those four inept fools who had come with him up the stairs?

'Forgive me a moment, excellency...' said Petrucci.

He glanced out of the study and saw before him Jacopo Bracciolini, dressed for battle, wandering along the corridors of the building.

'Good lord,' he exclaimed, 'who the hell is that? Guards!' Then he turned back to Francesco Salviati.

'Do you know anything about this, excellency?'

★

Francesco de' Pazzi was walking towards home. He had tried to mount his horse but the wound in his leg was too painful, so he had set off on foot. What a fiasco, he thought. Lorenzo was still alive, and he had a deep cut in his thigh from which blood gushed forth, leaving a red trail along the road. In a desperate attempt to stop the bleeding he had used his belt as a tourniquet, but it didn't seem to have had the desired effect.

What the hell had he been thinking? Had he lost his mind? If someone had asked him what had happened in the last hour, he wouldn't have been able to explain it. His desire to kill had been so powerful that he had lost all sense of the world around him. What he had felt as he stabbed Giuliano was inexplicable – an irresistible thirst for blood that couldn't be quenched, and so he had continued until he had actually managed to stab himself. And at that point it was as though he had awakened from some kind of trance.

He felt weak. If he didn't hurry, he might even collapse before he got home.

He accelerated his steps, and traversed Via del Proconsolo in a single breath, arriving at his door just in time.

When the servants saw him, they carried him immediately to his apartments.

He was stripped and washed with ice water, and his brother Giovanni, seeing the state he was in, immediately sent for a surgeon to tend his wound.

As he lay on the fine linen sheets of the bed, Francesco could only gasp a reply when Giovanni asked him what had happened, and pray that their uncle Jacopo had managed to do what he had not. He cursed himself for not having been clear-headed enough and for not having been able to help him in the difficult task of taking control of the Palazzo della Signoria. Now it was all in his hands and in those of Archbishop Salviati.

He hoped that, despite his age, his uncle had enough presence of mind and good luck to succeed in the undertaking.

He sighed. He had made a very serious mistake. He, who had been the one who most wanted an end to the Medici.

The palace guards had intervened without delay and Cesare Petrucci was rapidly reorganizing the defences. When he had seen Jacopo Bracciolini coming up the stairs he had instantly grabbed Bracciolini's long hair, pulled out the dagger from his belt and sunk it into Bracciolini's side. A stream of blood gushed from the wound and Francesco Salviati, who had emerged from the study, shrieked like a frightened old maidservant.

Without releasing Bracciolini, who thrashed about hysterically as he tried to free himself and cried out with pain at the bleeding gash in his side, Petrucci turned and put his unsheathed blade to Salviati's throat.

'So, Archbishop,' he hissed, 'is this why you came? To take the palazzo and overthrow the Republic?'

'Please,' stammered Salviati, slumping to the floor with his back against the door frame, 'don't hurt me...'

'You should have thought about that earlier!' snapped Petrucci.

Meanwhile the voices on the stairs grew louder.

'Signor Gonfaloniere!' called the captain of the palace guards as he raced up the stairs. 'A group of armed men under the command of Francesco Salviati and his brothers have occupied the lower floor, and at least fifteen other mercenaries have locked themselves in the chancellery!'

'They've what?'

'Yes, my lord,' continued the captain. 'I realize it sounds absurd but they entered the chancellery and closed the door behind them, but they don't have the key so they can't get out because the door to the chancellery only opens from the outside.'

Petrucci smiled. Fortunately, they were dealing with a gang of fools.

'Well,' he said, looking at Jacopo Bracciolini, who was now moaning in agony, 'you certainly came up with a grand plan. Captain, deal with this scum while I take care of the men in the chancellery.' He looked first at Bracciolini and then at Salviati. 'Then call the Eight of Guard immediately and take these traitors to them. Tell them to get the papers ready so that the trial can be carried out immediately. I will be there with you for the verdict. We will deal with the lower floor later.'

After giving his orders, Cesare Petrucci let go of Jacopo Bracciolini, who collapsed to the floor like an empty sack, and headed straight for the chancellery, a large contingent of guards behind him.

46

The Colours of Revenge

When Giuliano de' Medici had fallen, the faithful inside Santa Maria del Fiore had fled in all directions. At first, Jacopo de' Pazzi hadn't been able to understand what had happened to Lorenzo, but had begun to loudly shout 'People and freedom!' in an attempt to stoke the flames of the bloody rebellion they were enacting.

After the first moments of exaltation, though, he realized that there were few responses to his cry, and this became even more obvious to him when he saw his nephew, covered in blood and with a deep cut in his thigh, racing at breakneck speed through the crowd of people which, blinded by panic, was pouring out of the doors of the cathedral in a torrent of heads and outstretched arms.

Francesco was running so fast, he was little more than a blur.

After that, Jacopo found himself in the churchyard. A little to one side, a handful of men loyal to him awaited him on horseback, ready to move on Piazza della Signoria.

'This way, Messer Jacopo,' one of his men shouted, handing him the reins of a large horse.

Without hesitation, the old banker climbed into the saddle and, riding through the swarming crowd that filled the streets of the city, he led his men towards Piazza della Signoria.

There were no more than thirty of them. Well armed, of course, but would that be enough? Niccolò da Tolentino and his troops were waiting outside the walls to intervene but first the rebels had to take possession of the building.

Jacopo hoped that the archbishop had completed his part of the plan.

The city seemed suddenly to be sinking into hell. During the ride, he saw a crazed whirlwind of tattered robes and faces streaked with tears that only made him feel more confused.

His nephew had disappeared. So had Bernardo Bandini. The priests who had been supposed to kill Lorenzo had failed and now there was no trace of them. Young Ricci had been killed by the guards with Francesco Nori.

Only he and Salviati were left, along with the squad of mercenaries who, in theory, should have taken control of the Palazzo della Signoria. He laughed, more out of desperation than anything else. Girolamo Riario, the mind behind this great conspiracy, had been careful not to participate in person, as had Giovan Battista da Montesecco. The Pope had given the evil deed his blessing but, of course, had remained in Castel Sant'Angelo, conferring honours and positions upon his relatives.

And now the whole thing fell upon his shoulders. He, who more than anyone else had said he was against it. He, who had certainly not wanted the slaughter and had tried in every way he knew to dissuade the gang of fools from going through with their plan.

He guffawed. At this point, he didn't care any more. By now it was clear that the outcome of the revolt depended on him and Salviati. Let them all go to the devil – the Medici, Riario, the Pope, even those idiot nephews of his who hadn't even had the guts to see it through.

He tried to focus his thoughts. He hoped that the hatred felt for the Medici would prove to be their best ally. The whole plan relied upon it.

As they approached the square, Jacopo heard an uneasy rumble that sounded almost like the roar of the ocean growing louder. Whatever it was, they were heading towards it.

When the square came in sight, an incredible spectacle presented itself to the eyes of the man who had dared challenge the Medici.

It was when the crowd tried to force the door that it happened. Jacopo Salviati, Francesco's brother, stood a little apart from the mercenaries. He was no man of arms and had little idea what to do with the short sword he held in his hand, so while he waited for his brother's confirmation from upstairs that the palazzo had been taken, he stayed in the courtyard.

Suddenly, from behind him, he felt the air moving, and there was a horrible, disgusting sound. It was a strange noise – a loud crack followed by something fleshy-sounding, as if someone had trodden upon a giant snail.

For a moment he was afraid to look, but he summoned his courage and, tightening his grip on the hilt of his sword, turned around.

The square was packed with people, above them banners bearing a coat of arms that Jacopo de' Pazzi knew all too well: six balls on a golden background, five red and the sixth bearing the lily of France. The Medici's supporters were like a roiling ocean, and roared in anger as if only awaiting a signal to attack like a pack of rabid dogs. Some of them had gathered around the door of the Palazzo della Signoria in an attempt to force it. For the moment they had not succeeded.

As soon as they saw the conspirator arrive in the square at the head of a host of soldiers clad in armour and carrying swords, they exploded like an army of the damned. There were men of every rank, but for the most part peasants and commoners, and they went at Jacopo de' Pazzi and his men with their knives and sticks.

At first, the soldiers had the best of it as they rode through their attackers, standing in their stirrups and swinging their swords at them, but the crowd, enraged even more by the dead and wounded who fell to the ground, soon surrounded its enemies. Separating and isolating the soldiers, they pulled them down from their horses one by one and slaughtered them.

Jacopo saw the massacre taking place before his eyes. He had neither the time nor the courage to try and stop it.

He watched as a group of men and women encircled a wounded soldier, pulled him to his feet and then butchered him with clubs. Blood and brain matter flew in a crimson cloud.

Jacopo felt his stomach turn and his mouth fill with the sour taste of terror. He managed not to vomit but the show of calmness he had been trying to maintain crumbled.

Wool carders, butchers, peddlers, tinkers, beggars, whores, pimps, criminals and who knew what else launched themselves against him and his soldiers with fury in their eyes.

Jacopo saw a man with tired eyes, his face devoured by jaundice and his mouth full of broken teeth, approach, stick in hand, and attempt to grab the reins of his horse.

In a moment of courage Jacopo de' Pazzi snatched them from his hands and spurred his horse, turning it around and sending it racing back out of the square. As soon as he had managed to put some distance between himself and the crowd, he spurred it into a gallop and, together with a few of his men, headed towards the San Gallo gate in a desperate attempt to escape lynching.

Behind him, angry voices and shouts, weeping and the gurgling of slit throats sounded in counterpoint to his cries as he urged on his horse to reach the gate as quickly as possible.

47

Inside the Palazzo

Dead bodies were raining down from the balcony. Jacopo Salviati watched speechless as the soldiers who had accompanied his brother Francesco upstairs came crashing down to the ground.

He looked at his men. When he saw how terrified they were, he felt his urine soak his own hose.

The thuds of falling bodies followed one another ceaselessly and the floor of the courtyard was soon drenched with blood.

When the mercenaries from Perugia who were guarding the door noticed what was happening, they began to shout, but their cries of horror were drowned out by the sound of bells. Someone was ringing them just as they used to when the people were summoned to fight in times of war.

The first floor was lost; the palace guards had evidently succeeded in neutralizing the soldiers who had been with his brother Francesco.

In the meantime, the attempts to ram the main gate grew stronger, each one accompanied by a sonorous thud. Judging by the intensity of the blows and the shouts that were growing increasingly loud and frightening, the square outside must have filled with a crowd of people, and it was easy enough to guess what it would do once it was inside the building. It would certainly not be merciful to the Pazzi, or to their allies, to judge from what Jacopo could hear.

Soon enough his fears became reality: someone managed to force their way in through the gate and, as in some awful nightmare, he saw a crowd of commoners armed with sticks rushing towards them.

Angry and threatening, they advanced as fearlessly as if they cared nothing about dying. They were farmers, wool carders, carters, servants and shepherds who had the Medici to thank for the fact that they were able to scrape a living together at all: the Medici who were the only ones who had welcomed them into their palazzo and attempted to understand their needs and fears. Jacopo shook his head: he realized what a terrible mistake it had been not to take those people into consideration, not to try and guarantee their support. But it was too late now. His supporters would be wiped out, because poorly paid and ill-motivated mercenaries had no chance against people who resented the fact of their very existence depending upon the whims of nobles and knew only one aristocratic family which was more enlightened than the others, the family which had given them the opportunity to hold their heads high and rebel against the established order. And what would those men and women do to protect that family now that it was threatened? It was easy enough to imagine.

The palace guards had decided to launch their attack from the large staircase leading to the first floor.

Jacopo saw them descend in a rapid and compact group and, thanks to their speed and the element of surprise, overwhelm his men. The few who managed to escape the massacre were forced straight in the arms of the angry commoners, who butchered them without mercy.

Blades pierced throats and he saw three men pounce like a pack of dogs upon on one soldier who was on his knees and finish him off with blows from their cudgels, his blood spraying out as they caved in his skull.

He felt something cold against his cheek and blood spurted from his face, splashing on to the marble of the columns. Then something else hit him in the back and he fell face down upon the gravel of the courtyard.

*

Naked, Francesco lay in bed.

The white sheets were stained with blood. It had taken the surgeon longer than expected to stop the bleeding.

He tried to move his leg but intense pain flowed in cruel waves from his thigh up the side of his body. He felt the cold sweat that beaded his forehead and gasped, his hands clawing at the bedclothes. Spasms passed through his body, making it as taut as a bowstring, his sight dimmed, and the armchairs, caskets, paintings and the fabrics on the walls of the room became indistinct, blurring into a confused fog. Finally, the agony subsided, fading into a slightly less intense throbbing pain.

He tried to think through what had happened but it was pointless because his mind kept returning obsessively to the way he had received his wound. It was the demonstration of his total failure and further confirmation that he was incapable of controlling his instincts.

He had let them take over and deprive him of lucidity and detachment and it was an error that now risked costing him dearly. He was still lost in his thoughts when he heard a noise from outside. The rhythmic thud of approaching feet. Francesco would have liked to get dressed, grab a sword and prepare to fight tooth and nail, but he didn't have the strength.

He awaited his destiny, and when they entered, he grimaced.

The captain of the city guards stood before him in full uniform.

'Francesco de' Pazzi,' he thundered, 'I declare you under arrest for the murder of Giuliano de' Medici and for high treason against the Republic. You will be escorted to the Palazzo della Signoria and there be judged by the Eight of Guard. If found guilty, you will be executed on the spot.'

Francesco pushed himself up on his elbows and with a supreme effort, managed to get out of bed and stand up.

He was completely naked.

'I am coming like this, then,' he replied disdainfully, 'because this is how much respect I have for your trial, for the Eight, and for Florence.'

The captain seemed genuinely taken aback and for a moment struggled to answer.

'So be it,' he proclaimed, finally having found his voice, 'but whatever happens, you only have yourself to blame!' He turned to his men: 'Take him and lead him, as he is, to the Palazzo della Signoria!'

Laura was weeping. In the now empty cathedral, among the corpses and overturned pews, she cried her last tears. Everything was lost.

She hadn't been able to defend Ludovico when the two guards had sunk their daggers into him. Laura had watched him die before her eyes: he had fallen to the ground with his innards spilling out of his belly and his eyes staring desperately into the crowd as they tried to find her to say one last goodbye.

She hadn't been able to do anything except fall to her knees as the crowd overwhelmed her. And they had trampled her like a rag, denying Ludovico even the comfort of a last farewell.

Now, covered with cuts and bruises, she was dragging herself towards her only child, the only hope she'd had left.

It took her a seemingly infinite amount of time, but she eventually managed to get to her feet and found that, despite her spinning head and the feelings of nausea, she was able to walk.

She felt beaten.

Beaten by the great plan of death, which had once again mocked her, refusing to take her but tearing from her breast that which she held dearest.

It wasn't fair, it wasn't *fair*, she thought, that a mother should survive her child. There was nothing more vile and mean. She had already had to watch the love of her life die, why had it had to happen again? Why hadn't death taken her? She, who deserved it more than anyone and even saw it as a reward for all that she had to suffer. Was death not yet tired of playing its games with her?

Oh Death, you son of a whore!

But the thought gave her no satisfaction; on the contrary, it only multiplied the tears that began to stream down her cheeks like rain.

A desperate scream filled her throat and emerged in a broken gurgle but not even that gave her relief.

The large empty space of the nave disoriented her. The cathedral had been crowded, but now there was a silence that not even her screams could fill. She had seen the young cardinal Raffaello Riario hiding trembling under the altar, waiting for the massacre to end. If she had been able, she would have killed him with her own hands.

The one man responsible for that slaughter was hidden away like a dog behind the walls of his castle, without having lifted a finger. At that moment he was probably mounting one of his whores. If she'd had the strength, Laura would have spat. She felt emptied and dried up, almost as though her soul had been torn from her body.

If vengeance had once been the ice with which she had frozen her heart and her love for Ludovico the fire with which she had warmed her passion, all that was now left was ashes.

She went over to him.

She was afraid to touch him because she knew that when she did she would know with absolute certainty that he was dead.

She cast her mind back to when, many years ago, she had washed and prepared the body of her murdered lover, Reinhardt Schwartz. The same thing was happening again.

No amount of tears would be enough. What did death have against her? Why had it punished her like that, all her life? Why did everything she touch end up dead?

She placed her index finger on Ludovico's forehead. It was already so cold! Laura closed his eyelids. She couldn't just leave him there in that pool of blood; she would take him with her.

She had no idea how to transport him, though, especially since his body had been torn to pieces: the gash which had torn open his belly was so deep that it had almost touched his spine, and his organs, which had partly spilled out, covered the marble floor of the cathedral with dark, glossy humours.

She wouldn't be able to keep his body. Time passed and the pain and anger began again to pulse in her veins as though they had taken the place of her blood. She decided that she would not give up. Little by little, one thought began to fill her mind.

One word: justice.

48

The First Horrors

'In the light of what we have heard, Francesco de' Pazzi, Jacopo Bracciolini and Francesco Salviati are hereby found guilty of the crimes of which they have been accused, and, in the name of the Eight of Guard, the judiciary of the Republic of Florence responsible for criminal matters, I therefore sentence them to death by hanging. The sentence is to be carried out immediately.'

Cesare Petrucci read out the verdict and then called for the guards.

Impassive in their red robes, the Eight stood watching as the three men were led to the window of the Palazzo della Signoria to be hanged.

The Archbishop of Pisa was sobbing. He tried to resist, but he was a feeble man and could do nothing to stop the palace guards dragging him by the arms over to the window. There, the executioner put the noose around his neck and secured the other end of the rope to an iron ring. Then he picked the archbishop up and threw him out.

Salviati's scream echoed through the sky.

Below, the teeming crowd in Piazza della Signoria looked upwards and cried out with joy when they saw the Archbishop of Pisa flying through the air. As he reached the end of the rope, silence suddenly descended, and the sound of his neck snapping was as loud as a wooden staff striking the hard rind of a pumpkin.

A moment later, Francesco Salviati's body bumped against the facade of the building, his purple tongue dangling in a final obscene grimace.

Before it had time to swing, Jacopo Bracciolini and Francesco de' Pazzi followed it in a carnival of death, the latter still as completely naked as when the guards had taken him from his palazzo.

At the sight of the corpses swinging like garlands in the wind, the people in the square screamed with anger, aroused by the macabre spectacle and a lust for revenge that spread through the crowd like leprosy.

'Death to the oppressors!' someone shouted.

'Death to the Pazzi,' cried someone else.

Hell had fallen upon the earth, and that was the signal. As though obeying a silent but irresistible order, some of the men who had gathered in the square turned away and began forming gangs with others. Their intention was to patrol the city in search of the traitors who had endangered the fragile equilibrium which Florence had won for itself after years of internecine strife. They were tired of uncertainty and they wanted peace, and this was the perfect opportunity to obtain it.

They would wipe the slate clean, eliminating all those who were allies of the Pazzi and against the Medici, and would hand the city over to those who had always taken their side and granted rights to those who had none. And if accomplishing that required crime and violence, all the better.

It was Lorenzo di Credi who told him.

'The Pazzi,' he shouted, 'the Pazzi are killing the Medici like dogs!'

When he heard those words, Leonardo abandoned his work and tore off his paint-stained apron.

He grabbed his friend by the shoulders and stared into his eyes with a look so cold and determined that it almost made Lorenzo tremble.

'Where?' he asked.

'In Santa Maria del Fiore.'

Without waiting another second, Leonardo rushed into the glaze room, where he had left his belongings. After what had happened to him, he had taken to carrying a small crossbow of similar design to the fast-loading one he had once given to Lorenzo. It was handy, quick and lethal. He hung it from his belt, tied to his arm a quiver full of darts which were no less deadly despite their small size, and hurried towards Santa Maria del Fiore. He rushed down Via Malborghetto, then raced along Via Ghibellina as fast as he could until he reached Via del Podestà and the Porta Guelfa. From there he ran down Via del Proconsolo at breakneck speed towards Santa Maria del Fiore.

When he arrived in front of the cathedral, he saw Lorenzo walking with difficulty, supported by Lucrezia and Braccio Martelli. On his neck was a blood-red scratch while a gash in his arm had been roughly bandaged. His eyes were sunken and dark and he looked exhausted. Glistening with sweat, his hair hung down over his face like wet twine and his pale face was suffused with a sickly hue. He looked ten years older. Lucrezia was gazing at him adoringly.

When Lorenzo saw him, his face lit up.

'Leonardo,' he said, 'my friend, you're here...'

'I came as soon as I heard what had happened. I feared the worst.'

'They killed Giuliano.' There were tears in Lorenzo's eyes.

Leonardo come over to him and embraced him, and in that moment realized that his friend's strength was at its limits.

'You must take him to safety,' he said. Braccio Martelli nodded.

'My friend,' murmured Lorenzo, 'can I ask you a favour?'

'Anything.'

'Could you make sure Lucrezia gets home safe and sound? I don't think I can manage it.'

'I'm coming with you!' she whispered softly.

'You can't, my love, and you know it well. We could be attacked on the way to the Palazzo Medici. You and Leonardo will attract less attention. But you have to move fast. Florence is a powder keg, and it will soon become a cemetery. The mob wants blood. That's why I want Leonardo to watch over you. There is nobody who is dearer to me than you two... and I trust Leonardo...' His words grew fainter, and he seemed almost to lose consciousness.

'Hurry!' said Leonardo. 'If we stay here we'll become a target.'

'Promise me you'll watch over her,' whispered Lorenzo. The words seemed to cost him his last energies.

'I swear it!' his friend replied. 'But you have to get out of here now, do you hear me?' Leonardo turned to Braccio Martelli, whom he held in high esteem. 'Get him home safe and sound.'

Lucrezia kissed Lorenzo. 'I can't... I can't leave you, my love.'

'Come on, let's go,' said Leonardo, taking her by the hand. She tried to resist but he dragged her with him. 'You're only making it more difficult for him – what matters now is getting to safety as soon as possible.'

They set off. Leonardo decided to head for his workshop. There they would be safe, for a while at least. Nobody cared about some mad painter, he thought.

The events had brought them all back together, he reflected. And no matter how insane and absurd the circumstance that had reunited them, he would not waste the occasion.

Doubts, lies and betrayals could finally be swept away.

Their friendship would go back to being what it had once been. Leonardo needed that desperately, and so did Lorenzo. Not to mention Lucrezia: he knew how much she had suffered from the consequences of her courageous actions.

Leonardo owed a great deal to both of them.

He smiled, thinking how generous nature and destiny were when they gave men new chances to do good and to make peace.

He was happy.

Lucrezia took one last look at Lorenzo. 'He saved my life. It almost cost him his.'

'I wouldn't have expected anything less from someone like him,' said Leonardo.

Upon hearing those words, Lucrezia burst into tears. Because it was true. She wept in silence – the cool air would dry her tears a little at a time.

Despite the tragedy, for a moment she almost felt

happy. But then the thought of Giuliano and the horrible way in which he had been killed returned, and she felt ashamed.

She hurried off with Leonardo through a city that would soon be ready to devour its children. Yet she was not afraid, because she had rediscovered love and friendship, and nothing in her life could be more important than that.

49

Clarice's Plan

When she saw Lorenzo wounded and with his arm covered in blood, Clarice was afraid.

That Easter morning she had not gone to Mass, knowing that the function was simply an occasion to celebrate the friendship between Lorenzo and the young cardinal Raffaello Riario, about whom she could not have cared less.

Religion and faith were all that she had and since the early morning, she had retreated to pray in the Palazzo Medici chapel. Her relations with Lorenzo had certainly not improved over the last year and therefore she had no intention of gracing him with her presence in public. She wouldn't give him the satisfaction, and neither would she allow the Florentine ladies to voice their sympathies or humiliate her with gossip about her husband's continued infatuation with Lucrezia Donati.

But when she had seen him being carried up the stairs by Braccio Martelli and Agnolo Poliziano, she had been rendered speechless. Only for a moment, though – immediately afterwards she had ordered the servants to quickly bring basins of cold water and white linen cloths to their lord's chambers. Then she had ordered all those who had entered to leave her husband's room so she could be alone with him.

She had laid Lorenzo out on the bed and removed the improvised bandage that had been wrapped around the wound on his arm. As soon as the servants had brought what she needed, she had cleaned away the clotted blood and humours that had formed in the meantime and wrapped it with very fine linen bandages.

Next, she had attended to the cut on his throat.

When she had finished, she looked Lorenzo in the face. For all that time he had remained silent, giving himself over to her care.

'Thank you, my love,' he said. Then he added in a whisper, 'They killed Giuliano.'

'What?' said Clarice, thinking she must have misheard him.

'This morning in church, Francesco de' Pazzi and Bernardo Bandini murdered Giuliano in cold blood.'

Clarice raised a hand to her mouth and stood up, her head spinning. Her stomach clenched and for a moment she thought she was going to vomit. Lorenzo tried to get up but she held him down and then sat in a chair facing the bed.

'My God,' she said, 'tell me what happened.'

Lorenzo told her about the conspiracy: how Giuliano had died right in front of him, and how he was miraculously alive thanks to the intervention of his friends who had helped him reach the sacristy of the cathedral. And how in so doing so, some of them, like Francesco Nori, had tragically lost their lives.

Lorenzo spoke in a faltering voice. Clarice stared at him, so upset that she couldn't even shed tears. For the first time she had actually been close to losing her husband, and the possibility had frightened her. She embraced him and stroked his thick black hair.

She made him drink some hot broth and begged him to rest, but Lorenzo insisted on talking to his friends and allies in order to thank them and to recommend prudence. He didn't want this tragedy to be the excuse his supporters were seeking to wage war in the city.

Clarice kissed him on the mouth.

And now what would she do?

She had her husband forever. In spite of everything, in spite of her humiliations and her indifference, at the bottom of her heart, she felt that she loved him.

She looked at herself in the mirror. For some time now she had stopped inflicting punishment upon her body – the cuts on her chest had healed and now only a few pink scars remained. She decided she must keep Lorenzo as close to herself as possible. She hadn't succeeded before but now she would use this tragedy to remove him from politics and force him to dedicate himself to his family. With Giuliano's death, his presence was indispensable.

Poor Giuliano! He, who had never hurt anyone, who was considerate to all and who had never been overly involved in matters of government.

It was then that Clarice cried.

She cried for the unhappiness that had befallen them, because an innocent man had been killed like a dog. She cried because Giuliano was a kind man and because despite his faults, her husband didn't deserve to be murdered. As she reflected on these tragic facts, she felt a profound anger begin to grow inside her. Almost instinctively, she sent for one of her ladies-in-waiting: Viola, whom she trusted implicitly. As she waited for her to arrive, an idea began to form in her heart. At first it was nothing more than a sensation, but it gradually grew into something stronger. But by the time she heard the knock on the door of her rooms, Clarice had conceived a plan.

When the young woman came in, Clarice decided that what she was about to do was right – in fact, it was clearly the only thing she could do to truly make Lorenzo safe.

His infatuation with Lucrezia Donati had exposed him to dangers that she could not even imagine, not to mention Leonardo and the trial for sodomy. In the end Leonardo had been acquitted, but Clarice was sure there was an element of truth to the accusations, and perhaps his strange way of painting people was not only brilliant but also dangerous. He had seemed harmless to her when she had seen him on the Ponte Vecchio, but there was no denying that he was outlandish.

Clarice knew that Leonardo had a workshop in Oltrarno. She didn't know exactly where, but the right man could certainly find out. And she was sure that not far from there she would also find Lucrezia Donati. So why not pay some mercenary and a few of his minions to go and tell them to leave the city, under pain of death? She wouldn't have to kill them, just frighten them.

That way, time would give her back her husband. That was all she asked for.

Viola came in. Clarice knew she – with her cornflower-blue eyes and honey-coloured blond hair – was the right person to convince a mercenary to handle the business, especially since her escapades were legendary among the ladies of Clarice's entourage: they all knew that on her days off, Viola loved visiting fourth-rate inns.

Clarice did not care in the slightest, because Viola always behaved impeccably and was twice as intelligent as any of the other women who served her. There was, therefore, no person more suited to the task. To be sure of success, she would equip her with a purse full of florins.

The girl looked into her eyes with that mischievous expression of hers.

'You wished to see me, my lady?'

'Yes, my dear. Let me tell you about a project I have in mind that will bring you the money to buy whatever you like and me a satisfaction I have been seeking for a long time.'

And so saying, Clarice motioned for her to sit down.

'Make yourself comfortable,' she said, 'and I'll tell you what I want you do to.'

50

Lorenzo's Words

Lorenzo was tired, and it wasn't just the physical pain of his injuries that prostrated him.

There was something more, something worse, something unjust and treacherous that for too long had been forcing him to be something he was not, at least in part.

Before him stood his men. They too were in part the cause of the change he had accepted long ago as a necessary evil.

A change which now weighed heavy on his shoulders.

He sat in his study in a velvet-lined armchair. Around him, Gentile de' Becchi, Braccio Martelli, Antonio Pucci, Agnolo Poliziano and other friends had already spent too long cursing fate for Giuliano's tragic end.

Too long, because Lorenzo sensed a hint of hypocrisy in their show of anger. At least in some of them.

He felt the tension mounting. It would have been imperceptible to those who were not familiar with politics and the atavistic hatreds between the city's various families, but it certainly was not to him. He knew that feeling of waiting until something brutal and bloodthirsty manifested itself all too well. Because it was clear that many wanted to use what had happened to justify the violence that was about to take place.

The Pazzi's conspiracy had led to the death of Giuliano, but now his men were demanding that the price be paid in blood. They wanted to turn Florence into a slaughterhouse.

And they would, of course, succeed.

But, by God, they would not have his endorsement. Too much blood had already been spilt. He knew that he had grave responsibilities in that regard, and could no longer carry all the horror and suffering on his shoulders. He had borne it for ten long years. Yes, he had accepted the investiture and used it to his advantage, but it had been a way to survive – the only way he'd been able to think of.

But he wouldn't allow it to happen again. Giuliano's death had changed everything.

He had always wanted peace but in the name of peace he had legitimized monstrous acts. This time he would refuse.

'I know what you are thinking,' he said. 'That the Pazzi must be punished, they must be plucked out like weeds.'

'We cannot do otherwise, Lorenzo,' replied Gentile de' Becchi. 'To leave a crime like this unpunished is dangerous as well as unjust.'

'I understand that, but I will not authorize a massacre. As far as I am concerned, the Pazzi can be exiled. I don't want another bloodbath.'

'I think Lorenzo is right,' said Braccio.

For a moment they all were silent. They knew that Braccio Martelli was married to a Pazzi, but that was not enough reason to desist.

It was Becchi who broke the silence. 'I disagree,' he insisted, 'we cannot show weakness now.'

'Exactly,' chimed in Antonio Pucci. 'Now more than ever we must teach them what terror is. Cesare Petrucci awaits only a signal.'

'I owe Cesare a great deal,' said Lorenzo, raising his head. His eyes were sunken and his face hollow, and the suffering in his eyes was clear for all to see. He raised a cup of hot broth to his lips. He needed to rebuild his strength after what had happened. 'He held out against Bernardo Nardi and helped to return Prato to our control, and my gratitude to him is immense, but despite all that has happened, you will hear no words of hate from me. I already know that all hell will be let loose, but let it be clear that I won't be the one to encourage it. Today, on the day my brother was killed, I have no intention of legitimizing a massacre: you must take responsibility for your own actions. I have seen enough blood flow to drown ten men. Have you already forgotten what Giuliano's body looked like? And Francesco Nori's – he too slaughtered before my eyes? Do you really believe that I want more blood? Do whatever you want, but don't come here and ask that of me, not now!'

'Calm yourself, my lord, or you will hinder your healing,' advised Becchi, putting a hand on his shoulder.

'Leave me,' Lorenzo snapped angrily. 'I want to be alone with the memory of my brother. Is that too much to ask? Have I not already given you enough? For once, Florence will have to do without me. Have I made myself clear?'

Becchi fell silent. No one else dared speak.

Lorenzo's words hung in the air. His men had been given precise instructions but, perhaps for the first and last time, they had no intention of following them.

In silence, Becchi, Poliziano, Antonio Pucci and the others left. Only Braccio remained. Since the day when Lorenzo had won the tournament, they had been friends – as close as brothers.

Martelli squeezed his hand and Lorenzo, his eyes tearful, looked up at him.

'I saw how much they wanted blood, Braccio,' he said. 'I will ensure that at least Guglielmo de' Pazzi, who is married to my sister Bianca, is spared. I could not bear it if he weren't. Try to do everything you can for Florence.'

'I will do as you ask, my friend, even though I already know what they will say.'

'Are you referring to your wife?'

Braccio nodded. 'She's a Pazzi. It'll be a miracle if I manage to save her.'

'Now go,' said Lorenzo. 'I want to spend the next few days alone with my pain and with my thoughts.'

Braccio understood perfectly how Lorenzo felt. Without answering, he left the room.

He too had seen the rage in the faces of the others. In his own way, each of them wanted to use the conspiracy as a cover for taking revenge.

They might unleash hell on earth – but at least no one would be able to blame Lorenzo de' Medici for it.

Leonardo knew that the journey to Oltrarno would not be a short one, especially as he was sticking to quiet side streets. He tightened his grip on the crossbow for a moment as if it were a lucky charm.

Behind him Lucrezia was thinking how unbelievable it was that sooner or later fate, as it wove its threads, always reunited her with Leonardo and Lorenzo.

An apocalypse seemed to be descending upon the city: doors were barred and the deserted streets were gradually filling up with gangs of idlers and troublemakers loyal to the Medici, who were clearly on the lookout for those friendly with the Pazzi, with the intention of killing them.

They saw a man whose throat had been cut by a gang of youths. He was on his knees in the middle of the street, his eyes glassy and tufts of white hair sticking out like plumes from his shiny bald skull. One of the youths pulled back his head, showing the others the deep red smile the dagger's blade had carved there, and another kicked the man between his shoulder blades with a snicker. The old man fell forward, his face in the mud.

Dead.

Lucrezia barely held back a cry.

'This way,' whispered Leonardo.

They were heading towards Santa Croce. Leonardo had chosen to take a longer route so as to avoid the areas that would certainly be filling up with more cut-throats and thieves, ready to exploit the growing confusion and turmoil.

As soon as they had passed the Albizzi quarter, they heard loud screams coming from Piazza della Signoria and from the nearby piazza of San Pulinari.

They had to hurry, or it would be too late – the only solution was to take shelter inside the walls of Leonardo's house.

It was then, as they were walking along a narrow

alley, that a gang of youths clad in ragged, dirty clothes appeared before them.

There were about half a dozen of them: skeletally thin, with prominent cheekbones, long hair and huge eyes which seemed to bleed out of their gaunt faces. They held knives and clubs and the tallest one, who was clearly the leader, had a long gash across his cheek. They were barefoot and stank like a colony of rats.

The tall one pointed to Leonardo.

51

The Gang

'You, sir,' said the tall one, 'you look like a wealthy man. Not to mention that the woman with you could whip our cream for a day, if you follow my meaning.' Just to make sure they did, the youth grabbed his crotch.

There was ragged laughter from the rest of the gang. Leonardo said nothing, and continued to advance towards them.

He knew there was no other choice. If he hesitated, they would think he was afraid. When they were a few steps apart, the leader came towards him.

'Did you hear me?' he snapped.

Leonardo's calmness had irked him. Some of the other members of the gang, who were obviously inebriated, began shouting threats and insults and growing increasingly agitated.

Imperturbable, Leonardo continued to advance, grabbing the gang leader's arm and twisting it back, eliciting a moan of pain.

With his other hand he aimed the small crossbow at another member of the gang in whose hand the blade of a knife glinted. Leonardo pulled the trigger and the small dart pierced the lad's palm. With a cry of pain, he dropped his dagger and fell to his knees as he attempted to staunch the flow of blood from the wound.

The leader with the scarred cheek cradled his broken wrist and Leonardo quickly took another dart from the quiver tied to his forearm, put it in place and cocked the weapon. The cord tightened, ready to fire.

'Now,' said Leonardo, 'do the rest of you want to try your luck?'

The gang leader moaned while the other boy wailed from the pain of the dart sticking out of his hand. The four remaining youths stood staring in shock.

Lucrezia too was speechless: Leonardo had moved with astonishing speed, and there had been an elegance in his movements that had nothing soldierly about it. It was as though he were executing some deadly dance.

The other members of the gang decided to cut their losses and moved aside to let Leonardo and Lucrezia pass.

At that moment the bells of the Palazzo della Signoria began to ring out a frantic alarm to the people of the city.

'Now we're in trouble,' said Leonardo between gritted teeth.

'Why?' asked Lucrezia.

'Did you see the gang that attacked us?'

She nodded.

'Worse ones than those will soon be taking to the streets. Agitators will start whipping up the crowds against the Pazzi and murderers and thieves will take advantage of the confusion to go about their nefarious business. And if we don't hurry, we will find ourselves right in the middle of it.'

'God will have mercy on us!'

'They've moved fast – too fast. I'd hoped the institutions would have waited a little longer before plunging the city into anarchy.'

'Do you think Lorenzo ordered it?'

'No! He has certainly made mistakes in the past but despite what some say, Lorenzo is no bloodthirsty tyrant. My guess is that he is too grieved and weakened to deal with the situation and that his allies will use it for their own ends.'

'My God!'

'We need to stop talking and start moving.'

Messer Jacopo de' Pazzi had just come in sight of the Porta di San Gallo when he heard the bells ringing out the alarm. He knew then that all was lost, and that when Niccolò da Tolentino heard that sound he would realize that the conspiracy had failed and would return to Rome, abandoning Jacopo to his destiny.

At that point, there was no time to warn him without getting himself killed. In a few hours at most, the streets would be full of those loyal to the Medici, out to kill and mutilate anyone judged to be an ally or even a supporter of the Pazzi. Jacopo had been incredibly fortunate that he had managed to slip out of the city before the Palazzo del Podestà and the city guards got themselves organized.

As soon as he passed under the stone arch, he spurred his horse into a gallop, so as to put as much distance as possible between Florence and himself.

There was nothing else Laura could have done.

Her heart felt as though it were being torn out at the thought of it, but at least she knew Ludovico was with her.

In the deserted cathedral she had managed to find a cloak which someone must have abandoned in the chaos. It had hurt to put it on, because of the injuries she had sustained when she'd been lying on the floor of the church. She had pulled the hood down over her face. Now nobody could see who she was, though that was no great advantage: the Medici partisans would attack all those whose loyalties were in question, and a woman walking the streets of Florence alone was an irresistible invitation.

When she finally left the cathedral, the carriage that had brought her to the Mass that morning was gone. The coachman must have decided to leave when he had seen the turn events had taken. If Laura discovered that he had abandoned her out of mere cowardice, she would have him whipped when she returned to Imola.

She needed a horse.

She set off in the direction of Via del Castellaccio. She knew that it would take her to the Balla gate, and from there, one way or another, she could continue to Fiesole, and then continue on to Imola. But she could not do it on foot.

She carried with her a strange bundle that she attempted to keep concealed in the folds of her cloak.

She turned into Via dei Fibbiai, because Via dei Servi, the most direct route to the Balla gate, would be crowded with Medici loyalists, and Laura wanted to avoid any unpleasant encounters. She noticed that the shops were all closed: the traders had obviously decided that the wisest thing to do was to lock themselves up in their houses.

As she wandered along the streets, she finally had a stroke of luck. Right in front of her, someone had left a horse tied to a wooden pole. They must have abandoned it as they hurried to get to safety.

Laura smiled. Finally she had a chance. She approached slowly, raising her index finger to her lips as though the animal could understand her, and caressed its glossy coat. It was a fine beast, with a copper-coloured mane.

She whispered something in its ear and, seeming to understand her intentions, the horse gave a subdued whimper of approval. It stamped its hooves gently while Laura untied it.

She was no horsewoman, but she knew enough to put her foot firmly into the stirrups and thrust herself up with enough momentum to climb into the saddle. It hurt like hellfire, because of the bruises and wounds, but she had no intention of letting that stop her.

She had promised herself that she would reach Imola and complete the task she had set herself, and she certainly wasn't going to be prevented from doing so by saddle pains. The horse was a sign from destiny not to give up.

She trotted up to the gate.

The guards had already gathered in large numbers around it. It wouldn't be easy to get through but suddenly an idea occurred to her. She turned the horse around and went back to where she had found it. Near to the pole it had been tied to, she noticed some fresh horse droppings. She dismounted, picked up the dung in her hand and rubbed it on to her cloak and tattered clothes. It was disgusting, and she did a careful job, making sure that every part of the fabric was impregnated with the fetid stench of the animal's excrement. Once she was sure she was sufficiently repellent, she remounted her horse and headed back towards the gate.

As she approached, she made sure to lower her head so the hood almost completely concealed her face.

A city guard approached her. He was a sturdy man with inquisitive blue eyes, who smelled of wine and roasted meat. Long black hair emerged from the sides of his visorless helmet and there was a dagger on his belt.

'Let's see what we have here, then,' he said with a sneer that promised nothing good. But as he was about to touch the horse, he was overwhelmed by the powerful stench of ordure.

'Jesus!' he said disgustedly. 'You stink!'

'I'm sorry, my lord!' cried Laura, reaching out to touch the guard. 'But if there's anything I can do for you...'

'Stay away from me, you damn beggar!' he snapped, pinching together his nostrils as best he could. 'That stink of shit will kill us all!'

'What's happening, Capponi?' a guard sergeant shouted out to him. He was inspecting a family that was about to leave the city. There were four of them and they were carrying all sorts of household goods and luggage which they had piled on the back of a mule that was so thin it looked as though it would break under the weight.

'Nothing, my lord, just a miserable pilgrim who stinks of shit.'

'Let her pass, then, and free us of her presence as soon as possible.'

'That was just what I intended to do.'

And without another word, the guard raised his arm and motioned Laura through.

52

Hell on Earth

'**M**edici! Medici! Medici!'
The Medici loyalists crowding the now-dark streets of the city shouted the word obsessively. The Gonfaloniere of Justice, the Eight of Guard and the Podestà had ordered all the gates to be closed. Florence had become a gigantic prison, where those loyal to the Pazzi would be hunted down and exterminated: from the first to the last.

Legions of rats filled the alleys, which were flooded with humours and waste and illuminated by the rust-coloured light of the torches. The doors of the buildings were bolted, but that didn't stop the Medici's supporters. Everywhere there was shattered glass, torn hinges, broken bolts; and everywhere they went they brought death.

Rain began to fall, and the blood from the bodies that filled the streets swelled into a carmine river that flooded the whole city. The peasants said it was a curse that would devastate the crops – even as they raged against the Pazzi.

It was a hell on earth.

Gangs of criminals and thieves descended upon the centre like swarms of locusts, looting corpses, killing pilgrims and raping women. Florence had become a gigantic latrine, a no man's land where anything could happen and where even the most awful crimes would never be condemned as such as long as they were directed against the Pazzi.

The conspiracy had become the ruin of Messer Jacopo's family, and was gradually transforming into a triumph for the Medici. A triumph, though, founded on murder and pain.

Gentile de' Becchi, Antonio Pucci, Cesare Petrucci and other leaders of the party had taken advantage of that temporary power vacuum to inflict their apocalyptic vision of revenge upon all those who might prove to be opponents of, or even unfaithful to, the Medici. Giuliano's corpse had become a symbol of martyrdom upon which to found a new Florence – a Florence which was entirely favourable to their interests.

And in his infinite pain, Lorenzo had shut himself away from all of them.

Justice had lost all its dignity and become retaliation, principles had been turned into dogmas, rigour into cruelty and discipline into violence, and that world of horror and fear was making the citizens' lives a waking nightmare.

After also having condemned to death Jacopo de' Pazzi, who was soon hanging from the windows of the Palazzo della Signoria, the orgy of anger had not subsided but had rather exploded into mass insanity where each crime was more bloody than the one before.

A handful of Medici partisans had penetrated the abbey of the Benedictine monks in front of the Palazzo del Podestà and, after having ransacked it, had found Antonio Maffei and Stefano da Bagnone, the priests guilty of the attempt on Lorenzo de' Medici's life.

They had been dragged by the hair out into the street and left to the mercy of the crowd.

From the crowd of assembled tinkers, whores, peasants, artisans, beggars and adventurers, a man with long silver hair came forth. He was a sort of people's leader whom they called 'Greyhair' because of his unmistakable appearance. In the past he had been part of several bands of mercenaries, and now, reduced to being a simple good-for-nothing, he had taken advantage of the chaos to do a bit of looting and dispense a bit of violence.

As he approached the two terrified priests, he pulled a long, sharp knife from his belt and ran his tongue over his lips as though looking at some appetizing dish. He walked behind Maffei and kicked him in the back of his knees, sending him sprawling to the ground.

The priest began to cry desperate tears.

Greyhair spat at him in disgust, then raised his left hand to the man's head. He let the blade of his knife glisten in the light of the torches and braziers and then, with a sudden movement, sliced off the ear of the poor unfortunate who huddled at his feet in a puddle of piss and tears.

The crowd cried out enthusiastically at the scene – they clearly wanted more. People shouted out for Greyhair to go on and, so as not to disappoint his bloodthirsty public, he cut off the other ear, which fell to the ground.

Carmine blood dripped down Antonio Maffei's face.

At the sight of the torture to which his fellow conspirator was being subjected, Stefano da Bagnone began to shriek. Some in the crowd laughed while others shouted insults at him, promising him an exemplary punishment.

The almost hysterical mob swarmed around the priests and a couple of the most violent of the Medici partisans began to kick them. Soon at least a dozen men were cudgelling the two unfortunates. Their bones snapped like eggshells beneath the hail of blows.

The cheerful smile and malevolent expression upon his face showed how pleased Greyhair was by that horror.

Once the beating was over, nooses were placed around the necks of the two conspirators and the other ends of the ropes were tied to the saddles of two horses that Greyhair and another man then mounted. They spurred their animals into a gallop, pulling the two priests behind them. As the two unfortunates were dragged to the gallows, their bones were broken, their teeth smashed and their tongues bitten off while the crowd roared once again in jubilation.

When they reached the Gate of Justice, Greyhair and his companion halted their mounts and left Antonio Maffei and Stefano da Bagnone with the Eight of Guard. In a macabre parody of a trial, the magistrates condemned the two priests to death by hanging, and the mob of men and women watching burst out in a roar of approval and applause as the city guards dragged the two priests to the gallows.

A flock of crows flew croaking up into the sky and stray dogs snarled as the inarticulate screams of Antonio Maffei and Stefano da Bagnone filled the air.

The executioner put the nooses of two strong new hemp ropes around their necks and waited until the Gonfaloniere of Justice gave him the signal.

Taking advantage of the confusion, some in the crowd began throwing rotten fruit at the two condemned men. The fruit splattered against their bodies and faces, smearing them with yellowish slime. Dripping with tears, mucus and malodorous fruit pulp, Antonio

Maffei's face resembled a monstrous mask, the bleeding holes where his ears had once been adding a macabre detail which deprived the priest of any final trace of dignity.

The Gonfaloniere of Justice nodded and the executioner pulled the lever that opened the trapdoors.

The condemned men's feet trod air and their legs thrashed manically as their faces contracted in grimaces of pain, their gurgles choking in their throats. Antonio Maffei died almost immediately but Stefano da Bagnone took longer, his face swollen and his eyes staring as though they were about to burst out of their sockets. The crowd shouted abuse at him while his body, by some incomprehensible caprice of fate, attempted to fight against its mortal nature. It was as if God was angry with humanity for its actions and wanted to make of him a supernatural example of resistance to injustice.

Eventually, Stefano da Bagnone too died after atrocious suffering, but his dramatic dance with death had so impressed itself upon the eyes of the crowd that more than one began to tremble, as if, for the first time since that madness had begun, they had realized what had actually happened.

53

The Day of Reckoning

The pleasure that peasant girl gave him drove him wild.

When he mounted her it was like possessing an animal. Her submissiveness made her a docile filly, perfect for providing him with all manner of erotic satisfaction, and the fact that she didn't resist him but accepted whatever he did to her entranced him. He could punish her, whip her, penetrate her every orifice, and still she welcomed him with the same docile submission that he demanded of a woman.

When he was with Anna, he truly felt like a lord: he could taste it like a sweet fruit. She offered herself to him with a disarming naturalness, allowing herself to be violated without asking for anything more in return than a plate of soup and clean sheets. It wasn't just the physical side of it that excited him; it was also her simple-minded gratitude and her absolute subjection to him. He had such power over Anna that he was captivated by her: it was the perfect demonstration of the superiority of his noble birth, exercised in its most primordial way. The right of the fittest.

But it was becoming a problem: sex with her was so gratifying that Girolamo Riario could no longer do without it. He wanted it again, and again; he could never seem to get enough of her. He took her at all hours of the day and night, and she was always ready, never complaining but responding with surprising energy.

With her soft curves, her full breasts and that face of hers, so expressionless it was almost foolish, and yet seductive precisely for that reason, Anna was the very essence of sex. Despite what he might tell himself, Girolamo Riario worshipped her like a goddess: her vulva gave her control over him, enveloping his will and sucking him in. Girolamo was lost in an erasure of the self where the world melted into nothing more than an orgy of lust – a sensation of freedom where he felt light, unburdened by thoughts and worries.

Just as he did in this moment.

Sitting on his knee like a little girl, she gave an irresistibly naughty cry as he gently opened her lips, as soft and wet and red as cherries, with his index finger.

'Suck!' he said, moving his finger in and out. Anna wrapped her lips greedily around it, and immediately felt his member harden against her backside.

His penis almost unbearably hard and swollen, Girolamo Riario also inserted his middle and ring fingers into that beautiful mouth which oozed with pleasure. After she had sucked his fingers, Anna knelt down in front of him, resting her hand on his glans and gently teasing it before starting to masturbate him. She did it slowly, languidly, almost distractedly, and the lord of Imola felt his desire for her almost overwhelm him.

How was she able so innocently to make him both her slave and her master? he asked himself. Anna masturbated him at length until, sensing that he was about to come, she turned around and got down on all fours, proffering her haunches to him. He came over her, flooding the dimples on the diaphanous skin above her backside with semen. She took some on her index finger and put it into her mouth along with Riario's three fingers.

He moaned with pleasure.

He was about to take Anna over to lie down on the bed when he sensed the appearance of something cold and malign in the room – something which made the flames of the candles flicker.

'And so this is how you awaited news of the outcome of the conspiracy, is it?'

He knew the voice but in that moment, his brain clouded with erotic ecstasy, he could not connect it to a face. It should be obvious to him, he was certain. Who the hell was it?

'Are you so overwhelmed by the pleasures this farm girl gives you that you cannot even remember who I am any more? Are you really such a fool? I should have realized it, idiot that I am!'

'Laura...'

'Ricci!' said the voice behind him.

'Wait...'

'I have already waited too long, don't you think?'

Girolamo Riario felt something cold pinch at his throat. The gleaming blade of a dagger.

'Tell your woman to leave us alone,' said Laura.

'You can go now, Anna,' he said, without waiting for Laura to repeat her order.

The girl nodded and, her sweet eyes lowered to the floor, retrieved her clothes and trotted to the door.

'It is a mystery to me what you see in such a dull and ordinary woman,' said Laura when she heard it close.

Riario was careful not to reply.

'Now,' Laura said, 'you will remain still, naked like the worm you are, and you will do something for me.'

'Very well,' he confirmed.

'I don't need your worthless permission,' snapped Laura, pressing the blade against his throat. Drops of blood emerged from the shallow cut it opened. She took a bundle out from beneath her cloak, which she placed on the bed in front of her prisoner.

'Untie the knot and open it.'

Knowing that hesitation was more than his life was worth, Riario did as she ordered.

It appeared to be a sphere which had been wrapped in clothes. The strange and disturbing object gave off an almost unbearably powerful smell.

Riario loosened the knot and began unwinding the long piece of white cloth, which was drenched with some black fluid. As he proceeded, the nauseating odour became unbearable, and he gagged as the food he had eaten a few hours before rose in his throat.

In the innermost part, the white cloth had become entirely black and his hands were now covered with the stuff, which was partially congealed into dark crusts: dried blood.

As he finally finished the awful task, the suspicion which his reason had refused to accept was proven to be accurate: when the fabric was completely unwound, a head rolled out onto the bed, its eyes wide open, its matted hair like revolting tentacles and what had once been a face now an awful mask.

It was Ludovico Ricci.

Girolamo Riario could fight it no longer: he fell to his knees and vomited up the contents of his stomach.

Laura gave him a vicious kick in the ribs and Riario collapsed to the floor, smearing himself with his own spew.

'My son!' cried Laura Ricci. 'I was such a fool. The only time I actually should have consulted the tarot, I refused to for fear of the answer I might receive. And now here I am.' She spoke with a bitterness that seemed to come from the remotest recesses of time, as though she had nurtured it over the years in order to free it at precisely that moment.

'Please...' he said again.

'Be silent,' she hissed.

She looked at her victim, huddled on his knees, and yet did not seem to see him at all. It was as though her eyes were veiled – as though she were not really there at all but imprisoned in some distant dimension.

In a sense, her life had ended with the death of Schwartz. Her son had given her a joy she had barely believed possible, but Ludovico had still been a simulacrum of life – a vision of something she had lost forever and that not even he had ever managed to restore to her.

She had projected on to the boy everything that she had lost, had made him her only reason for living, the sole object of her affection, her comfort, her joy, even her love.

And now she had lost him too, in this squalid way.

Once again, the person she loved had been killed, confirming her failings first as a woman and then as a mother. She could not protect the men who loved her, and she hated herself for it.

She turned her dull, lifeless eyes upon her victim and reflected that she was tired, and that even if she killed him it would give her neither Ludovico nor the love of her life back.

Girolamo Riario crouched on the floor in a pool of his own vomit. He was pathetically weak.

The air in the room was unbreathable.

Laura looked at Riario one last time and then raised the blade of her dagger to her throat.

'Look closely, you accursed bastard. I'll show you how a real woman dies.'

And without another word, Laura plunged the blade into her throat and pulled it in a semicircle, slicing deeply into her flesh. Her blood sprayed out over the white sheets of the bed, the wolf skins that covered the floor and the puke-covered face of Girolamo Riario.

The dagger fell from her hand and Laura looked at Girolamo Riario one last time before slumping on to the bed. Slowly she slid down to the floor, dragging the sheets with her, the gleam in her dark eyes dimming.

Her life was ebbing away, but at the exact moment in which her soul abandoned her body a smile came to her lips.

Finally, after so long, she had found peace.

His eyes wide with terror, a weeping Girolamo Riario stared at her.

Then he began to scream.

54

Daydreams

A whole day had passed since they had arrived here, yet Lucrezia still could not get used to the marvellous place Leonardo had brought her to. The old building that housed his workshop was in Oltrarno, and it was incredible.

She remembered being surprised and even a little upset when, several years earlier, she had discovered the drawings, plans, blueprints of machines, studies of the human body and Lord knew what other devilries covering the walls of the cellar, but now that she had seen the rest of the house, she felt a sense of absolute wonder. Every single corner of it seemed to have been shaped by new and incredible ideas. Leonardo had built a sort of machine, which he called an 'elevator', to go up more quickly from one floor to another of the building and which allowed him to move heavy and voluminous equipment that could never have been carried by hand up a ladder. It was worked through a complex system of pulleys which, by means of a winch, allowed the elevator to move from top to bottom and vice versa, and was controlled by a crank inside the device which Leonardo turned in one direction to rise and in the opposite direction to descend.

The room in which she found herself was lit by strange lights: large boxes of treated wood inside which candles had been placed. In one of the four sides of each box Leonardo had set a large glass lens, and the result was that these strange devices gave off much more powerful illumination than a normal lamp.

She looked around her: not far away, a magnificent lyre seemed to be observing her. Leonardo had built the musical instrument within a fantastic creature made of bronze. The animal held up the lyre with its legs, the instrument seeming to have been constructed inside the beast's jaws, which were covered with scales and fangs.

But the thing that had most amazed her was the mirror room.

It was composed of eight walls, entirely covered with mirrors. While the glossy, perfectly smooth and transparent surface in front of her showed her image, the other seven mirrors allowed her to see every other facet of her person without her even having to move.

It made Lucrezia dizzy.

She had returned to that room several times, drinking in the wonder of it until she was breathless with amazement.

She wondered how many other inventions Leonardo was working on. Some called him a painter, but anyone who had seen this place would have realized that he was much more.

He was a genius.

Lucrezia couldn't think of a more apt definition.

'Messer Leonardo, you amaze me,' she said, looking at the handsome young man with long blond hair and a faint beard of soft fluff that barely covered his sunken cheeks.

He lowered his eyes in embarrassment.

'Come, my lady, it's nothing. Just some foolish toys upon which I pass the time.'

'You are too modest.'

'No, I am not. And yet, for all my arrogance, I can get nowhere near what I truly dream of doing. All that you see, Lucrezia, is nothing but a pathetic attempt to study reality.'

'And what is your true dream?' she asked, charmed by the man's prodigious imagination.

'What has always been man's greatest dream?'

Lucrezia did not know.

'Love?' she asked. 'Peace?'

Leonardo laughed. 'Love, of course! Peace, absolutely! How right you are. And yet I doubt that a man would answer that way. Which shows, once again, the superiority of the female intelligence.'

Leonardo stood for a moment absorbed in his own thoughts, as though her answer to his question had touched him deeply.

'How nice to hear you laugh again,' she said. 'I remember the last time I was here – you seemed the shadow of the man you have once again become.'

'The credit for that belongs entirely to my friends,' he replied.

'And who might they be?'

'Can you not guess?'

'I can, but I'd like to hear you say it.'

'You, Lucrezia, and Lorenzo de' Medici.'

'There, Leonardo! That wasn't so difficult after all, was it?'

'What?'

'Expressing your true feelings for once! The joy of friendship. Sharing a little affection with those around you. It was long overdue.'

'Yes,' he said with a smile, 'you're right.'

Lucrezia nodded.

'But to return to my question,' continued Leonardo. 'Considering what has been happening in Florence these past few days, do you think that men truly care about things like love and peace?'

This time Lucrezia said nothing.

'I did not intend to darken your mood, my lady,' he said, realizing too late the implications of his words, 'but I think the answer to my question is that they do not. Though when I asked you that question, I was referring to something simpler.'

'To what?'

'Flying.'

Lucrezia's eyes widened.

'Really? Do you believe it possible?'

'I am totally serious,' replied Leonardo. 'It is complicated, of course. But the answer, Lucrezia, is in nature, just as it always is. Come,' he continued, 'I want to show you something.'

They climbed onto the elevator platform and Leonardo turned the crank, and soon they found themselves in the cellar.

Leonardo led her through a labyrinth of machines and devices until, suspended from a tangle of ropes, Lucrezia saw something that took her breath away.

A pair of wings – or rather, a kind of machine on to which wings had been grafted. Actual wings.

Leonardo sensed her amazement and, like the born performer he was, decided to continue his show. With what seemed to Lucrezia like magic, he slipped into a sort of rigid bodice built of wood and leather and through a series of levers began to operate the large membranous wings, which started to beat the air.

Her eyes opened even wider.

'Does it work?' she asked.

'It's not finished yet. I'm still working on it but sooner or later I'll find the courage to try it – and then you'll be the first to know.'

'It would be magnificent,' she said with a smile. 'It would be one of humanity's greatest achievements.'

He nodded absently, as though showing her his invention for even a moment had already drawn him back into that world which only he could perceive.

'I have decided to call it an Ornithopter, because, as you can see, it is based upon the flight of birds – in particular on the black kite.'

'Why the kite?' asked Lucrezia.

'It's a long story,' replied Leonardo. 'One day I will tell it you.'

Greyhair waited for the boy to come back. He was rail-thin, his teeth were black and his face was sooty, but he was as agile as a cat and no one was as skilled at climbing along balconies and through windows as he. He moved quickly through the night that had fallen on Florence like an inky rainstorm. The odd torch lit the streets here and there but in Oltrarno, the darkness was almost total.

When, the night before, the blond-haired girl had paid him to do the job, it had occurred to him that he could well just take the money and run. After all, who would check up on the outcome? But when she had told him that he would receive as many florins again when the job was completed, his greed had taken over. And anyway, what was it to him? All he had to do was put the wind up a half-mad painter and get him to tell them where Lucrezia Donati could be found. Frightening a man like that didn't sound as if it would be a particularly taxing undertaking, so Greyhair decided that he'd had a nice stroke of luck. It was the ideal moment for it too, because Florence had descended into total anarchy. Families had shut themselves up in their homes and there was always someone shouting or screaming somewhere as the partisans of the Medici continued to hunt down the allies of the Pazzi.

That thirst for blood was dragging the city down into an abyss and the institutions were doing nothing to stop it. In fact, in some ways they were actually encouraging it, and now the homes of supposed enemies of the Medici were being sacked by the gangs of mercenaries and thieves who filled the streets.

He smiled, because he was one of them.

He'd made a notable contribution to the rampant madness, and having the chance to earn something from that state of affairs was a real blessing. He was not planning on missing out on the opportunity to earn another five thousand easy florins.

At the end of the day, the orgy of violence to which the city was being subjected was the only method for rebalancing the destiny of its population by taking money from the rich and giving it to the poor so that they were a little less so. Greyhair didn't know of another way. The nobles and the wealthy were greedy and, in spite of all their talk and good intentions, they would never dream of giving anything to the lower classes. And thus rebellion and subversion, even for a short period, took on the form of a ritual of collective purification. For this reason, Greyhair hadn't hesitated to fan the flames of the madness, and he hoped that it would last as long as possible so the poor and the derelict could adequately vent their anger at the many abuses and insults they had been forced to suffer over the last few years. Only then would they go back to accepting an everyday life made up of persecution and injustice.

He looked up at the crescent moon which lit the night sky like a yellow sneer. As he waited near the house opposite, he heard the barely perceptible patter of his scout's feet. He opened his voluminous cape for a moment to allow the light of the lantern he held within to be seen.

'There are two of them,' murmured the boy.

'Are you sure?'

'Yes. A man and a woman.'

'You saw them?'

'As well as I see you now.'

'Good.'

The boy gave a cough.

'What is it?' asked Greyhair.

'Are you sure that man is a painter?'

'Why do you ask?'

'Because I saw loads of weird machines. I couldn't tell you what they are, but I doubt they have anything to do with painting.'

'Have you ever once painted in your life?' asked Greyhair mockingly.

'Me? No, never.'

'So what the hell do you know about it?'

'I ask your pardon.'

'Never mind. Go and call the others.'

'Very good,' replied the boy, and raced off towards the end of the street.

Greyhair looked around him. Everything was perfect: stray dogs were growling around a corpse, there was the flickering of fires and there were screams coming from a nearby street. It was the ideal situation, because nobody would be paying any attention to him. Getting into that house would be child's play – and once he was inside, anything could happen.

55

Nocturnal Fracas

Leonardo had been keeping an eye on them for some time.

He had seen the boy climb up on to a balcony and peer inside his house. The youth had been so skilful about it that he almost hadn't heard him, and when he'd realized he was being observed, Leonardo had continued to demonstrate his work to Lucrezia. He'd wanted to avoid alarming her for as long as possible, but when he had noticed that the young spy was leaving, he'd also seen a glimmer of light on the opposite side of the road. It had lasted only an instant and then the darkness had returned, but the beam of light had sufficed to illuminate a face that promised nothing good.

Without wasting any more time, he had told Lucrezia to prepare herself for a busy night. He feared that some of the looters and thieves who were roaming the city under cover of the reprisals and violence which had erupted intended to take advantage of the situation to help themselves to the valuables contained in his home. He had no idea why, and he certainly didn't have time to find out if there was something else behind it – all that mattered at that point was getting ready.

Leonardo didn't imagine that they intended to kill them, but they would almost certainly try to rob him, and he had every intention of trying to stop them. Without hurting them, if possible – he had a couple of tricks up his sleeve to frighten them with.

He had seen the boy taking orders from that man with the long grey hair and then run away down the street.

When the others finally arrived, Greyhair had been ready for a while. They had brought a ram to break through the heavy oak door of the painter's house, and many of them were carrying stones to hurl at the windows.

They were so busy organizing themselves that they almost didn't realize that the first floor had suddenly been illuminated.

It was at that moment the most extraordinary and incredible thing Greyhair had ever seen happened.

Someone opened the windows. Light flooded the street and incredible objects began to rain down from above.

Were they birds? When he first saw them, it seemed to Greyhair that they must be, and indeed their shape and the beating of their wings made them appear such. But they made a strange noise, a sort of threatening buzz, and appeared to be in the throes of the most absolute delirium. Some flew upwards and then fell back down while others crashed to the ground. Others still swooped at them, making a deafening racket.

Greyhair's men started crying out in panic. A couple of them held in their hands one of those bizarre contraptions, which continued to beat their wings. Shouting hysterically, they dropped those little monsters of wood and springs and who knew what else crashing to the ground.

As Greyhair tried to restore order, darts began to rain down on them. An impressive number of darts, as though an entire legion of guards were barricaded in the house.

Whoever was firing the crossbows, they were clearly no marksmen, since none of their bolts hit their targets – but perhaps their intention was simply to scare them: one of the bolts missed Greyhair by a whisker, and scare him it did.

He looked around for the idiot boy who had assured him that there were only two people in there.

He spotted him just in time: he was hiding behind a water butt and was now looking for a way to sneak away and avoid ending up spitted like a thrush.

He seized him by the neck.

'What the hell did you see, you useless little bastard? There must be at least ten of them in there!'

'L-let me go, sir, please! Didn't you see those wooden birds? There's a demon in there!'

'Gah.' Greyhair spat out a lump of phlegm. 'These devilries don't frighten me – but if we now find ourselves under this hail of darts, it is thanks to you.'

And as he said this, a dart implanted itself in the water butt with a dull thud.

'We'll end up dead if we hang about here,' shouted the boy, who looked to be crazed with fear.

'You're right,' admitted Greyhair. He was about to grab hold of the youth when he heard a clatter of hooves coming down the street. For a moment he looked up and, taking advantage of that moment of distraction, the boy slipped from his hands and raced away.

'You little bastard!' shouted Greyhair.

Indistinct shapes were approaching, becoming clearer as the horses galloped forward.

He couldn't stay where he was or he would end up in one of the cells of the Palazzo del Podestà – or, perhaps, with a nice noose around his neck.

Never mind, he thought, he had at least pocketed the florins of the advance, and his hide was worth more to him than the payment he'd been promised on completion.

Without waiting another moment, he set off in the same direction as the boy.

Lorenzo had waited three days. He had remained in his home and had his brother's body prepared and then had buried him with full honours in San Lorenzo. It had been a time of pain and recollection, of desperation and of explanations. Not that anything had actually been explained, since no meaning could be found in a death like the one which had been inflicted upon Giuliano. Not even if he dedicated the rest of his life to looking for it.

The truth was that he felt guilty for having survived, because his brother had been the only truly innocent person in that whole story. He'd held no political position, nor had he attempted to twist the course of events for the benefit of his family. He had never betrayed anyone, nor had he ever even tried to. None of the wars unleashed by Florence bore his name – indeed, as far as he was able, he had tried with all his strength to avoid them.

Yet it had been he who had fallen under the daggers of a handful of traitors.

The cold evening air slashing at his face as he spurred Folgore on, Lorenzo tried to accept the idea that there was no longer anything he could do about it, but it was pointless. He must at least try, though, to be worthy of the luck that had left him alive, he thought.

At the end of the third day he had left the palazzo with an escort and set off across the city. He was shocked to see the state Florence was reduced to: it was like a vast bonfire of pain and madness. Houses burned, stray dogs devoured broken bodies left to rot along the streets and gangs of young criminals descended like flocks of crows to sack the smoking ruins of the buildings. The horrors he had witnessed combined into an apocalyptic vision that Lorenzo would never have imagined seeing with his own two eyes.

While they were trying to get to Leonardo's workshop, he and his men had stumbled into gangs of self-proclaimed Medici loyalists who were enjoying themselves by having a kick-around with some severed heads. When they saw him, they fled like the cowards they were.

Over a few days at least a hundred people had been hanged from the windows of the Palazzo della Signoria or beheaded on the gallows. Who could tolerate such insanity and cruelty?

His gloomiest predictions had come true.

When he finally halted Folgore in front of the door of the building that housed Leonardo's workshop, he was praying that he had arrived in time.

As he dismounted, he was stunned to see that the road was dotted with the carcasses of strange wooden objects in the shape of mechanical birds and that innumerable crossbow bolts protruded from a nearby rainwater butt.

Lorenzo ran over to the entrance and slammed the ring of the door knocker furiously against the wood.

'Leonardo!' he shouted. '*Leonardo!*'

He looked up and saw that the windows were open and a bright light was shining out of them. At that moment, his friend peered over the balcony. 'Are you trying to knock the house down?' he asked.

'So you're alive?' cried Lorenzo. 'Oh thank God! And what of Lucrezia?'

'It's open,' replied his friend laconically, 'come up and see for yourself.'

Instructing his escort to stand guard outside the entrance, Lorenzo pushed open the heavy door, which he would never have expected to find unlocked, and went inside.

In front of him he found a strange wooden frame which he didn't remember having seen before – a sort of platform. There were no stairs and he had no idea how to get up to the next floor, because it was clear that it was there that Leonardo was to be found.

'Climb on to the elevator,' said Leonardo's voice from above. 'Then turn the crank clockwise to come up.'

Lorenzo stepped forward and saw a wheel at the top of a wooden pole that served as a backrest. He began to turn it as Leonardo had ordered, and after a few moments realized that he was moving. He saw wheels and gears turning and the platform started climbing upward. As it began to rise, he felt himself overcome by a faint sensation of dizziness. He leaned against the backrest and soon found himself on the upper floor. The platform stopped with a creak, docking into a groove carved into the floor.

It was then that he saw Lucrezia.

Her eyes were bright and her hair fell like a river over her shoulders; there was a smile upon her face.

There was no need to speak. They threw themselves into each other's arms and, in a moment, everything – the unspoken words, the broken promises, the tears and the pain of recent days – was forgotten.

A smile on his lips, Leonardo looked at them in silence.

SEPTEMBER 1479

56

Love Does Not Forget

For once it was he who had come to her. It had been such a long time since he had been to her home.

As soon as he entered he smelled the scent of cornflowers, that marvellous essence which had bewitched his heart.

He entered the elegant salon. The large windows were open, as though wanting to embrace forever the last glimpse of summer, and the sunset made the sky above Florence red. All around, coloured candles burned, speckling the first shadows of evening which darkened the room with points of light.

A mischievous breeze caressed her splendid glossy hair, which shone like the purest silk from Venice and the Far East.

Lorenzo stood looking at Lucrezia for a long time, because he wanted to let his eyes fill with her beauty for one last time: her blood-red lips, sun-bronzed skin, high cheekbones and those magnetic, impudent eyes – black pearls in which the light of the candles sparkled together with the red flame of passion.

When he was standing in front of her he was struck by man's inferiority: woman was a creature infinitely more beautiful, proud and honest; woman seemed to fly far beyond the tawdry events of the earth and the ephemeral miseries of fame and power.

And Lucrezia was the very essence of the infinite and fascinating mystery of woman.

He could not speak. There were a thousand things he wanted to say, but his gaze was lost in the enchanting dress she wore, of a blue so intense that it looked like a clear sky. The pearls threaded to its ocean of velvet caught the light; its deep neckline emphasized her perfect breasts and her naked, seductive shoulders seemed to capture the last rays of the sun. Brocade sleeves with braided laces studded with precious stones ran down to her beautiful hands.

Lucrezia was a vision.

Lorenzo thought about how much he had desired her, loved her, and then betrayed and lost her, and then – miraculously – found her once more. And now, as he looked at her, he realized that he feared disappointing her again, almost as though by touching her he might not only harm her splendour but also the integrity of her person.

Because she had been sincere and honest with him, always; even when she had lied to him, she had done so to save his closest friend.

What was between them could never be more beautiful than that, he thought.

Whatever happened could only adulterate those moments of pure beauty.

'You've come to say goodbye.' It was not a question, but the plain truth. After all that had happened, after the overwhelming passion, after the expectations and the words, after the blood and the forgiveness, now it was time to say goodbye.

But it was not a final farewell, and the bitterness of when they had found themselves strangers in that farm hidden in the woods had gone. There was not even the distressing need to know the fate of the other which had haunted them when they had separated after the Pazzi conspiracy.

Lucrezia instead felt a sense of peace and reconciliation. Lorenzo was almost afraid to speak: words were traitors, children of a moment and of a state of mind, while love... love was forever.

And now in his dark eyes she could finally see everything he felt for her. She saw that despite everything that had happened over those years, despite the joys they had given each other and those of which they had deprived one another, his great, kind heart had never died.

He had put his own life at risk to save her.

Was there anything more beautiful that a man could do for a woman?

'If I stand here today watching this sunset from the salon of my palazzo, I owe it to you,' she said finally.

Lorenzo sighed.

'What will become of us?' asked Lucrezia.

'Every time I think of you, my eyes and my heart are doused with a rain that I cannot explain. When I try to write for you, the ink dries up and the words are like fallen leaves, the tired ghosts of what I can express only with my eyes, with the love that dwells within me, and that love no pain, no promise, could ever describe.' Lorenzo paused and took a deep breath, as if gathering together what he wanted to say from the deepest, most hidden folds of his soul. 'Waiting and denial make love stronger,' he continued, 'and I think that I want you now more than I ever have... And everything I once said was so true that I only now realize that I traded happiness for a life without you, and I curse myself for it. And not because we had so little time together, but because I let politics and power take everything without giving anything in return.'

As she listened, Lucrezia began to cry. Tears of joy and at the same time of regret for what had been lost and for what could still be.

'Time will tell if we deserve to love each other again. I don't want to make promises that I cannot keep. But I know that there is a light which, despite all that has happened, will never go out. It is like your music, that sense of the infinite over which I discovered I could for a moment hover. Do you remember?'

She nodded.

'I was young then,' he continued, 'and a better man than I am today. But if life has taught me anything at all, I owe it to you, because I see in everything you've done an integrity and a courage that I will never have, and that is why I admire you.'

'You always knew how to choose the right words to make me cry,' she said between sobs. 'No one knows me better than you, nobody else has ever been able to explain to me who I am. No one except you – and that is why I have loved you, and will always love you.'

And so saying, she stepped away from the window, sat down in an armchair and took up her lute.

The notes began to emerge, perfect cadences, like the greatest promise of love ever written.

Lorenzo stood listening to her play and letting the melody cradle him in the impalpable arms of her grace, just as he had so long ago.

It was true.

Love would never die, and would never forget.

57

The Old Friends

Two men were sitting on the top of a hill watching the impossible trajectories of bird flight.

There was such stupendous unknown perfection about their movements, thought Lorenzo. He looked over at Leonardo: his friend was staring rapt at the sky.

For a moment he felt as if he were back ten years before when, on this very hill, Leonardo had shown him his first fast-loading crossbow. He had built many others since then, but Lorenzo always carried with him the one he had received as a gift that day.

The time of madness and death had passed. Nothing could give him back his brother, just as nothing could erase the horror and mayhem the men loyal to him had perpetrated after that bloody Easter. He knew he had many faults, but he had also learned that the only way to survive power and responsibility was to do good.

He couldn't say whether he had become a better man in recent times, but he was certain that he was trying.

Florence was finally enjoying a period of peace and all of his efforts were now unequivocally aimed at making the city increasingly beautiful.

He hadn't been responsible for the conspiracy, nor for the reprisals that had taken place after it: he had ordered his men not to use the death of his brother as an excuse for committing even worse crimes, but he had been ignored.

After it was all over, he had removed many of them from positions of power and had them replaced.

'What are you thinking about?' Leonardo asked. He wasn't looking at him – his eyes were gazing up at the white clouds that glistened in the sky like sugar crystals.

'About everything that has happened since that day.'

'The day when I gave you the crossbow?'

Lorenzo nodded. It was incredible how well his friend could read his thoughts.

'Exactly,' he said.

'What do you think... of us?'

'What do you mean?'

'I mean, as friends. Have we managed to become good friends over time? Despite all our mistakes and our fallings-out?'

'I think so,' answered Lorenzo.

'I think so too. It wasn't easy for me. I have a disagreeable character and I tend to push people away whenever I have the chance.'

'So I've noticed.'

'Yes,' said Leonardo. 'But in any case, I still believe what I told you a long time ago.'

'You do well to do so – you were right and I was wrong.'

'Of course, it's hard to be clear-headed at a time like that: it's easy to be an idealist when you don't have the responsibilities of running a city on your shoulders.'

'I've made so many mistakes,' confessed Lorenzo. 'I think that if I had acted differently, some things might not have happened. I think perhaps I would be at peace with my conscience.'

His long golden hair blowing in the summer breeze, Leonardo shook his head. 'There's no such thing as conscience, my friend. There is only what we do.'

Lorenzo sighed. He felt that there was much truth in those words. It was precisely what he had done that tormented him.

With its vivid, vibrant colours, the countryside looked back at them.

'Nothing is comparable to nature,' said Leonardo. 'I think that if we want to be happy, we should just abandon ourselves to it and try to replicate its secrets and formulas.'

The sun shone high in the sky. It had torn through the blanket of clouds and now bathed the hill in its light.

'I have a job for you,' said Lorenzo. 'I know that you owe Florence nothing and that, if anything, Florence owes you, but I'd like it if you accepted.'

'What is it?'

'I would like you to start painting again. I know that many things engage your interest, and I have no wish to tell you how you should spend your time, but when I look at that painting...'

'The one of Lucrezia?'

Lorenzo nodded. '... I see your talent at capturing her grace and her sense of heavenly peace, of a beauty that feeds on the blues and greens, and I would like the opportunity to contemplate more such masterpieces. And so I wondered if you could consider accepting a commission.'

Leonardo smiled. 'I'm not sure I can.'

'Perhaps you could think about it. Take some time and tell me what you decide. In the meantime, if you like, why don't you show your face at the art school of Bertoldo di Giovanni in the San Marco Garden? I know him well, he is an excellent sculptor and who knows, maybe you would find it amusing.'

'What would the subject of the painting be?'

Lorenzo seemed to think for a moment.

'I'd rather only tell you if you agree to do it.' He smiled. 'In any case, I have something else in mind for you too.'

'Really?'

'Yes. If you accept my proposal, I would like to send you to my good friend Duke Ludovico Maria Sforza in Milan. There you could give full rein to your talents and represent Florence as its most brilliant herald and artist.'

Leonardo was silent.

'I'll think about it,' he said, and then pointed to a bird gliding through the blue sky as though it were the only master of the air. 'See that?'

'What?' asked Lorenzo.

'That black kite. It flies as no other bird can.'

'I didn't know.'

Leonardo's eyes returned to the heavens.

'He's an old friend,' he said as a tear ran down his face. 'Just like you.'

Author's Note

As my historical trilogy dedicated to the Medici approaches completion, I feel as though I have engaged with a fascinating and intriguing period and themes. Among other things, this second novel attempts to depict two historical figures of vast import: Lorenzo de' Medici and Leonardo da Vinci. At the mere thought of it my feeble mind faltered, and I therefore decided to use the unconscious as the narrative key.

My own unconscious, evidently.

In short, I tried to depict Lorenzo and Leonardo without being overly influenced by the clichés regarding them; trying, where possible, to highlight some lesser-known aspects of their lives. Without forgetting that, despite what we might believe, the Renaissance was also one of the darkest and most violent periods of history.

Some elements were of considerable help: certainly one of these was the fact that Leonardo was at the time not yet a genius at the height of his fame but an eclectic artist in search of his direction, and that in the years the story covers – from 1469 to 1479 – he was therefore intent on understanding what his true passions and interests were.

A very young, enigmatic Leonardo who, between 1474 and 1478, actually stopped painting and was also accused of sodomy, but also a Leonardo who was an apprentice, hungry for learning, who undertook his training in Verrocchio's workshop.

As I did my research for the drafting of this second volume of the trilogy, the thing that always struck me was how much effort the great artist from Vinci put into the study of nature, and his gargantuan efforts to recreate its solutions. For this reason I have tried to make room for episodes like that of the kite on one hand and some simple construction techniques on the other, trying to imagine a hypothetical night of awaiting the setting of the golden ball on the lantern of Santa Maria del Fiore, commissioned by Andrea del Verrocchio.

In short, it is a deliberately fractured narrative that attempts to render a contradictory and enigmatic figure through fragments which show the absolute ineffability of the character – as ineffable as the gazes of the figures at the centre of several of his masterpieces.

And Lorenzo?

He was no less problematic.

From the many documents and writings I examined, a much darker, more pragmatic and cynical figure emerged than I would have expected: I am thinking of the war against Volterra or of the law that prevented Beatrice Borromeo, wife of Guglielmo de' Pazzi, from inheriting the immense fortune of her father, or even of his complicated relationship with his wife Clarice Orsini, when his love was all for Lucrezia Donati.

But on the other hand, while I was forming an opinion on this personage whom I was to depict in fiction, I also realized how terrible it must have been for Lorenzo the Magnificent to face the inner torment of having to embrace the power and guidance of a city like Florence against his will.

And this is perhaps the key to my vision of Lorenzo: namely, that of a man torn between love and the duty, indeed, the need, to exercise power – because he, and no one else, was asked to become the lord of Florence as soon as his father Piero passed away.

Lorenzo, who had already been forced to agree to lose Lucrezia in order to marry Clarice in the name of an alliance between the Medici and the noble Orsini family, would have had no intention of becoming the new champion of those appointed to govern the city, at least not at twenty years of age, and yet that was exactly what everyone expected from him.

He was given no choice or chance to play for time: that was the way it was. And so this inner conflict, this fatigue, this weight soon turned him into a character of light and shadow, a figure which at times had something of the tragic about him, of the character that fascinates precisely because it stands on the tenuous and difficult boundary of right and the unjust, and therefore of good and evil.

In terms of narrative modalities, I thought it appropriate to tell the story through a series of scenes, so as not to lose its dramatic continuity. For the reader, it will be possible to read this novel as a self-contained story or, if you prefer, enjoy it after finishing the first volume in the trilogy so as to have a more complete fresco of an era. I have chosen, once again, to shape the backbone of the work upon Niccolò Machiavelli's *Florentine Histories* and Francesco Guicciardini's *History of Italy*, reliable and priceless guides to remaining upon the straight line of verisimilitude so as to create a literary narrative which contains as much historical fact as possible.

Once again, I did not skimp on my Florentine 'pilgrimages', nor could I have done without my conversations with my good friend Edoardo Rialti, a profound connoisseur of Florence and a refined scholar of letters, whom I thank deeply.

Much inspiration came from the most painstaking – and most frenzied – study of which I was capable. This involved the reading of many sources, of which it is only right that I should mention, *in primis*, *Lorenzo de' Medici: Scritti scelti*, edited by Emilio Bigi, Turin 1996; Ingeborg Walter's monograph *Lorenzo il Magnifico e il suo tempo*, Rome 2005; Jack Lang's *Il Magnifico:*

Vita di Lorenzo de' Medici, Milan 2003; Ivan Cloulas's *Lorenzo il Magnifico*, Rome 1988; Dimitri Mereskovskij's *Leonardo da Vinci: La vita del più grande genio di tutti i tempi*, Florence 2005; Bruno Nardini's *Vita di Leonardo*, Florence 2013; Frank Zöllner's *Leonardo da Vinci, i disegni*, Cologne 2014; and *Le macchine di Leonardo: Segreti e invenzioni nei codici da Vinci*, edited by Mario Taddei and Edoardo Zanon, Florence 2004.

These and other readings were then accompanied by the study of innumerable texts for a proper reconstruction of the Pazzi conspiracy. I should mention at least Lauro Martines's *La congiura dei Pazzi: Intrighi politici, sangue e vendetta nella Firenze dei Medici*, Milan 2005; Franco Cardini's *1478: La congiura dei Pazzi*, Bari 2014; and Niccolò Capponi's *Al traditor s'uccida: La congiura dei Pazzi, un dramma italiano*, Milan 2014. The dynamics of the conspiracy required in-depth study in order to provide an orderly chronological exposition of the events. The considerable number of characters in play and the speed of their actions forced me to prepare the long sequence of the Pazzi conspiracy with infinite care, and this led to a good number of failed attempts, with the consequent 'reassembly' of the third part of the story in order to obtain a functional narrative, as well as dramatic progression which would be clear and comprehensible for readers.

It was certainly the most difficult sequence I have ever had to write.

For the same reason, the novel accelerates as it approaches its finale: to try and convey, also in terms of perception, how the story of the conspiracy ended in an orgy of violence and anarchy that condemned Florence to ten days of pure cruelty from which the city only recovered after a long time and with difficulty.

Of course, even in the conspiracy you will find historical characters – most real but some invented – who were important for guaranteeing continuity between the two novels, the first engaging in a certain way with the second, just as Alexandre Dumas's *The Three Musketeers* does with his *Twenty Years After*... Think about Milady de Winter and you will understand what I mean.

In fact, the *feuilleton* is perhaps the primary reference point for this book of mine which inevitably drinks from the same well as the serialized novel. I am thinking in particular of Alexandre Dumas, Robert Louis Stevenson, Théophile Gautier, Edgar Allan Poe, Victor Hugo and Emilio Salgari, and therefore of that genre which I love so much and which I read regularly with great pleasure, attempting to blend it when I write with the shadings of *noir*, in the style of the great lesson provided by Emilio De Marchi, in particular his *Il cappello del prete*.

As with the previous novel, I could not have satisfactorily dealt with the duels and battle sequences without historical fencing manuals and I must therefore mention once again my essentials: Giacomo di Grassi,

Ragione di adoprar sicuramente l'arme si da offesa, come da difesa, con un Trattato dell'inganno, & con un modo di essercitarsi da se stesso, per acquistare forza, giudicio, & prestezza, Venice 1570, and Francesco di Sandro Altoni, *Monomachia: Trattato dell'arte di scherma*, edited by Alessandro Battistini, Marco Rubboli and Iacopo Venni, San Marino 2007.

Thanks

We have arrived at the second novel of this trilogy. I have made some calculations and by the time it is finished I think it will be about 1,100 pages long. I don't think I could have faced such a challenge without knowing that I had Newton Compton on my side. I say this without rhetoric or panegyrics: they have been the perfect partner because they have always believed in the potential and value of popular literature – that literature which has continued to offer readers extraordinary stories and memorable characters and which, through similar tools, is today destined again to shape the collective imagination.

I don't know if this will be the case with my book, but I hope that I have done a good job. The characters inspiring the book were formidable but if conditions turned out to be optimal, the credit is entirely due to my publisher.

As I mentioned in the first novel, I had wanted to publish a trilogy with Newton Compton for a long time. Between the ages of ten and fifteen, I grew up with the novels of the magnificent Newton Ragazzi series but also with their *Mammut*, those large, elegant volumes with retro covers which led me to rediscover the classics and to read them again, for example in the amazing trilogy of *The Three Musketeers*, *Twenty Years After* and *The Vicomte of Bragelonne*, published in 1993 in an extremely elegant large-format double-volume edition with an introduction by Francesco Perfetti. I remember the covers of two tomes showing *Soldiers Playing Backgammon* by Gerbrand van den Eeckhout and *The Portrait of a Gentleman with the Order of the Knights of Malta* by Michiel van Mierevelt. And therefore my deepest and most sincere thanks for this second novel go to Dr Vittorio Avanzini, one of the great founding fathers of Italian publishing, for welcoming me to such a prestigious catalogue. Once again his suggestions and advice proved central to the writing of the novel.

I will be forever grateful to Raffaello Avanzini, who promoted and supported this mad project every step of the way with commendable attention and rigour. Working side by side with him in an extraordinary, ongoing dialogue is a truly magnificent experience. Thank you once again, captain.

Together with my publishers, I would like to thank my agents, Monica Malatesta and Simone Marchi who, as always, were by my side studying the details, offering solutions and finding the perfect answers to all my needs and requirements. We have always been united by a love for literature and for dialogue. I am a very lucky novelist.

Alessandra Penna is an incredible editor: it's a privilege to spend time on my books with her, working on the words until they 'sound' right. And now we are sailing with the wind behind us towards book number three.

Thanks to Martina Donati for all of her advice, suggestions, enthusiasm, care and elegance.

Thanks to Antonella Sarandrea, who is in the trenches every day working to give the maximum visibility to my work. You're the best, hats off!

Thanks to Carmen Prestia and to Raffaello Avanzini, because the number of countries this trilogy has been published in is truly amazing.

Finally, I want to thank the whole Newton Compton Editori team for their extraordinary professionalism.

Thanks to Edoardo Rialti, genial man of culture. Without him I would know Florence much less than I do and I would not have had those precious suggestions of his which opened up new perspectives in the narration of this novel.

Thanks to Patrizia Debicke van der Noot for writing some magnificent novels about the Medici family.

I would like to mention, in this second chapter of the trilogy, two Italian authors who provided reference models for my work: Umberto Eco and Sebastiano Vassalli.

Naturally I want to thank Sugarpulp, who have never failed to give me support and energy: Giacomo Brunoro, Andrea Andreetta, Massimo Zammataro, Isa Bagnasco, Matteo Bernardi, Valeria Finozzi, Piero Maggioni, Chiara Testa and Martina Padovan.

Thanks to Lucia and Giorgio Strukul for helping me become what I am.

Thanks to Leonardo, Chiara, Alice and Greta Strukul: always with me, when it really counts!

Thanks to the Gorgis: Anna and Odino, Lorenzo, Marta, Alessandro and Federico.

Thanks to Marisa, Margherita and Andrea 'the Bull' Camporese, who read my books at supersonic speed and always want more.

Thanks to Caterina and Luciano, because they have always been and will always be an example.

Thanks to Oddone and Teresa and to Silvia and Angelica.

Thanks to Jacopo Masini & Dusty Eye: without your photos it wouldn't be any fun.

Thanks to Marilù Oliva, Marcello Simoni, Francesca Bertuzzi, Francesco Ferracin, Gian Paolo Serino, Simone Sarasso, Giuliano Pasini, Roberto Genovesi, Alessio Romano, Romano de Marco, Mirko Zilahi de Gyurgyokai: because you are a tribe of writers to share the paintings of battle and the colours of friendship with.

To conclude, infinite thanks to Alex Connor, Victor Gischler, Tim Willocks, Nicolai Lilin, Sarah Pinborough, Jason Starr, Allan Guthrie, Gabriele Macchietto, Elisabetta Zaramella, Lyda Patitucci, Mary Laino, Andrea Kais Alibardi, Rossella Scarso, Federica Bellon, Gianluca Marinelli, Alessandro Zangrando, Francesca Visentin, Anna Sandri, Leandro Barsotti, Sergio Frigo, Massimo Zilio, Chiara Ermolli, Giulio Nicolazzi, Giuliano Ramazzina, Giampietro Spigolon, Erika Vanuzzo, Thomas Javier Buratti, Marco Accordi Rickards, Daniele Cutali, Stefania Baracco, Piero Ferrante, Tatjana Giorcelli, Giulia Ghirardello, Gabriella Ziraldo, Marco Piva a.k.a. il Gran Balivo, Paolo Donorà, Alessia Padula, Enrico Barison, Federica Fanzago, Nausica Scarparo, Luca Finzi Contini, Anna Mantovani, Laura Ester Ruffino, Renato Umberto Ruffino, Livia Frigiotti, Claudia Julia Catalano, Piero Melati, Cecilia Serafini, Tiziana Virgili, Diego Loreggian, Andrea Fabris, Sara Boero, Laura Campion Zagato, Elena Rama, Gianluca Morozzi, Alessandra Costa, Và Twin, Eleonora Forno, Maria Grazia Padovan, Davide De Felicis, Simone Martinello, Attilio Bruno, Chicca Rosa Casalini, Fabio Migneco, Stefano Zattera, Marianna Bonelli, Andrea Giuseppe Castriotta, Patrizia Seghezzi, Eleonora Aracri, Mauro Falciani, Federica Belleri, Monica Conserotti, Roberta Camerlengo, Agnese Meneghel, Marco Tavanti, Pasquale Ruju, Marisa Negrato, Serena Baccarin, Martina De Rossi,

Silvana Battaglioli, Fabio Chiesa, Andrea Tralli, Susy Valpreda Micelli, Tiziana Battaiuoli, Erika Gardin, Valentina Bertuzzi, Walter Ocule, Lucia Garaio, Chiara Calò, Marcello Bernardi, Paola Ranzato, Davide Gianella, Anna Piva, Enrico 'Ozzy' Rossi, Cristina Cecchini, Iaia Bruni, Marco 'Killer Mantovano' Piva, Buddy Giovinazzo, Gesine Giovinazzo Todt, Carlo Scarabello, Elena Crescentini, Simone Piva & i Viola Velluto, Anna Cavaliere, AnnCleire Pi, Franci Karou Cat, Paola Rambaldi, Alessandro Berselli, Danilo Villani, Marco Busatta, Irene Lodi, Matteo Bianchi, Patrizia Oliva, Margherita Corradin, Alberto Botton, Alberto Amorelli, Carlo Vanin, Valentina Gambarini, Alexandra Fischer, Thomas Tono, Ilaria de Togni, Massimo Candotti, Martina Sartor, Giorgio Picarone, Cormac Cor, Laura Mura, Giovanni Cagnoni, Gilberto Moretti, Beatrice Biondi, Fabio Niciarelli, Jakub Walczak, Lorenzo Scano, Diana Severati, Marta Ricci, Anna Lorefice, Carla VMar, Davide Avanzo, Sachi Alexandra Osti, Emanuela Maria Quinto Ferro, Vèramones Cooper, Alberto Vedovato, Diana Albertin, Elisabetta Convento, Mauro Ratti, Mauro Biasi, Nicola Giraldi, Alessia Menin, Michele di Marco, Sara Tagliente, Vy Lydia Andersen, Elena Bigoni, Corrado Artale, Marco Guglielmi and Martina Mezzadri.

I have probably left someone out... As I keep saying, you'll be in the next book, I promise!

A hug and infinite thanks to all the readers, booksellers

and promoters who put their faith in this historic trilogy so full of love, intrigue, duels and betrayals.

I dedicate this novel and the entire trilogy to my wife Silvia, because every day she watches over me with the courage of a warrior and the beauty of a starry sky.

This novel is also for my brother Leonardo, who honours me every day with his affection and his esteem.

About the author

Matteo Strukul was born in Padua in 1973 and has a Ph.D. in European law. His novels are published in twenty countries. He writes for the cultural section of *Venerdì di Repubblica* and lives with his wife in Padua, Berlin and Transylvania.